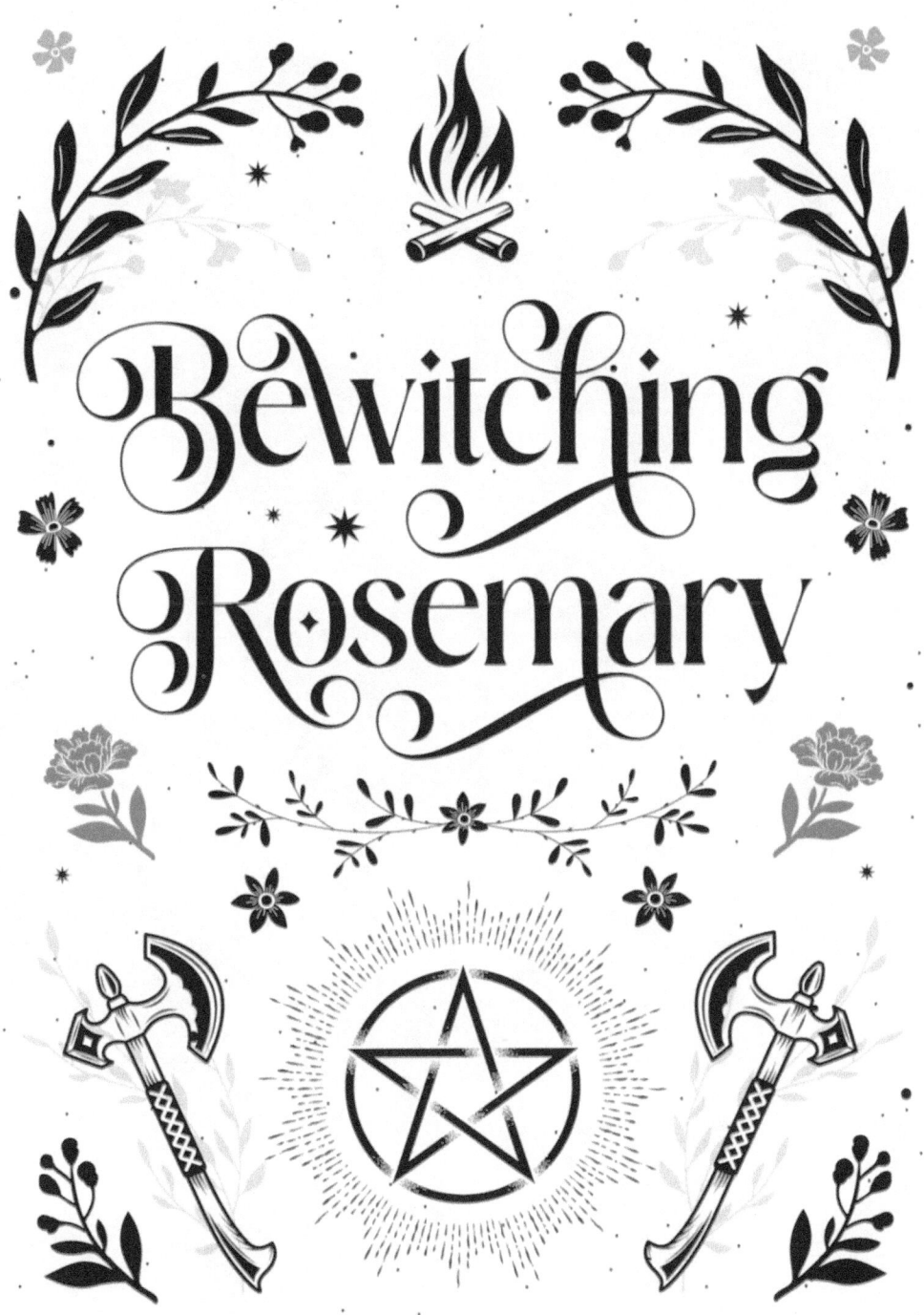

Bewitching Rosemary

COLLEEN DELANEY

Bewitching Rosemary

COLLEEN DELANEY

CITY OWL
PRESS

BEWITCHING ROSEMARY
The Witches of Star Island, Book 2

CITY OWL PRESS
www.cityowlpress.com

Cover Design by MiblArt. All stock photos licensed appropriately.

Edited by Tee Tate.

For information on subsidiary rights, please contact the publisher at info@cityowlpress.com.

Print Edition ISBN: 978-1-64898-505-8

Digital Edition ISBN: 978-1-64898-506-5

Printed in the United States of America

To Mr. Mustache, Moose, Bones, Bird, and Bug
You five are my whole world. Now, go outside so I can get some work done.

Praise for Colleen Delaney

"Delaney casts a spell with the first in *The Witches of Star Island* paranormal series. The love story is endearing and the supernatural twists propel the story forward at an exciting clip. The ending leaves many questions unanswered... but Delaney's sturdy worldbuilding ensures this series has plenty of places to go. This is a strong start." — *Publisher's Weekly*

"Family relationships, soulmate relationships, past lives, and incredibly well done magical elements keep you turning the pages of this one." — *HJ Reviews*

"*Finding His Mate* is an interesting story in a dystopian future where different paranormal creatures rule the world. The characters are so damaged and so resilient, and the next book promises more of the same. Highly recommend for fans of shifter romance with fated mates, especially if darker backstories are your thing." — *Jaycee Jarvis, author of The Hands of Destin series*

"*The Hedge Witch* is a fast-paced and delightful read with a heavy dash of spice as well. I recommend this to fans of a good witchy romance, particularly if you enjoy a suspenseful plot to go along with it." — *Your Book Friend Blog*

Also by Colleen Delaney

THE WOLVES OF LUVEN

Finding His Mate

Waiting for His Mate

Stealing His Mate

Protecting His Mate

Aching for His Mate

THE WITCHES OF STAR ISLAND

The Hedge Witch

Bewitching Rosemary

Hauntings and House Witchery

Chapter One

"Whoever might be out here, listening in on this slightly drunk garden witch's musings," Rosemary began as she clipped some thyme, "thank you. You know I don't hold much stock in good and evil; no one sees the villain they are. But you kept the Bays safe, and we are grateful."

She rubbed a few soft leaves between her fingertips until the earthy fragrance drifted through the air.

"Perfect," she hummed. The three glasses of wine she'd downed in the last hour had her feeling deliciously magical. It was a good night for spells, and acts of gratitude, especially after the day the Bay sisters had. Her younger sister, Laurel, had been attacked by the witch Morana as she tried to steal the Bay's magic. Laurel had nearly died before managing to trap Morana in the Hedge World. Gratitude was in the forefront of her mind.

Rosemary headed back into the house down the white stone path. She loved this walk—wildflowers creeping between the stones, her herb garden in the distance. The air was warm and breezy against her skin, carrying the scents of mint, basil, and chamomile. Summer on Star Island had a wild sort of magic about it that Rosemary loved. Her plants were at their strongest, and so was she.

Laurel would be heading out soon—out of their house and into her new life with Owen. The prophecy had started; each of their soulmates were coming and Laurel's happened to show up first. The book of their young adulthoods was closing, and Rosemary couldn't be more excited. She'd wished for her soulmate since she was sixteen, dreamed of what he'd look like, and even what he'd taste like. She wanted to know what it would be like to wrap her legs around his hips and show him everything she'd learned—and see what he might bring to the table. Or the shower. Or the earth under the full moon. She couldn't wait to tell him everything about herself and learn everything there was to know about him. It was like waiting for the best sort of best friend. One who she'd fall madly in love with.

In the kitchen, Lavender, the oldest Bay sister, had a beef and carrot stew simmering. It was a bit heavy for summer, but there was nothing like a dangerous afternoon to put a true hunger in one's belly.

Rosemary was about to sneak a quick taste when a heavy knock at the door made her jump out of her skin. It was very late for a social call on Star Island. The population liked to keep old-fashioned hours in every sense. After the afternoon they'd had, Rosemary steeled herself. Another magical battle could be on the horizon.

"Who the hell is at the door at this hour?" Rosemary called as she walked into the dining room. "I swear to all the goddesses—"

She stopped talking and the bundle of thyme she had been holding slipped through her fingers and bounced on the floor.

"Oh, fuck." Her entire body felt like it was on fire, and her fingers and toes buzzed so violently she thought they might vibrate off her body.

Rosemary took one look at the police officer taking up the entirety of her doorway, turned around, and walked straight out of the parlor. She didn't stop as she marched into the kitchen, out the screen porch, and past the herb garden. She kept going into the darkness to the deeper parts of their property, because there was no way this was happening.

Rosemary Bay, garden witch and sex magic enthusiast, was not soulmates with a cop.

Yes, he was handsome. His face was perfectly constructed and would be welcome buried between her breasts. The bright eyes that didn't leave her face could probably bore right into her soul. Even beneath his beard, she could tell that he sported a jawline that could cut glass. Yes, her heart slammed into her stomach and then her throat and then against her ribs the moment she saw him. Which paired with the full-body explosion of heat and electricity was an undisputable sign of a soulmate. And finally, yes, he was the size of a small tree and could probably carry all one hundred and seventy-five pounds of her without breaking a sweat and transplant any tree or shrub she wanted moved without complaining of back pain.

But no.

No amount of tree transplanting or bosom-nuzzling would change the cold, hard fact that Rosemary was not suited to the idea of having a cop as her partner. Forever.

She kept walking, paying little mind to the fact that her abrupt exit in the middle of a visit from local law enforcement probably looked suspicious. There was also that pesky detail that her sister, Laurel, had just bound an evil witch to another realm and therefore made her an accessory to a missing person case. But that did not stop her from stomping away from the house.

"Rosemary!" Lavender hissed into the darkness.

"Walled garden," she yelled to her sister and did not slow her pace.

Rosemary continued on her way, following the loose stone path lined by her perfectly chaotic wild flowers. She took a few deep breaths. The flowers should help her calm down, or at the very least help her to regain some sense of self. She was a garden witch; she was most powerful when surrounded by *her* garden. She needed those plants to start working for her.

The Bay property had several different gardens tucked and spread throughout their land, courtesy of Rosemary. The herb garden, rose garden, walled garden, as well as a few other collections of aesthetically pleasing groups of blooms were Rosemary's territory. But while she may have sown the seeds, blessed the ground, and poured her love into the plants, once the flowers got started, there was no stopping them. They had their own wild, inherent magic. Rosemary just gave them a little push.

She walked under the arch into the walled garden and found her favorite bench, the one with the archer carved into the side, forever shooting an arrow into the night sky, and sank down until she hit the cool stone. It was one of her favorite places on their property, and she was a strong believer in a comforting environment helping a person through a hard time.

Her soulmate was here. And somehow, after a month of being ready for him to come and fifteen years of waiting impatiently for him to show up, she was unbelievably and completely unprepared.

"What is wrong with you?" Lavender broke into her thoughts. "It looks extremely suspicious that two of us disappeared into the night when the new sheriff came asking about Morana. Are you trying to arouse distrust?"

"Did he follow you? The cop?" Rosemary kept her eyes buried against her hands, not yet ready to face her sister.

"I doubt it, but I wouldn't yell anything, just in case."

"That cop," Rosemary paused and took a deep breath, "that man in our parlor talking to Laurel about Morana Stoch, is my soulmate."

Lavender burst out laughing.

"Stop it, Lavender, it isn't funny," Rosemary spat. She crossed her arms over her chest and grimaced at her sister.

"Funny? No, it's damn hilarious. Your soulmate is in the parlor, Rosemary. *Your* soulmate. You've been talking a big game for the last month. Hell, you've been doing it for years. 'Once my soulmate shows up, we'll spend three days between the sheets. I can't wait until he gets here so we can have sex under the full moon. The second I see him, I'm attacking him like a spider monkey. We're going to do so much sex magic,'" her older sister mocked her. "Look at you! Just as scared as Laurel was. And you didn't even have the decency to talk to him first, just immediately hid in the garden. I would have thought you'd be crawling up him right now or dragging him to your bedroom. Or worse, taking your clothes off in front of all of us." Lavender chuckled.

A few weeks earlier, their younger sister Laurel's soulmate, Owen, had appeared on Star Island. It took her a little while to be accustomed to the idea of her soulmate suddenly in her life, and Rosemary had teased her on more than one occasion.

"Lavender, my soulmate cannot be a cop." Rosemary gestured wildly with her hands. "Do you know how many hallucinogens I currently have growing on our property? Seven. I did Witch's Eyes two weeks ago. I go to the Women's March every year in Boston. I'm a registered member of the Green Party. I cannot be soulmates with a stick-in-the-mud cop!"

"Just because the majority of the cops on Star Island have arrested you for public indecency doesn't mean this one will be like that. Maybe he'll love having a crazy little nudist as a life partner. And wait, you are growing illegal substances on our land and didn't tell me? Are you insane?"

"Lavender, focus. There's no one more well-versed in botany on this island than me. Unless this new guy used to be on a drug taskforce specializing in mind-altering drugs of the pre-modern period, he won't recognize anything. And pot is legal now, so I can't get in trouble for that."

Rosemary wasn't a *heavy* drug user. She smoked pot once in a while and saved the stronger stuff for spells. She grew everything; it was in her nature. She had an entire garden of baneful herbs tucked away in a corner of the land no one used, and they were far more dangerous than her patch of Witch's Eyes.

"Do you want to go talk to your *soulmate*? Get his phone number and send him a dirty text? Ask him out to dinner? Or go back to his place and fuck him senseless, considering that was what I thought you would do as soon as you saw him?" Lavender leaned against one of the magnolia trees and absentmindedly ran her hand over the bark.

"No. I think I'll sit out here for a little while." Rosemary closed her eyes and blew out a breath. What a mess.

Lavender nodded. "I'm going back to the house so I can answer any questions he might have. Hopefully I'll come up with something believable about why you disappeared into the garden on my walk back." Lavender rubbed her fingers against her brow. "I'm so tired." She sighed, then turned and walked under the arch and disappeared into the darkness.

Rosemary tipped her head back and stared at the stars. She wished it was daytime. She needed to garden, and not just cut a few flowers and rub a few herbs between her hands. Rosemary needed to move bushes, plant a few new trees, and maybe redesign an entire new garden. She had been considering putting in some peonies in a spot just outside the walled garden. She could probably take a quick trip to the mainland this week and grab a few tubers to get it started. A big project would help her accept the fact that her soulmate was probably a pretty buttoned-up police officer. Maybe he'd surprise her and be really into landscaping. She could hope.

She whimpered. Someone being a cop didn't necessarily mean he would be a rule-follower, right? She grumbled. Cops enforced rules. It was sort of their life's work.

It wasn't like Rosemary wanted a criminal for a soulmate. She followed ninety-five percent of the laws in place. She just wanted someone to get into a little mischief with. Or someone that would turn a blind eye to some of the questionable things she did. Like aiding her sister in trapping a witch in the Hedge World.

Oh well. She would have to figure out a way to make it work. Because there was no way Rosemary Bay, garden witch and sex magic enthusiast, was tamping her spirit.

"Oh shit." She laughed. After all that, she had forgotten to get his name. So, for now, her soulmate would be known as tall, bearded cop.

When Rosemary finally ambled back to the house, tall, bearded cop was gone, as were Laurel and Owen. They'd headed to Owen's rental for the foreseeable future with a promise to text in the morning. Lavender and Sage were both sleeping, but Verbena was at the dining table taking notes.

"I didn't expect you to still be here." Rosemary pulled out the chair next to her.

"Well, you know Lavender and Sage turn into pumpkins if they stay up too late. Besides, I wanted to make sure you were okay."

"Just some disappointment that manifested as panic. I'll be fine." Rosemary paused. Verbena sat beside her, but she couldn't ignore the fact that her sister felt hundreds of miles away.

"Related," Rosemary shook out her hands a bit to clear her thoughts, "do you have any houses on the market right now that could use a few new trees in their yards? I'm going to be gardening all day tomorrow, and I don't know if Sage would appreciate me transplanting her entire apple orchard. I need to do some heavy work."

"Not particularly. I do have a house with a fifty-percent-dead pine out front that could use some serious pruning. Care to hack away at dead branches?"

"Better than nothing. Text me the address. I'll be there in the morning." Rosemary settled into her seat, wondering if she should make a cup of tea or eat an entire cake. It felt like that kind of night.

"I'm going to head home," Verbena said, pushing in her chair and grabbing her purse.

"You could stay?" Rosemary offered. "We still haven't touched your room, you know. Sage and I are fine sharing."

"Thanks, but, you know me, I like to keep my routines. Helps keep me sane." Verbena forced a smile. "Try to get some sleep tonight. It's going to be okay."

"I know it's going to be okay." Rosemary mustered a small smile in return. "I was just hoping it would be extraordinary."

After Verbena left, Rosemary made herself a cup of tea. There was no cake to be found in the fridge—a true tragedy when living with a baker—so she settled for a chocolate chip cookie the size of her palm. The tea, Don't Let the Bedbugs Bite, was one of her own creation. She and Lavender both dabbled in the tea world, and this one was a simple blend of chamomile, vanilla, and orange, plus a little bit of spell work.

Rosemary finished her tea and cookie, then headed to her bedroom. She carefully opened the door, to not set off a deafening creak, and tiptoed past the already snoring Sage. Their twin beds were situated on either side of the room, just as they had been for nearly thirteen years. Their room still looked like a couple of teenagers lived there, each with their own style. Sage's wall was sparse, only a *Farmer's Almanac* calendar hanging on it, while Rosemary's had close to thirty small pictures pinned up with thumbtacks. Between their beds was a dwarf clementine tree and a lush fern. Neither wanted to be too far away from plants while they dozed.

Rosemary slunk out of her dress, a simple pale green sundress with permanent dirt stains around the edges, and pulled on an oversized T-shirt and boxer shorts. She climbed under her covers, fidgeting with the pillows and tossing around until she got comfortable. She finally settled on her back and stared at the dark ceiling.

This was not the way she pictured spending the night after seeing her soulmate for the first time. She had expected a lot more passion, a lot less clothes, and a lot less fear.

This wasn't like her. Rosemary didn't back down from a challenge. She grew in-ground succulents in the north Atlantic, for Gaea's sake. She could handle anything.

She decided right then it *was* going to be okay. Maybe it was her fate to draw him out of his shell. Maybe he needed to break free from society's constraints. Tall, bearded cop just needed a wild witch by his side, and in no time, she'd have him sky clad under the full moon, a student to her every desire.

Hopefully.

Chapter Two

Asher Evans was having a very weird day.

He started his shift around two in the afternoon. The schedule was still an absolute mess. He worked nine to five three days a week, second shift once a week, and rounded it all out with a solitary, miserable third shift. The previous sheriff of Star Island had made a big point during the interview process that he liked to spread out the third shifts so everyone in the small department had a few days of normalcy. Asher didn't want to change anything immediately, so he was stuck working nights one day a week. It was no secret the cops of Star Island hadn't wanted an outsider coming in and running things, so keeping some remnants of the last sheriff seemed like a good idea.

Asher got to work that afternoon and had seventeen sticky notes on his desk from the office administrator, Jane. She was a seventy-eight-year-old woman who had been working that exact job since 1977. No one knew the office like she did. In truth, Jane Mulchum ran the Star Island police department, no matter what anyone else's title was. If she were a police officer by trade, she would have been the obvious choice to replace Sheriff Martin, but her true calling was administrative work.

"Jane? Are these all messages from the same person?" Asher called from his door. He was met with a firm jaw and raised eyebrow.

"Yes. Ivan Stoch has called thirty-eight times since nine o'clock this morning. He seems insistent he speak to you directly and would not talk to any of the other officers. I only wrote seventeen messages because at that point he became very rude, and I no longer wished to assist him in anyway. But be assured, there was no new information."

"Rude? To you?"

Jane looked side to side, then got up from her desk and crossed the room, bringing her voice down several octaves.

"If it were up to me, I would call the local law enforcement wherever he is. That man sounds like he has been taking drugs. And not the easy-going type. He sounds like he's on cocaine." She pulled a disapproving face. "His number is from a small town in Montana. I Googled it. I also looked up the number to the local police station if you would like it." She slipped an eighteenth sticky note into his hand.

"Thanks, Jane. I'll call him back first."

Asher walked back into his office and closed the door. It was the only room, other than the holding cell, that had a door in the department. He settled into the chair he was still getting accustomed to, grabbed one of the sticky notes, and punched the number into his keypad.

"What?"

"Hello, is this Ivan Stoch?"

"Yeah, why?"

"This is Sheriff Evans of Star Island. You've left me some messages."

"About time. My sister is missing on that island of yours."

Missing? None of the sticky notes said anything about a missing person. Asher grabbed a pen and slid his notebook under his hand.

"When precisely did she go missing?"

"I don't know, yesterday? Maybe the day before? I haven't heard from her and she's not answering her cell. She was supposed to check in."

"Let's start at the beginning. What's your sister's name?"

"Morana Stoch. I told your secretary that the first time I called. You really should have her replaced. Complete hag."

Asher ignored him. If working in public service had taught him anything, it was that people were allowed to be rude when they were worried about a loved one.

"How old is she?"

"Eh, twenty-eight. Maybe twenty-nine. Wait, twenty-six."

Odd, Asher thought. If Asher forgot how old his sister was, she would never let him live it down.

"When did she get to Star Island?"

"Few days ago."

"Do you know exactly when she got here? That would be helpful." Even though it was high tourist season, most people got to the island via the ferry. If he could pinpoint a day and time, it would make tracking her much easier.

"I don't," he snapped. "Your spit of land isn't easy to get to. And she doesn't fly."

"Where is she staying?" Asher continued.

"Staying? I don't know. She was supposed to find, or meet up with, someone that lives there. Laurel Bay. If you ask me, it's a bad idea to meet up with people you've never met in real life."

"They had never met before? How did they know each other?" Asher scribbled "Laurel Bay" into his notebook.

"Online, I guess. Look, I just want to know if my sister is okay. Laurel Bay is probably a good place for you to start."

"Thank you for the lead. It would be very helpful if you remember where she was staying."

"Just find her," he insisted.

"I'll do my best. Could you send a recent picture of her with a clear shot of her face to the department here? It would help to circulate an image of her. It's a small island; someone is bound to have seen her around the last few days."

"Yeah. I'll call you for an update in a couple hours," he added.

"How about I'll call you tonight if I need any other information or if I get any leads. Otherwise, let's plan to check in via email every morning around ten a.m. Eastern time."

"Fine."

Asher hung up the phone and quickly read over his notes. An overbearing brother was in search of his adult sister who was supposed to meet up with someone on the island. If the brother's demeanor was any indication, this sister might have just wanted a break from him. He'd wait until the picture came through, then make his way over to wherever Laurel Bay lived and see if he could put this Ivan character at ease.

After stacking the errant Post-Its in a pile, Asher grabbed a folder out of his drawer. He labeled it "Morana Stoch" and set it aside. Hopefully, he'd be crossing that name out soon and replacing it with something inane like "missing ducks."

Asher rubbed his forehead a couple times. He thought trading Buffalo for Star Island would mean less heartrending police work and a lot more getting cats out of trees. He hadn't expected a missing persons case in his second week.

He drew in a long breath. He would stay focused, and he would get through the day.

Asher didn't get out to Laurel Bay's house until almost eight in the evening. He felt odd, calling so late on someone who may or may not have anything to do with a person who may or may not be missing, but he wanted to give Ivan an update the next morning. While he had been rude and persistent, he was a worried sibling.

Asher took one of the patrol cars to the center of the island, between the Vega and Sirius peninsulas. The properties here were larger than those on the coast, some stretching across acres and acres of woods and twisting roads, and quieter than the beachfront property. He hadn't had a chance to fully explore the island since he'd started his new job. Over the course of the summer, Asher planned to learn the roads, coasts, and wilderness of Star Island better than the last neighborhood he had worked in.

He pulled into the gravel drive, a pleasant crunch beneath the wheels of his car. There was something settling about creating such a racket when entering someone's property. He liked that no one could happen upon the residents completely unaware. Well, unless they traveled through the tangled mess of wildflowers and hedges that lined this particular drive, but those plants looked like they might have sinister plans for anyone who stomped on them.

Asher parked the car, grimaced while he gave his shoulder a quick roll to loosen it, and climbed out of the driver's seat, taking a moment to gather his surroundings. The house was picturesque, as many of the older homes on the island were. It looked like it had been dropped out of a sweet fairy tale, not one of the stories where children get eaten. This particular yard was different, mainly because there were flowers everywhere. Asher had never seen a yard so overtaken by plants in his life. It reminded him of the "after" in *The Secret Garden*. His sister had watched that movie a million times when they were kids.

Asher climbed the stairs, surprisingly devoid of creaks, and rapped on the door.

A young woman and man opened the door almost immediately, both with furrowed brows at his appearance. He wore his uniform, and would continue to do so until he was a recognizable fixture on the island, but still, he was a stranger in a tight-knit community.

"Good evening, ma'am. I'm looking for Laurel Bay," he began. He guessed this woman was Laurel Bay, but he didn't want to presume.

"That's me," she answered. Her eyes narrowed, and the man next to her took a step closer, his hand going to her waist.

"Perfect. Have you by any chance seen Morana Stoch lately? Her brother called the office after she didn't check in. Said she was planning on visiting you here on Star Island." He wanted to keep things light and non-accusatory.

"I'm sorry, who are you?" Laurel looked slightly put off, but he couldn't place exactly why.

"I'm Officer Evans, the new sheriff. Haven't gotten a chance to introduce myself to all the year-rounders, and I'm sorry to be meeting you in such an odd circumstance." He shook both their hands, hoping to lessen the tension.

"Owen Davies," the man said as he took his hand, still wary but a little friendlier.

Asher heard footsteps coming from one of the other rooms and glanced over Laurel's shoulder, hoping he might see Morana come out of the shadows. That would be the perfect ending to his first missing person's case on Star Island. He could even draw a bow on the folder.

"Who the hell is at the door at this hour? I swear to all the goddesses—"

Asher's throat went dry.

The most beautiful woman he had ever seen was standing in front of him, her mouth like an O and her eyes wide. She dropped a bundle of flowers that had been in her hands and locked gazes with him She looked at him like he was some long-lost friend reappeared from beyond the grave. His chest felt tight and hot—as if he'd been underwater way too long and needed a sweet sip of air. He balled his fists and stared at her. Her wavy brown hair was loose on her shoulders, and he was fighting the urge to bury his hands in it. What the hell was going on?

"Oh fuck," she said, then turned around and walked out of the room.

Asher moved to follow her. He *had* to follow her. He didn't get her name. Who was she? Did she live here? Where was she going?

He cleared his throat and stilled his feet. He was not about to barge into someone's home to chase down a complete stranger. He looked back at Laurel, hoping for answers.

"Sorry, that's my sister, Rosemary. She's...strange."

Asher took one more glance at the space Rosemary had disappeared from and then back to Laurel.

"Right." He needed to focus on his current inquiry, not let his mind wander to the pretty woman who'd popped in and out. He was a professional. He could keep his mind in one place. "Morana. Have you seen her?"

"I'm sorry, I haven't. I've never met her. Her name sounds vaguely familiar. I'm in a lot of online groups for tarot cards readers and mediums. She might be in one of them."

Asher couldn't stop a small grin spreading across his mouth.

"What?" Laurel asked. "Don't believe in psychics?"

"Hm, I will plead the fifth on that question."

"Well, I do readings for everyone on the island. If you need some guidance, feel free to make an appointment." She smiled and Asher suddenly felt like he was receiving a sales pitch.

"I'll think about it." He reached into his breast pocket. "Here's my card. Please call if Morana does reach out to you or if you remember anything about her that might be useful. Her brother is very worried."

"Thanks, I will."

Asher nodded and turned to leave. He briefly considered taking a peek into the backyard to get one more glimpse at Rosemary but quickly decided against it. He was an officer of the law, not a lovesick teen. It was a small island. He'd find time to introduce himself to her properly in the next few days.

Later that night, Asher couldn't sleep. It wasn't strange for him to have a hard time sleeping, especially when he worked an off-hours shift. He'd gotten home around eleven, had a bowl of cereal, and turned on some mindless TV, hoping to drift off around midnight. Instead, he was wide eyed and tossing around his bed like a restless wave at two in the morning.

Rosemary Bay.

He could not shake her from his thoughts. He hadn't even spoken to her, but he felt drawn to her. He didn't understand it. It was like she was the porch light, and he was the moth; there was no fighting it.

He rubbed his chest where he still felt the effects of seeing her. He was hot and achy, like he was coming down with something or pushed himself too hard in a workout. The closest feeling he had to this was five years earlier when he'd done a sprint triathlon with barely any training and then felt awful for a few days.

She was beautiful, obviously, but it was more than that. He didn't understand why he would feel like this after one glance. It had been a long time since he'd slept with someone. He racked his brain, thinking about the last time he actually spent romantic time with a woman. It was coming on fifteen months.

Yikes.

He was probably just crazy horny. After all, he didn't know her from Eve. She could be cruel. Or married.

That put a pit in his stomach. No, she wasn't married. He felt it in his bones. She was available, for him.

He also felt like she was in danger.

Asher groaned. That feeling had gotten him into trouble before. He couldn't stop it. Sometimes, that instinctual need to protect someone took over every fiber of his being and he had to act. Usually it ended up good for both parties, but the last time he was overcome with it... Asher rubbed the scar on his left shoulder.

He didn't want to think about that.

This overwhelming need to protect had steered his entire life, the good and the bad. He had come to Star Island to try and outrun it, but it looked like he didn't go far enough.

He padded out of bed and walked to the bathroom, rummaging through the medicine cabinet to find his prescription for clonazepam. It had been two months since he'd taken one, but he wanted to get on top of it. No use going down that terrible path if he could stop it before it began.

Asher got to work the next morning, tired but functional. The clonazepam had done the trick, and he'd drifted off to sleep not long after. He still felt a little off though. He could have used another three hours of sleep. He swung by the local bakery to grab a large coffee and ended up getting a cherry scone that was probably the best thing he'd ever eaten.

"Jane, could you come in my office?" he called.

She took off her reading glasses and let them hang on the chain around her neck before getting up and coming into his office.

"Is this a door-shut conversation?"

"What? No." He waved his hand. "I wanted to ask you about the Bay family. I met Laurel and Rosemary last night. That persistent caller from yesterday insists his sister was visiting Laurel Bay, but she said she didn't know her."

"Let's see. The Bays came to Star Island...must have been at least twelve years ago. Sad story. Their parents were both killed in a car accident. The oldest sister took on the role of guardian for the rest of them. At that point, Sage was in middle school, Verbena and Laurel were in high school. Lavender and Rosemary really raised those girls."

"Wait, how many Bays are there?" Asher was trying to keep track in his mind, but at this point it just sounded like Jane was listing off herbs.

"Five. Lavender is the oldest. You have her coffee right there, so you probably saw her this morning. Then there's Rosemary. She works at the florist shop around the corner. Then Laurel, the witch, Verbena, the realtor, and Sage, the farmer."

"I'm sorry, the witch, the realtor, and the farmer?" That sounded like a set-up for a joke.

"That's how they are known. Laurel's the psychic; Verbena is the best realtor on Star Island, she's really turned around the market, brought a huge influx of new people in; and Sage has a small farm on their property. The farmers' market starts next week. You should check out her stall. No one's produce is as good as hers is."

"There are five Bay sisters, and the one I am supposed to be looking into is referred to by locals as a witch. This case just took an interesting turn." Asher had been expecting some small-town quirks when he moved from Buffalo, but he wasn't prepared for a town witch.

"Laurel Bay is harmless. She's basically entertainment for the bachelorette parties that stumble down the street hammered after they've missed their ferry for the second night in a row. Plus, she's always right. I don't hold much stock in psychics, but she did tell me to be wary of my daughter-in-law, and let's just say, she's not my daughter-in-law anymore. And if the accuser is that jerk I talked to yesterday, I wouldn't think twice about believing Laurel over him."

Asher didn't like to jump to conclusions about anything. He wasn't going to let Laurel's occupation and reputation color his opinion of her, nor would he do the same with Ivan's erratic behavior.

Was Ivan a worried brother? Did Morana even come to Star Island? He wasn't sure of the answer to either yet, but he'd be figuring it out soon.

Asher needed to canvass town, check out the hotel, motel, and campsite, and get Morana's picture circulated. Hopefully, she'd turn up, and then he could focus on boring cases. Like the case of the sheriff introducing himself to the florist.

Chapter Three

Rosemary was gardening. Furiously.

It was not her usual mode of gardening. Normally, Rosemary liked to commune with her plants while she worked with them. She took time to run her fingers between the fragrant stems of cilantro, bury her hands into her thyme and deeply inhale the beauty of it. She cherished every new rosebud, danced her hands over the petals on the flowering trees, adored the black-eyed Susans, the forget-me-nots, and the gladiolas that lined the paths that led further into the property. She loved her ornamental shrubs, treated her potted plants on the porches like pets, and never left without a meticulously designed bouquet for the dining table. On a normal morning, there were songs and words of gratitude mixed in with her tender hands.

Today, her brain couldn't do anything that wasn't heavy, chaotic, demanding work. So when she finished cutting back the spruce at Verbena's listing, she went home and moved eight boxwoods for no reason other than she needed to. Then she pruned back a few gangly branches on the white oak that were getting dangerously close to the kitchen window. Finally, she moved a few dogwood shrubs to the side of the house to make room for a new flowerbed.

By noon, she could barely lift her arms.

She let herself collapse in the herb garden, lying straight down between the rows of basil and marjoram. She stretched her arms above her head and fluttered her eyes closed. Beads of sweat trickled across her forehead, down her sides, and over her knees. She needed to stop before she passed out from exhaustion.

But it was the only way to keep herself calm.

Rosemary wasn't just a garden witch. It was her foremost specialty, but she had spent a good portion of her twenties honing her sex magic. She wasn't a sex addict, far from it. She had a reputation to maintain on Star Island, therefore any sex magic she took part in was conducted solely on the mainland and only with reputable warlocks, and on two occasions, a very nice animan from New Hampshire. There was an entire subculture in the witch community surrounding sex magic, and they all shared information: which partners were respectful, powerful, and easy on the eyes didn't hurt. She would never throw herself into a sex spell with any old warlock who raised his hand and volunteered.

But she liked it. She liked deriving power from one of the strongest acts available to humankind. Sex was like stripping the soul raw for another to see, and there was a lot of magic and even more power to be gained in it.

Rosemary hadn't done a sex spell since before Beltane when the big *something* told all the Bays their soulmates were en route. She didn't want to mess up meeting her soulmate by leaving Star Island and spending the weekend between the sheets with some academic warlock to bring about something frivolous like a rainstorm. She'd taken a break.

She was regretting it right now.

Because after seeing Sheriff Asher Evans (a quick text to Laurel and Google search had clued Rosemary in to his name) taking up nearly the entire doorway, Rosemary needed to have sex. And she had a feeling this itch was one only her soulmate could scratch. With what she hoped were adept fingers.

She rubbed her hands over her face and let out a muffled scream. How on earth was she going to introduce a police officer to sex magic? There was no way she was giving it up. Once you harness the power of the full moon through an orgasm, there really was no going back. She wasn't even sure he'd believe she was a witch. Had witches ever been admitted to mental hospitals upon telling their human soulmates what they were? Or worse, had witches ever kept their power secret from their soulmates their entire lives? Rosemary didn't think she could do that. She was an open person. Her sisters might complain she was too open when it came to certain details. She couldn't imagine keeping the biggest part of her life hidden from her soulmate.

She slowly rolled up to sit and took a deep breath. She would do some calming herb magic on herself, take a shower, probably masturbate, and then try to think about something other than Asher Evans for an hour. There were about fifteen books Lavender had suggested she read. Maybe it was going to be an afternoon for studies.

"What the hell happened to the boxwoods?" Sage asked as she walked into the kitchen. Her feet were bare, her boots and socks discarded on the screened porch where they would not offend anyone. She went straight to the sink and started to wash her hands.

"I needed to move them." Rosemary was sitting at the dining table arranging her fresh herbs into a neat line. She would start an incantation for a good night's sleep in a few minutes. The spell she had done over a cup of her Slow Down tea for calmness had taken the edge off the rest of her afternoon, but she would need something stronger if she hoped to sleep tonight.

"Are you freaking out over that cop that came last night? He's not going to suspect anything. Remember, Morana's body and soul are trapped in the Hedge World. No human in their right mind could even conceive what that means." Sage dried her hands and pulled a pitcher of iced tea out of the fridge. "Is this caffeinated?"

"No, and Sage, did no one tell you? That cop, Sheriff Asher Evans, is my soulmate."

"Oh, shit," Sage started, then couldn't contain a chuckle. That chuckle quickly spun out of control, and she had her hands on her knees and was wheezing with laughter. She popped back up and crossed her legs. "I'm going to pee my pants."

"It's not funny." Rosemary was beginning to feel very put out by her sisters' reactions. At least Verbena had the decency not to laugh at her.

"Rosemary, it's hilarious. Fate is obviously pulling your leg. Pot smoking, sex magic practicing, running around naked under the full moon Rosemary's soulmate is a cop? That's like a primordial joke."

"Okay, well I don't find it funny. What if your soulmate is...I don't know, an oil tycoon?"

Sage's face went serious. "That isn't the same thing. You're worried your soulmate is going to be too uptight for your bohemian lifestyle. I would have to take down an oil tycoon out of principal, soulmate or not. I would destroy him, mind, body, and soul."

"Cool it, vigilante. It just isn't what I expected."

"Have you even talked to him? Maybe he's not a strait-laced cop. A lot of cops do plenty of illegal things, though they usually aren't as harmless as consuming some things that grow out of Mother Earth. Maybe he's involved in some shady cover-ups. Or steals drugs out of evidence? Or plants evidence? You can dream." She pulled a glass out of the cupboard and poured herself a hefty serving of iced tea.

"Sage! That's worse! I don't want to be saddled with some asshole cop with no morality. There are just too many things that could go wrong here." Rosemary groaned with frustration. "I want to talk to Mom. Or Grandma. Or Aunt June. One of them must have some advice. Or better yet, I want to talk to Dad. How on earth did he handle being human and surrounded by witches? And how long did Mom wait until she told him? Did she just let the floodgates open all at once, or was it a gentle introduction?" These pangs of missing her parents would never go away, but Rosemary was feeling overwhelmingly homesick for her parents right now.

"I don't know. Maybe ask one of Mom's brothers?" The Bay witches rarely talked to their non-magical relatives. They saw them at Thanksgiving maybe every five years, but the witchy sisters celebrated Yule rather than Christmas and didn't really want to have that conversation with their cousins who didn't know magic existed. Both their mother's non-magical brothers had married non-witches who followed Christianity, and neither of them had seen fit to let their wives or children in on the secret of witchcraft, seeing that it didn't affect their daily lives anymore.

"Maybe." Rosemary's mind had already turned to another idea.

"Nope," Sage cut in. "We're not raising any more of our relatives. I still haven't defiled the grave of Jonas Fortworth after the last set of Bay witches visited us." The sisters had raised a trio of Bay witches from the eighteenth century when they needed some information a few weeks ago. Sage had promised revenge on the warlock who had murdered them and placed a curse on their bloodline, but she had yet to find the time to visit Baltimore and go through with the spell. The curse over the Bays stated that if a warlock or witch collected the blood of all living Bay witches, they would absorb the power as their own. So the sisters also had that sword hanging over their heads.

"And," Sage continued, "I don't want to mess with Mom or Grandma or Great-Aunt June. They deserve some peace before they enter their next life, if they aren't currently chilling in bliss at the moment."

"Mom might not be chilling in bliss." Rosemary raised an eyebrow.

"Rosie, she was hit by a very human drunk driver who is still in prison. I think that's vengeance enough for now."

"Don't you miss her?" Rosemary pushed.

"Shut up, Rosemary, of course I miss her. But playing on my heart strings isn't going to make me agree with you on that. There's got to be another spell that could make you telling the cop about your powers go smoothly. And are you even sure he's human? Laurel couldn't tell that Owen was a sonofawitch right away. Maybe he's a warlock or an animans or even a shifter."

"If he was a warlock, I would have been able to smell it. He's my soulmate. I know I'm not terribly deft with my sense of smell, but as far as I could tell, he was a plain old human." Rosemary had done a little work to hone her sense of smell. She wasn't one of those witches who could smell magic from across a crowded room, but she could smell Sheriff Owens across the parlor. He smelled very good, but he didn't smell like magic.

"Well, you'll figure it out. Mom and Dad did. Now, I have to take a shower. I'll be down for dinner in a bit. Any idea when Lavender is getting home and what she is making?"

"She texted that she'll be back in thirty minutes. And she picked up burgers and fries from the diner. The bakery was crazy today and she didn't want to cook."

"Yum. I could use a burst of greasy calories." Sage pushed her chair away from the table and headed upstairs.

Rosemary leaned back in her chair and sighed. She was stuck.

Her cell phone buzzed in her pocket, and she pulled it out.

"Hey, Therese," Rosemary answered. Her boss at the florist had a habit of calling Rosemary all hours of the day and night, even on her days off.

"Rosemary. We got a second wedding request for the weekend of August eighth. This one is Friday night. I know you have the Marshall-Zimmy wedding on the ninth, but I said yes because the bride was begging," Therese said quickly.

"The bride was begging? That's in less than two months. She didn't think to have her flowers sorted months ago?" Rosemary was the only florist on Star Island that was adept at weddings. Therese could pinch hit if needed, but Rosemary excelled at it, obviously. Nothing like a florist who could ensure happy feelings throughout their big day.

"Apparently, they've only been engaged for a month. Daddy pulled some strings to get the venue. You can do it though, right? I did already say yes," Therese reminded.

"Sure," Rosemary grumbled. She'd be up all night on Friday getting the flowers ready for Saturday afternoon. "But you need to help. All night. The Marshall-Zimmy wedding is huge. I think there are fourteen bridesmaids and five flower girls. You'll have to do the boutonnieres and help with all the centerpieces."

"Fine," Therese answered. "See you tomorrow."

Rosemary hung up and finished bundling her herbs with twine for her bedtime spell, then cleared the table of errant buds and leaves. She tried to shake away her annoyance at Therese. Rosemary knew she carried the business. Therese could run a perfectly nice, small flower shop on her own, but she could never, ever handle the wedding volume that Rosemary did. And with the growing popularity of Star Island as a wedding destination, Rosemary was bringing in most of the cash flow.

"Let it go," she commanded. Her brain would never relax if she started stressing about work.

"Sweetest dreams or dreamless night, I cast this spell with all my might." It was simple, but a little rhyming usually did the trick. Now all that was left was to put the bundle beneath her twin-sized bed and let the magic do its work.

She felt a twinge of sadness. Her soulmate was here, and no matter what that meant, life was changing. She wouldn't be sharing a room with her Sage anymore. She should have been glad of it, but she liked having her close by so she could keep an eye on her. In the winter, that girl needed to be reminded to eat. And shower.

Rosemary felt a little better remembering that Sage's soulmate would be arriving soon. Whoever he was, Rosemary hoped he had a will of steel to keep up with the resident harvest witch. Sage wasn't one to be trifled with.

Rosemary managed to get through dinner without falling asleep at the table but went to bed soon after. She would face tomorrow with a clear head and come up with a plan. After she went to work. It was July after all, and the brides of Star Island were expecting perfect bouquets. A little flower magic went a long way when it came to a wedding.

Chapter Four

"I'm going to do a quick tour of town before I head home for the night," Asher said to Claire, one of the officers. She was currently on desk duty and keeping track of any calls that came in.

"See you tomorrow, Sheriff," she answered blandly, keeping her eyes on her computer screen.

"Call me Evans. Or Asher. Not Sheriff. Makes me feel like I live in the Old West," he joked.

"All right, Evans. Have a good night." Claire still didn't look up.

Asher grimaced. He was still a little while off from creating good relationships with the rest of the department. It was his first job in a true position of authority, and he was pretty sure no one here wanted him to get the job, especially Claire, who had been deemed too young to run the department.

Truthfully, Asher wasn't even sure why he'd taken the job. All he knew was he was a cop, and he wanted to get out of Buffalo.

Asher left his patrol car in the parking lot and turned the corner down Gibbous Avenue. He enjoyed all the celestial names the island used for everything from streets to schools to businesses. His favorite so far was the local preschool aptly named Shooting Stars and Comets. The exterior of the building was done up with a night sky mural.

It was a beautiful evening, warm and clear, and many of the businesses had their doors propped open. The bakery was closed for the evening, the florist as well. Even though Solaris was a small town, the restaurants and bars stayed open past five, at least in the summer months. Asher was curious what it would be like to live here in January, when all the tourism stopped, and the ferry ran every other day rather than twice a day. His colleagues told him that most of the locals hunkered down from November until April unless vacation or obligation took them off the island. The North Atlantic was not a gentle sea in the winter months, so traversing it was no easy feat, especially if sea sickness was a problem. Asher wasn't too worried. Having lived through the 2014 blizzard in Buffalo, he could handle anything thing this island threw at him. He'd get worried if a hurricane managed to wind up this far north, but other than that, he'd be fine.

Asher wandered past the post office and toward the only bar in town, The Muse. He had stopped in last week and introduced himself to the proprietor, but now he wanted to ask about Morana Stoch.

The bar was hopping. There were still a couple hours until the evening ferry left, and a lot of the day trippers were getting one more drink in before going back to their lives. Asher caught the eye of Luke, bartender and owner, and waved hello. He grabbed a stool at the end of the bar and let his gaze sweep over the patrons.

The picture Ivan had sent of Morana was definitely helpful. The woman had hair like ice and looked like she never cracked a smile. She'd be easy to spot in a room full of boisterous vacationers. Hell, she'd be easy to spot in the middle of Times Square.

After a few minutes of looking, Asher resigned himself to the fact that Morana wasn't here. He was beginning to wonder if she had ever come to Star Island in the first place. Maybe she just picked a place on a map to tell her brother and disappeared into a new life. It wouldn't be the first time a person escaped from their family by simply vanishing. And with a brother like Ivan, who could blame her? Asher made a mental note to look for any domestic disturbances on either of their records.

"Can I get you something?" Luke asked, setting a napkin down on the bar in front of Asher.

"Still on duty. I have a question for you." Asher rummaged through his pocket and pulled out the picture of Morana. "Has she stopped in? In the last week or so?"

Luke took the picture and brought it close to his face, taking a good look.

"Oh, yeah, I remember her. Very odd person." He slid the picture back to Asher.

"When did she come in?" Asher pulled out of his pocket a small notebook he always carried and a pen.

"Three days ago, maybe? She came in early, like right when we open at ten. And she ordered four straight gins, no food. I don't think I've ever had anyone order that before. No ice or anything." Luke shuddered. "But she took them down no problem, used the bathroom, and left."

"Did she mention anything to you? Where she was staying, if she was visiting anyone?"

"Nope. Just drank her drinks and was out the door. No tip, no conversation, no thank you. As I said, she was odd."

"And you only saw her the one time?"

"Yeah, she never came back. I would try Lavender at the Immortal Cupcake. It's the only place you can get a to go coffee to go on the island, so a lot of the visitors hit her up in the morning. You want a Coke or a bite to eat?"

"I should be on my way, need to ask around a little more before I head home for the night."

"See you around." Luke shifted to the woman next to Asher, who looked like she was about to climb over the bar to get another drink.

"Thanks, Luke."

Asher headed to the small grocery store and did both his shopping for dinner and asked the cashiers on duty if anyone remembered Morana. One said she might have seen her but didn't ring her up or talk to her. So pretty much a dead end. But Asher walked out with a rotisserie chicken, some potato salad, and a six-pack of Miller Lite. He'd visit the other businesses tomorrow.

Asher's apartment was temporary, but well located in the center of town. It was a small one bedroom with a tiny kitchen, a shower he could barely fit under, and a bedroom that didn't have room for anything other than a bed and dresser. The plan was to buy a house, with a bit of land, once he figured out where on the island he should live. He wanted something he could really live in long term. His last home had also been a transient sort of apartment. He wanted to put roots down somewhere, and Star Island seemed a nice enough place. He was getting too old to keep living in short-term housing.

Asher sat on the couch, his food in front of him on the coffee table. There was no kitchen table or even seating at a counter here. But he dug into a warm meal, even if it wasn't home cooked. The deli at the market was surprisingly good for such a small place.

Just as he was licking his fingers clean after eating the last chicken leg, his phone buzzed on the table next to him. He quickly wiped the excess grease onto his napkin and answered.

"Hey, Natalie. How are you?"

"I should be asking you that! My baby brother moves to an island smack dab in the middle of the Atlantic Ocean and suddenly it's like he doesn't know how a phone works."

"First of all, it's a coastal island. Second, still older than you. Third, you should really come to visit. I moved to a vacation spot." Natalie always referred to Asher as her baby brother, even though he was technically seven months older than her, and a grade ahead in school. Their parents had adopted Natalie as a baby, but Asher didn't join the family until he was almost three. They had been preparing Natalie for a new baby, but when the social worker mentioned Asher, they felt like he would make their family complete. But ever since, Natalie had called Asher the baby.

"I will, I will. I'll be able to get some time off in September. Then expect to have me for at least a week while I take in the sea air like some sort of eighteenth-century heroine. I'll come home with better skin and a journal full of sexually confusing poetry."

Asher chuckled. His sister had a flare for the dramatic and honestly, he had missed it. Until a few weeks ago, they'd lived in the same neighborhood in Buffalo and saw each other at least once a week.

"So how is it? Do you like the island? What about the people you work with? Is everyone being nice to you? Do you have someone to sit next to at lunch?" She pummeled him with questions.

"It's good. I do like it here. It's nice and quiet and a good change of pace for me. The people I work with have given off good first impressions, but I will save judgment until I have known them longer. Everyone is nice to me, and I tend to eat lunch alone, but then again, everyone does." Asher always found it best to answer Natalie's questions in chronological order so he didn't forget any of them. "How's Sophie? Does she miss her favorite brother-in-law?"

"You are her only brother-in-law, and she's surviving. We'll see if she can swing getting work off in September and come with me." Natalie's wife, Sophie, was a high school teacher. While she had mountains of sick days saved up, taking time off in September was nearly impossible for teachers.

"Are you guys going to make me an uncle soon?"

"Asher! That is very prying. And I should be asking you the same question, since you are technically seven months older. Tick tock, buddy, that biological clock is ticking away. Before you know, you'll be an old maid with bad knees and no one will want your crotchety self and dried up testicles."

"I'm thirty-four, Nat. I could have children for the next thirty years. At least. I also don't have a willing partner."

"True, I have you beat in the spouse department." Natalie and Sophie had been married for just over two years but had been together close to seven.

"I miss you," Natalie said quickly. "I understand why you left, but you know I miss you. And if you come back, you can live in our basement for six to eighteen months depending on how often you do the dishes."

"I miss you, too. But..." He let his voice drift off.

"But?" she prompted.

"I think I'm here for the long run. Or as long as they'll have me. I can't... I can't be a cop in Buffalo anymore, and I don't know if I can be anything other than a cop."

"You're a good cop. Asher the protector. But it's not your whole identity." Natalie cleared her throat. "Star Island is lucky to have you. You'll take good care of those islanders."

"They refer to themselves as 'Celestials,'" Asher interjected.

"Oh, for Christ's sake, I was trying to be nice. These people sound ridiculous."

"Jury's still out, but I'll let you know what I decide."

"Is there even a place to get wings? Or pizza?"

"Eh, the wings are the grocery store variety. But pizza, yes. I'm still in the United States."

"You're not in the contiguous forty-eight, so I don't know what to expect."

"This is why you have to come visit. I'll get you loving the Celestials in no time."

Natalie took a deep breath. "You up for a serious conversation?"

"Is everything okay?" Asher sat straight up, his mind immediately going to how quickly he could get to Buffalo.

"Yes, fine. Here's the thing. Mom gave me something for you and I'm not sure if you want it."

"What is it?" Asher's mom lived in Buffalo, too. It wasn't like they weren't in contact.

"It's a letter from your biological father."

Asher felt like he'd been kicked in the chest. His biological father was exactly that, and nothing more. A man who had given up a three-year-old and never looked back. No contact, no birthday cards, no hint of concern over whether Asher had landed in a family as good as the one he did. Asher hadn't thought about him in years.

"I could mail it, or scan it, or—"

"I don't want it right now," Asher answered. "Can you hold onto it?"

"Of course. If you change your mind, let me know."

"I will." Asher exhaled.

A few beats of silence passed as he tried to keep his mind off the letter and fifty percent of his DNA. Why was a letter coming now? The man had died a while ago, at least according to his parents. And it wasn't like Asher just turned eighteen and finally could receive contact no matter what.

"I bought a snake plant."

"You did what?"

"I bought a snake plant," Natalie repeated. "I am going to become a houseplant person. Sophie has low hopes. I think one year from now our townhouse will look like a jungle."

Asher chuckled. Just like that Natalie had him focusing on her inability to keep plants alive.

They talked for a little while longer, swapping stories of childhood back and forth until they were both exhausted with laughter. There was something about talking to Natalie that made Asher feel lighter. She was his annoying, prying, talkative younger sister, but she was his best friend.

"Verbena Bay." The woman answered the phone with a friendly sort of authority that put Asher's mind immediately at ease.

"Good morning, Ms. Bay. I'm interested in purchasing a house on Star Island and my colleagues insist you are the best realtor here." Asher fiddled with a pencil between his fingers. He'd had the job for less than three weeks, but he had a feeling. He wanted to make Star Island his permanent home, and that would include getting out of his short-term rental as soon as possible.

"That's what my website says! So, first, what's your name?"

"Asher Evans. I'm the new sheriff."

"Ah yes, you've met a few of my sisters." He heard some clicking in the background, like she was working on a computer. "What type of property are you looking for? Bedrooms, bathrooms, any particular amenities that are important to you? Is there a certain area you are specifically looking in?"

"Oh." Asher took a beat. He hadn't thought too much about anything other than wanting a house. In Buffalo, he'd lived in a mid-rise building with a gym, but that wasn't what he was looking for anymore. "Probably three bedrooms. Bathrooms are less important to me. One or two is fine. I want to have some space between me and the neighbors, I've been thinking about getting a dog or two, so space for them to run around would be good."

"Mmhmm." Now he could hear furious typing in the background.

"I haven't given much thought to where exactly I want to live. Right now I'm renting an apartment in one of the old, converted buildings in Solaris. I don't want to be in town though. The further out the better. And I don't care if I'm close to the coast or not. As far as I'm concerned, this entire island is by the beach."

Verbena laughed. "Isn't that the truth? Do you need a garage?"

"You tell me. How bad is the snow here? Keep in mind, I'm coming from Buffalo."

"Not as bad as Buffalo, that's for certain. But we have gotten some nor'easters that sit over the island some years. With a job like yours, one where you can't take a snow day, I'd recommend a garage and a place very close to one of the main roads. Steve, our only snowplow driver, does his best, but after major storms there are only about five streets that he can give good attention to. Some of those littler offshoots don't see a plow for days."

"Thank you for the advice."

"All right! I don't know if anyone mentioned this to you, but for permanent housing, not just a summer place, it can take a few months for me to find something perfect. I'll give a couple places a look-over the next few days that have been on the market for a while. There are a few families who have let me know they are considering moving but aren't on the market yet. I think we might have better luck with one of those places. Do you need to get in somewhere immediately?"

"No, my temporary housing is fine for now. I would like to settle down before Christmas though."

"Definitely. That shouldn't be a problem. Well, I'll be in touch! Give me a call if you think of anything else you would like to add to the list."

"I will. Nice talking to you."

Asher felt good. He'd taken another step towards his new home. Star Island was going to be good for him.

His mind flickered back to Rosemary Bay for a moment. He wondered if she was working at the florist today. He glanced at his watch. It was nearly lunch, after all. He was due a little time to stretch his legs.

There was something about her. It might not be a bad idea for Asher to lay some groundwork for a few dates and maybe a fling. She was really hot, after all. Like burning him up from the inside out. Wouldn't hurt to figure out if she could be interested, too.

Chapter Five

"Have you finished the centerpieces yet?" Therese called from the front desk.

Rosemary was up to her elbows in calla lilies, parsley, sage, rosemary, and thyme. They had a wedding the next day and the bride, Nell, was extremely superstitious. According to her, the centerpieces *and* bouquets needed to symbolize the perfect, happy marriage, with no room for error. Rosemary was used to brides who wanted to design their bouquet down to the very last herb, but parsley in a centerpiece was a little daunting.

"I have three left," Rosemary answered. "Should be done in about thirty minutes." It wasn't a big wedding, Rosemary only had twelve centerpieces to complete, but they were huge. The sheer amount of thyme going into each of these pieces had Rosemary hoping that no one had allergies.

The wedding was tomorrow morning, but Rosemary would finish everything tonight. Once the centerpieces were complete, she would move onto the bouquets, and Therese was delivering it all. Thankfully, the bridesmaids were only carrying three calla lilies tied together with twine, so she'd be done with those in a jiffy.

"You can head back there."

Rosemary pricked up her ears. Therese was talking to a customer, and from the sound of it, she was sending them back to the work room. She really hoped it wasn't Nell. She hated when brides came in to see the centerpieces in the back room. It usually led to them wanting to change something. No centerpiece looks amazing with the backdrop of a greenhouse surrounded by cuttings; they stand out in the wedding venue.

Rosemary quickly organized the pile of parsley in front of her to look less haphazardly thrown down and wiped her hands on her apron.

"Good afternoon."

Rosemary inhaled sharply and kept her mouth shut by sheer force of will. Sheriff Asher Evans was standing in the doorway of her work room. He had his hands on his hips and a friendly smile on his lips.

That man could fill up her doorway any day of the week.

She set both her hands on the table in front of her, giving her a bit of grounding. She would not attack this man at her place of work. She would not.

There was a good chance she would not.

She would *probably* not.

Today.

"Good afternoon, sir," she finally managed to spit out after what felt like ten minutes of silence. Sir? She called him sir? "How can I help you?" Her voice wavered like a teenage boy getting his new pipes.

"Please call me Asher. You're Rosemary, right? Rosemary Bay?"

"That's me." Her heart skittered. Was this an interrogation? Most likely. She shook her hands out and hoped it didn't look suspicious. Lots of people were anxious around cops, not just witches who were accessories to missing persons and using every bit of personal power to keep their clothes on.

Maybe he would take her back to the station. Put her in an interview room. Handcuff her to the table. Let her sweat it out for a while before coming back, shirtsleeves rolled up to expose his forearms—

"Sorry to drop in on your place of work unannounced. I wanted—"

"To ask me about Morana Stoch? That's her name, right? Sorry I ran out of the house the other night. I was in a weird mood. I get in weird moods sometimes. I'm a weirdo. But I don't know her, never seen her before, never met her. Wouldn't even know what she looks like. Have you had any luck tracking her down?" Oh, goddess, she was rambling. She turned back to the parsley, hoping that giving her hands something to do might stop her mouth from pouring words out of it.

"No, we haven't found her. Actually, I've had no indication that your family ever met the woman. And people around here speak very highly of all five of you. Jane at the office told me none of you could be involved." He smiled warmly and set his hands on her worktable. Damn, her soulmate was handsome when he smiled. She could get used to that face.

He was so relaxed. How was he so relaxed? Rosemary felt like she was about to jump out of her skin.

"Well, that's nice to hear. We haven't lived here forever, but it seems like thirteen years is long enough to make people see us as locals." She paused, stilling her hands. "If you aren't here to ask me about Morana, is there something else?"

He licked his lips, and she swore a slight blush rose to his cheeks, though it was mostly obscured by his neat beard. By Aphrodite, Frigg, Áine, Ishtar, Astarte, and any other goddesses that threw their hat in the lust ring, this man was gorgeous.

She was doomed.

"I've been trying to introduce myself to everyone on the island. Well, the year-rounders."

"Celestials," she interrupted.

"Yes, the Celestials. I didn't think our brief introduction the other night counted."

"I guess not." She giggled. He didn't seem too put off by her basically running away from him. "Nice to officially meet you, Asher."

"You too, Rosemary." He stuck his hand out across the table to shake hers. She glanced at it for a moment. She was terrified to touch him. She was at work, and it might open the floodgates, and after that, there would be no hiding anything from this man. Also, Therese would probably fire her if she caught Rosemary making out with a cop in the store. There had been an incident with a warlock swinging by a year ago that led to a very stern warning.

She took his hand though. It would need to happen eventually, why not now?

The moment their palms touched, Rosemary felt a reassuring buzz between them.

"Sorry," he said, jumping back from her. "I think I shocked you. In

June. That's odd." He glanced around the room, as if looking for some stray electrically charged shag carpet wafting in the breeze.

"Don't worry about it. Um, I have a bride that needs these centerpieces done, as well as four bouquets by tomorrow morning. I need to get back to work."

"Oh, of course. Good to officially meet you. I'll see you around," he said, and something about the cadence of his voice made Rosemary believe he really meant it.

"Bye, Asher."

"Goodbye."

She leaned to the right so she could watch Asher until he exited the shop. He gave Therese a short wave before disappearing through the door.

She couldn't wait to strip him out of those clothes and throw him on the floor and...

"Stop it," she chided herself. She knew better than to allow her mind to turn to deliciously lustful thoughts while working on wedding centerpieces. There could be unfortunate side effects of that, and they usually involved people having sex in the bathrooms at the wineries on the island.

"What are you doing?"

Rosemary popped her head up to get a view of the front door over the coffee table. Laurel was in the threshold, alone.

"Sit-ups."

"Rosemary," Laurel said as she shut the door and walked into the parlor. "Why on earth are you doing sit-ups? I've known you your entire life, and I have never once seen you do a sit-up."

"I have a little excess energy I need to work off, that's all. I thought a few sit-ups might be in order." Rosemary struggled to curl her abdomen up and touch her knees.

"I'm pretty sure that isn't how you are supposed to do sit-ups anymore. And you look like you are going to hurt your back. Why don't you try some yoga instead? I could go through a few sun salutations with you if you want."

"Actually, that sounds better." She climbed up to the couch and snuggled against a pile of pillows. "Sit-ups are not for me. I officially vow never to do a sit-up again. Why are you here?"

"I need more clothes. And my crystals. And tampons."

"The things a male soulmate does not have at his disposal in a rental cabin."

"Very true. We're in this weird place right now. I know we're destined to be together and we're totally in love and all that, but we're still, like, newly dating? I don't have most of my clothes at his house, and it isn't even his house. There's just a lot up in the air. We need a place that is ours, not mine or his. Something we can grow in together."

"How long does he have the rental for?" Rosemary asked.

"He only had it for two weeks, but the owner let him extend until mid-July. She already had a renter lined up for the rest of July. So we need a plan."

"A plan," Rosemary echoed. "Hey, will Nyx be moving when you do?" Laurel's familiar, a great horned owl with a penchant for terrorizing her own familiar, Verruca—who happened to be a toad—tended to stay close to her witch.

"Probably? It's up to her. She can still live in the woods here if she wants to. I'm not going to force her to come with us."

"Please take her. I am so sick of soothing Verruca after a particularly trying night being chased by your owl. I have better things to do with my time."

Laurel scowled, then stopped and raised an eyebrow. "Speaking of which, why on earth aren't you with Asher at this exact moment, screwing his brains out for four straight days? Wasn't that your plan? You said as much. Nothing but sex until you needed sunlight or got a urinary tract infection?"

"It's complicated," Rosemary answered curtly.

"Soulmates tend to be. Are you afraid?"

"Stop it, Laurel."

"I'm not asking to be mean or tease you. It's really fucking scary, the idea of a soulmate. Sure, it's great when you're thirteen and you know that someday your knight in shining armor is going to gallop into your life on the back of a steed the color of a raven, but it's not the same thing as actually meeting him or her. That's the scary part, looking at this person and knowing they are *your* person. Forever. It's crazy daunting. Like the most dangerous trust fall of your life."

"A steed the color of a raven?" Rosemary smiled.

"Oh, Rosie. You know I could never be soulmates with someone who would choose a white horse over a black one." Laurel smiled. "You'll figure it out. He will, too."

"I think he's a regular human," she admitted. That was the scariest part of it all; Rosemary couldn't imagine introducing someone into this world, but it was looking like she had to.

"Dad was human. Grandpa was human," Laurel reminded her. "Lots of humans end up with witches and do just fine. If it didn't work, you'd never have one as a soulmate."

Rosemary nodded but couldn't do a thing to quell the anxiety rising from her chest to her throat. "What if...what if he doesn't understand me?"

It was her worst fear breathed to life. Rosemary didn't have a lot of friends. She was friendly to every person she met, but very few people could handle her, even without the magic. She knew she was a lot. She was blunt and overly honest and said the wrong thing a lot and tended to tell people things about their sex life they didn't want spoken aloud. What if Asher was another in a long line of people that didn't get her?

"He will. But if, somehow, he doesn't, then I hope he will spend the rest of his life trying to."

"I guess."

"Now." Laurel clapped her hands together. "I really need a tampon. Good talk."

Rosemary's fears had quelled slightly since talking to Laurel, but not completely. She hated this limbo they were stuck in; she wanted him, physically if not anything else. And he had to feel the same way. She didn't think she could do this getting-to-know-each-other dance much longer.

She needed to put on her big girl panties—which coincidentally were bright purple, lace, and only covered about fifty percent of her cheeks—and face her soulmate head on. But she wanted a little certainty.

Long after Sage had started her steady snoring, Rosemary crept up the attic stairs. They were in one of the closets in their bedroom and very easy to hide from prying eyes. The attic was where the Bay sisters kept everything witchy. An entire library of books pertaining to the craft, space for spell work, instruments that weren't easily disguised as kitchen utensils, and cozy corners to snuggle down in made up the top floor of their house. They'd inherited many of their books from Great-Aunt June, but a handful had been their mom's, and Lavender and Rosemary did have a book of their tea recipes and the spell work that went along with the brews. Someday they'd make copies to give to other witches.

Rosemary walked straight to the bookcases. They were overstuffed, unorganized, and in desperate need of someone to put them in a workable order. But none of the Bay sisters had inherited the librarian gene, so they remained a mess.

She pulled a few of her favorites down and set them on the large oak table, itching to work a little magic tonight.

Rosemary loved spell work. She didn't have crazy innate abilities. There were garden witches on the Black Hat Haberdashery who could sink their fingers into the earth and draw tulips out of their bulbs a month early. For Rosemary, plants responded well to her touch, but she could turn a simple sprig of marjoram into a love spell with a few whispered words beneath a full moon, or a noon sun, or a total eclipse. She could hum over a bridal bouquet and all the bride's anxiety would dissipate into the ether. She loved yelling wishes into the darkness and reaping the benefits. Spell work was her favorite part of the craft.

She wasn't sure exactly what she was looking for tonight. But she would know when she saw it. Rosemary opened *He Loves Me, He Loves Me Not* and slowly flipped through the pages. She had done several spells from this book before, all with good results. She trusted the author, a witch named Catherine Beller from the early 1900s.

"Love spell, lust spell, Banishment, to harden a heart," Rosemary muttered as she turned the pages. Most of these spells had to do with matters of the heart, and while she wasn't looking to cast a love spell on Asher, anything to do with one's soulmate involved the heart, whether or not the witch intended it to.

"Trust." She flipped back to the previous page to scour it more carefully.

"To gain the trust of your lover." Rosemary played it over in her mind. It would be very helpful if Asher immediately trusted her. She could tell him about Morana without fear, let him know about her identity as a witch... explain they were soulmates. It would be wonderful to skip all the disbelief that would come with inviting a regular human into their world.

She glanced over the title again. They weren't technically lovers yet, but they probably had been in a previous life, so it might still count. She looked back down to see how difficult the spell was.

"Let's see. 'Under cover of night, go to your lover's bed.' That might be difficult, I don't even know where he lives," she muttered. "'Sing these words to the stars, then take your lover into your mouth, and ingest his seed.' Oh my goddess, Ms. Beller! You, saucy minx! Good for you." She giggled. "Get it, girl." Rosemary had been supremely unaware of blow job spells committed to writing before the 1950s.

She scanned down the page and found a quick incantation that needed to be recited before the act took place.

"'Within the hour, your love will trust you with all his heart, and doubt you no more.'" Rosemary mulled it over in her head. She had never done a sex spell where both parties were not aware of the spell. She had no idea whether or not it was immoral to do a sex spell without the consent of a partner. She had done spells on her sisters, and even her parents when she was a teenager, without them knowing about it. A month earlier she had done a very small spell on Lavender to get her to take a day off and relax. But this felt different.

"If it's done out of love and necessity," she mumbled. Would Asher really mind if she did a quick spell while giving him head? He'd probably just be happy about the head. And he would trust her, so she could explain everything an hour later. And then they could also move on past this awkward beginning and start really soul-mating together. Which hopefully involved a lot of naked time.

She was going to do it.

Chapter Six

"Did she by any chance mention where she was staying?" Asher asked. The man who worked the counter at the post office recognized Morana from stopping in to mail a letter earlier in the week, and Asher was praying that he finally had a solid lead.

"Sorry, no. She didn't buy stamps or anything, just popped the letter in the mailbox and asked the time. Weird person."

"How do you mean?"

"I don't know, she looked like she was trying to bore a hole into my skull with her eyes. Wouldn't be surprised if she was on...what's it called? From that TV show in Arizona? Meth."

"New Mexico," Asher corrected.

"Whatever. Desert, US."

Drugs. That was an interesting observation, especially since Asher had gotten the same feeling from her brother when talking on the phone to him.

"Thanks. I don't suppose there's any way to track the letter she sent?"

"No, it went out days ago. And even if there was, I can't do that without a warrant, Sheriff."

"Of course. Thanks for your time."

Asher walked out of the post office into the bright sunlight and rubbed the bridge of his nose. He was not looking forward to talking to Ivan Stoch again. He had no new information. He knew Morana was on Star Island for at least two days during the previous week. The ferry driver didn't recognize her at all, so she may have come and left again, with Asher none the wiser. With her striking appearance, Asher could only imagine she had come during peak times, and maybe left during them as well. He seriously hoped the next time he contacted Ivan, the brother had spoken to his sister, who had moved on to a different county.

"Asher!"

He looked up, surprised to hear his first name being called. So far, everyone on the island still referred to him as sheriff or officer, or at best, Evans. It would take time to gain the confidence and friendship of many of the islanders. Eh, Celestials.

Rosemary Bay smiled in his direction. She walked towards him, like a beacon of light in a yellow sundress and sandals. She was holding a huge potted hydrangea that on second glance, looked very heavy. He hurried in her direction and took the plant from her hands.

"Thanks, I did need a break." She laughed, pushing a few stray hairs out of her face and tucking them back. "I'm delivering it to Mrs. Rankel at the preschool, and it's not quite far enough away to drive, but whew, that was heavy." She reached her hand to his bicep and gave it a quick squeeze before letting her hand drop. Asher steadied his breath. "But I'm glad I caught you."

"You are?" Asher looked down at this beautiful woman and took in the sight of her. She had her hickory-colored hair piled high in a bun at the top of her head, bobby pins sticking out haphazardly in every direction. He'd never been this close to her before and noticed a spray of freckles across her tanned nose. Her sister Laurel hadn't had freckles, or skin that appeared to have seen the sun in the last three years. Rosemary looked like she bathed in the warm sunlight every chance she got.

And her scent—this woman smelled like the first day of spring. All flowers and grass and anticipation.

"Yes. I was hoping I might be able to swing by your office tonight, so we could talk." Her mouth twisted up in the corner, as if she was holding in a secret.

Asher snapped to attention. "Talk? About what?"

"I'd rather wait until we aren't out in the open, if that's all right. Won't take long." She flashed him a quick smile. "I promise it's nothing dire."

"What time?"

"I have a few things to finish up after hours in the shop tonight, is nine o'clock too late?"

"No, I'll make sure to be there." He would rearrange the entire police department's schedule if needed. He would not miss meeting with Rosemary.

"Perfect." She took the hydrangea back from him. Her fingertips brushed his knuckles as she shifted the weight of the pot back to her own body, and it was like she reached into his chest and grabbed his heart.

This woman was having a surprising effect on him.

"See you tonight."

"Looking forward to it, Asher."

She turned around and walked back from where she had come. Asher was stuck in his spot, trying not to ogle her backside as it swished her skirts back and forth. He failed miserably.

Running into Rosemary Bay was the highlight of Asher's day. While she would be a bright spot even on a perfect day, the rest of his morning and afternoon were less than ideal.

No one in town had any new leads on Morana. He had contacted several of the rental companies to see if anyone matching her name or description had secured lodging but with no luck. The singular campground on the quieter Vega Peninsula was free and had no official form for keeping track of campers, and no one currently camping there had been on site for more than a week. So it was possible she had been camping, but there was no one to corroborate that idea. Normally, Asher would have assumed Morana only came for a day, but he had conflicting information from people who had seen her. It seemed she was on Star Island for at least three days.

"Oh good," Jane said the moment Asher walked back into the police department. "You're back."

He'd spent the last few hours following dead ends and was hoping to get a bit of office work done, but by the look on Jane's face, that wasn't going to happen.

"Claire called in. She's working the Plumrose wine festival. There are a couple of unruly ladies she's dealing with and could use a hand with regular crowd control, just until it winds down at five. Mark is on a call, so I could send him once he's finished up,"

"No, I'll go." Asher ducked into his office to grab his patrol keys. His cell phone buzzed in his pocket. He was surprised he had a series of missed texts.

> Wil: Asher! How's life in the Atlantic?

> Brett: Hey, cowboy, how's being a sheriff?

> Toni: Evans—We miss you on the beat. Hope your new station is treating you well.

Asher shoved his phone back into his pocket. He hadn't been keeping in touch with his friends from Buffalo, but now wasn't the time to answer. He found his keys and headed out to the center of the island.

Asher pulled up to the winery expecting a couple dozen people needing directing to their cars. Instead, he found close to three hundred people jammed around a barn that looked like it accommodated fifty.

"Shit," Asher mumbled. He could feel his panic rising, swirling hot and cold through his chest. "Not now."

He sat frozen in his seat, hands on the wheel. He tried to focus on the tools his therapist drilled into his head so many months ago, but when the anxiety took over, it was like finding a key in the middle of a swamp. He couldn't see, and everything felt dank and rotten.

"Pick one thing," he whispered.

Touch. He could feel the steering wheel beneath his hands. The air conditioning blew cool air in his direction, ruffling his hair. Bead of sweat rolled down his neck.

Smell. There was a hint of grass in the air. A bit of mint, too, from the gum he'd stashed in the console.

Sound. The din of chatter from the guests was the only thing Asher could hear. But it wasn't panicked or stressed. It was pleasant. People enjoying their afternoon.

Asher risked opening his eyes. The crowd was still there, but it didn't feel as overwhelming. On closer inspection, Plumrose looked well equipped to handle a crowd this size. Asher noticed Claire talking to a group of women, all with their hands on their hips and severe haircuts. Oof. He was glad Claire was dealing with them. He donned his dorky reflective vest and headed out to do some crowd control and parking maintenance.

By six o'clock, Asher was back in his office. The wine festival hadn't been as bad as he thought it could be—he was basically a glorified security guard—but that is what he had signed up for. Asher came to Star Island to get away from the horrific crime he'd dealt with in Buffalo. Even though there still was the case of Morana Stoch niggling in his brain.

He finished his paperwork for the day and begrudgingly opened his email to contact Ivan.

Mr. Stoch-

Still no luck on finding new information on Morana. She was definitely here at some point, but I have no proof whether or not she simply left the island of her own accord. Did she mention if she was camping? No one at the campsite recognizes her, but there's no sign-in sheet, unlike rentals that have strict policies when it comes to visitors. I did have confirmation that she sent a letter while here, so please check your mail to see if she reached out to you and let you know if she was moving on.

I hope you've heard from Morana and that she has only continued on her vacation. I will of course still be looking for more information about her, but I am beginning to suspect she has moved on.

Thanks – Sheriff. Evans

Asher exhaled audibly. He wasn't giving up on Morana; he could never do that to any missing person. But it was truly odd. In such a close community, she didn't speak to anyone, had no lodgings, didn't meet with the person she told her brother she was going to, and that young woman claimed to have never met her. Maybe he needed to look further into Laurel Bay. He didn't think she had anything to do with it, but he might be letting his interest in Rosemary cloud his judgement on her sister. He truly hoped his morals wouldn't allow that, but taking a step back might be a good idea. Just a small step.

"Evans?" Jane's voice came over the intercom on his phone.

"Yes, Jane?"

"You have a call. I think it's the jerk from Montana." She sounded exasperated. "And he's upset."

"Thanks, Jane." Asher took a deep breath before picking up the phone.

"Sheriff Evans," he answered.

"How dare you give up on my sister?" Ivan spat.

"Ivan, I said I wasn't giving up on her. I am simply beginning to wonder whether your sister just kept her plans from you, unintentionally. A lot of young women don't feel the need to keep their brother up to date on their travel plans." Internally, he couldn't help but add she might be trying to escape you.

"She told me everything. She was on Star Island. She never would have left without seeing Laurel Bay. You need to look into that family. They did something to her, I just know it. She never goes this long without contacting one of us. Especially after visiting the Bays. If they did something to her..."

"They? I thought you said Morana was only visiting Laurel Bay. What do you mean by they?" Asher pulled out his notebook. This guy was all over the place, but maybe in some of the mess he might say something useful.

"The sisters. I know she's got a bunch of sisters, a weird group. Don't tell me you are so green in this position you don't know Laurel Bay has sisters. Should I be talking to someone else?"

"Yes, I know the Bay family, but I am surprised you do. Were you in contact with any other members of the Bay family? Have you spoken to any of them personally?"

"What? No. Stop turning this on me, you're the one who can't do your job." Asher could hear his sneer over the phone.

"I'm sorry to disappoint you," Asher said calmly. "I will continue my inquiries at a laxer pace, though know I will not give up the case. I truly do hope either you or I find your sister."

"Sure," Ivan answered before disconnecting the call.

Asher set his phone on the receiver and rubbed his temples. Now this man was accusing the entire Bay family? Who he had never met? Asher couldn't help but think Ivan was throwing out a huge net, praying he caught something, which was not how Asher did police work.

He glanced at the clock: seven-fifteen. He might as well take dinner now so he would be back with plenty of time to meet with Rosemary at nine.

At eight forty five, the office was all but empty. Charlie was covering the phones, Claire and Sam were patrolling, but Jane and the rest of the support staff had gone home for the evening. Not many people wandered into the Star Island police department for help after five-thirty. If someone needed them, they usually called, and tonight Charlie would send an officer to them. Asher would be in the office until his meeting with Rosemary was over, but then he would join Sam and Claire in patrolling until midnight when Mark came to relieve him.

He was still getting used to the constantly changing hours that came with this small station. His first two years on the force in Buffalo, Asher had third shift and was basically cut off from all normal human communication. But he did get to know all the people that worked the middle-of-the-night shift at Dunkin' Donuts really well, as well as everyone who opened a bodega at five in the morning. Switching back and forth was hell on his sleep schedule, but nights here were pretty quiet. So far, he'd only had one after midnight call, and most nights he patrolled to make sure no one was stumbling home drunk on a major roadway. Twice, he gently suggested both bachelor and bachelorette parties made their way home to their lodgings rather than bother the locals with their late night singing.

Asher tidied his desk, putting away all the notes he had taken on Morana Stoch's disappearance. His gut told him the Bay sisters were good people, but he couldn't risk letting any information out into the general public, especially the sister of his only lead.

"Yeah, he's in his office, you can head back there," Asher heard Charlie say. He couldn't stifle a grin from taking over his face. Seeing Rosemary Bay before going out on patrol was going to brighten his mood and probably give him a lot to think about while staring into the darkness waiting for a car to speed by or a call to come in.

God, that woman was gorgeous. And sexy. And had the best smile he'd ever seen.

"Asher?" Her voice was soft and low, like the best kind of secret and one he wanted to keep for himself.

"Come in," he answered, leaning against his desk.

His door slowly pushed open, until Rosemary stood in front of him. She leaned against the door until it clicked shut.

She looked amazing.

She'd changed out of the yellow sundress from earlier and now wore something black, low-cut, and very tight. He knew there were probably specific words to describe the way the fabric pulled over her breasts, waist, and thighs, but his mind was blank. All he could think was "HOT."

"Hi." Her voice was like honey, smooth and sweet and dripping.

He blinked hard, trying to focus.

"Rosemary. What can I do for you?"

Chapter Seven

Rosemary was ready. She had on her sexiest dress, no bra, black lace panties, and her best come-hither look. She looked irresistible, and that was the point.

She was ready to seduce her soulmate and do a teeny, tiny, barely noticeable spell to ensure he trusted her.

With a blow job.

"What can I do for you?" Asher asked. His voice was smooth like a steady stream in summer.

She could think of a million things he could do for her, but they all involved the two of them going back to his place, no clothes, and twenty-four to forty-eight hours alone.

He looked amazing.

He was in civilian clothes, black pants and a dark green button down with the sleeves rolled up to his elbows. His hair was brushed away from his face. He kept it longer than most cops, Rosemary noticed, and she was glad he did. Those waves didn't deserve to be cropped short. The light stubble he usually sported was a little darker tonight, and she liked it.

This was going to be the easiest spell Rosemary had ever done.

"How are you liking Star Island?" she began. While Rosemary was ready to throw her dress off and get down to spell-casting business, Asher might need more of a warm up.

"It's very beautiful here. Hard to complain, living on an island in the Atlantic during the summer."

"You can reserve judgment once we get a nor'easter and the ferry doesn't run for two weeks."

Asher's mouth ticked up in an amused grin. "I don't think you came here to talk about the weather patterns of Star Island," he began. "Is there something I can help you with? Police related or otherwise?"

There. That was her in. She knew he wanted her—first of all, she was hot as hell. But he was her soulmate, so the attraction was there. But she couldn't very well tell him right this second that she was a witch and knew they should be together. That was what this spell was for.

"Actually," she said while discreetly locking the door behind her with a satisfying click, "It's more like what we can do for each other." She took a couple steps towards him. "I'm...attracted to you."

"You are?" Asher cocked an eyebrow at her.

"Yes. Very. Since the first time I saw you. That's why I ran out of the room. It was definitely a strong, instant attraction." She paused, trying to read his face. He looked...intrigued? Not necessarily overcome with lust, but he didn't look like he was going to shoot her down.

Nothing she said was technically a lie. She was extremely attracted to him and did run out of the room. She just left out the whole part about them being soulmates and her being a witch.

"Tell me I didn't just embarrass myself and that you feel something too." Rosemary's confession hung heavy in the air as seconds, hours, days, and eons ticked by. It felt like an eternity until either of them breathed.

"I do," he finally answered, his voice confident. His expression changed in that breath. Asher wasn't looking at her passively or inquisitively.

He was looking at her like a wolf come to devour her.

Asher took a step towards her, closing the distance between them, and wrapped his arms around her waist. He roughly dragged her towards him until her breasts pressed against his abs. Her breath caught in her throat. She set her hands on his forearms, trying to find some semblance of balance. She needed to stay in control.

Oh, but it felt good to be in his arms. And comfortable and right and like she belonged there. It was like coming home after the longest trip of her life. This was the place: the man, the comfort, and the love of her life. Flashes of emotions bubbled up without context—passion, love, fear, loneliness, adoration.

Rosemary took a slow, deep breath. She reminded herself why she was there. She had to stay out of her head, and her heart, to go through with the spell. Rosemary Bay was a force to be reckoned with when it came to sex. She was a goddess of lust and would have him begging for a blow job in no time.

Rosemary snuck her hand to his neck, curling her fingers around it and teasing the spot where his hairline met skin. She was already on her tiptoes, but if he didn't meet her halfway, there was no way a kiss was happening.

Instead of bending down, as she suspected, Asher shocked her by grabbing her bottom with both hands and hoisting her into the air, guiding her legs to wrap around his waist. In the same breath, his mouth covered hers.

His kiss seared. It burned and teased and drove her mad with desire. There was no soft build-up or timidity to Asher's kissing. His mouth demanded Rosemary's lips part, seized her tongue with his own, and had her melting with desire. His mouth commanded hers, bringing her to his frantic pace, as if they would consume each other's entire beings.

Asher kissed like a drowning man searching for air.

He swung her around, setting her onto his desk, a few errant items falling to the ground, while he continued assailing her mouth with his own.

Rosemary tried to stifle a moan and attempted to keep her mind on the task at hand, but she did not accomplish either. Her soul was singing in triumph. Every fiber of her being screamed, "Yes! This is the one! You found him!"

She reached for the collar of his shirt, trying to find his buttons. She needed him naked. Now. She knew this spell called for head, but sex was probably good enough, right? Right? There were particulars of the spell she was forgetting but...screw it. All she knew was that her body needed his in the worst way possible. She'd deal with the consequences later.

Asher batted her hands down while his lips trailed away from her mouth and to her neck. His hands went to the straps of her dress, pushing them down her shoulders, pulling on the fabric until he managed to slide it over and away from her breasts. She'd gone braless, so nothing was blocking his touch or view, which he immediately took advantage of. Both hands covered her, and Rosemary couldn't help but moan again. Somewhere in her mind she remembered talking to another person in the office who might be able to hear them right now.

"Quiet down," Asher commanded before taking her nipple between his teeth.

Rosemary muffled her mouth with her fist. She didn't want to be interrupted now. She had to be quiet or else she might be falling off this desk trying to get dressed after someone knocked at the door.

With his thumb on one nipple and his tongue on the other, Rosemary could feel her mind turning to mush.

The spell.

She was doing a spell, wasn't she?

Focus, Rosemary, she chided internally. You can do this.

"Take your, oh goddess that feels good, take your..." She couldn't form the words to tell him what to do. She heard him hum with laughter.

"Lay on your back," he said, and she obeyed. He looked over her body, drinking in every inch of bare skin like he was about to ravish her. And by all the goddesses, she wanted him to. His hands traveled up her thighs, found her panties, and pulled them off as he pushed her dress around her waist.

Finally, Rosemary thought. She waited for him to lose at least some of his clothes.

"Open your legs."

He was still dressed, but she scooched her knees apart, the width of his hips. He had to be feeling as desperate as she was. Maybe he would just shuck his pants this time. She could wait to have him completely naked the next time they fucked on his work desk.

"Wider," he growled, his fingertips coming to her thighs and pulling her towards him.

She did, still waiting for some glimpse of his body. She'd settle for a blurry shot of skin just before he slid inside her.

Instead, he dropped to his knees and buried his face between her legs.

"Holy fuck," Rosemary moaned.

"Shush," he said, coming away for a moment before returning. Her hands flew over her mouth, trying to keep the sounds she couldn't help but make from escaping.

His tongue teased her into oblivion. Even the pressure of his fingertips against her thighs was tantalizing. She couldn't believe how good this was. It wasn't like a one-night stand. It was like being with someone who knew every favorite spot and exploited that knowledge to give her the best pleasure of her life. Her mind might have been a muddled mess, but her body knew him. He was the one she'd been searching for. He was finally here.

"Pinch your nipples. I want to watch you do that while you come."

"Oh, hell," Rosemary whispered, moving her hands from her mouth to her breasts. She loved listening to his commands, getting a jolt of pleasure every time he gave her another direction. Who knew she liked being bossed around? Usually, she was the boss.

"I'm going to come," she breathed. He hummed, his licks becoming long and purposeful, and snuck a finger inside of her, curling into a perfect crook.

She came, hard and violently, like nothing she had ever experienced before. Asher pressed his free hand against her belly to keep her from falling off the desk while she convulsed beneath him. She reached down and wound her fingers between his, needing even more connection with him.

When the waves of her orgasm finally subsided, Rosemary fluttered her eyes open. Asher was staring at her, his eyes like a wolf looking over its subdued prey. He bit her thigh once, letting her skin slowly escape the grasp of his teeth, then got to his feet. Her chest heaved as she tried to catch her breath.

Asher stood between her legs and grasped his hands behind her knees, drawing her closer to him. He released her legs and fumbled with his belt, releasing the buckle, then went for his zipper.

Finally, Rosemary thought.

"Sheriff?" A knock at the door accompanied the voice on the other side.

Rosemary froze. The door was locked, but if whoever was on the other side had a key, they were about to get a very intimate view of their neighborhood florist.

"Yes," Asher answered, his voice steady and his hands on her legs.

"Claire called in. She's got a domestic on Sagittauri and needs back-up. I told her I would send you."

"Of course. Let me finish up with Ms. Bay and I'll be on my way." Asher slowly fixed his pants, then stepped out of Rosemary's legs and gently closed them. He grabbed a paper towel from the top of his filing cabinet and wiped his face off.

"No," Rosemary whispered. The details of the spell came rushing back to her. She could still sneak a blow job in there. She could be fast. Just as soon as she could move the lower half of her body. She could probably roll off the desk to the floor and crawl to him.

"I have to go," Asher said, his voice slightly pained. "You were delicious. I'll tell Charlie you had to take a call and I gave you my office. No one will bother you. Leave when you are ready." He bit his lower lip and looked her over. "See you soon, I hope."

He turned and left.

Rosemary panted and looked down at herself, tits out, panties somewhere in this room, legs like jelly hanging over the edge of the sheriff's desk. There was probably an imprint of her butt on the desk.

"Oh shit." As her body slowly re-entered this plane of existence, so did her brain.

Asher had given her the equivalent of a blow job.

She needed a counter spell. Fast.

Rosemary pushed herself off the desk, every single muscle protesting. Goddess, she should have thought this through! If they'd been in his apartment, she could have definitely snuck a blow job in and then languished in post-orgasmic bliss in his bed. Or on his kitchen table. She hopped around the room, pulling her dress back on while looking for her panties. She found one of her shoes under the desk, but it was like her underwear disappeared into the ether.

She had to leave it. Asher or the cleaning crew would get a surprise sometime in the next week. With her purse in hand, she power walked past the front desk, giving a small wave and nod to the guy sitting there, and burst out of the police station. She needed to get home as quickly as possible.

Her bike was locked to a tree, but the second Rosemary attempted to sit on the seat, she knew that wasn't happening.

"Ahh," she squealed.

Nope, she'd be lucky if she could ride her bike to work in two days after that orgasm.

She racked her brain. Star Island wasn't exactly a place where one could hail a cab. They had to be called and usually took at least ten minutes. And no one Ubered here after seven. She knew every Uber driver on the island, and they turned off their phones after dinner.

It was after nine, but Lavender might still be in the bakery. It was her best chance. She took off in the fastest sprint her body could manage which, honestly, was close to a walk, even closer to a hobble.

"Lavender!" she yelled, rapping on the back door with her fist. The Immortal Cupcake closed at six in the evening, but Lavender often stayed late to get things ready for the next morning if she had a big order or wanted to sleep past four. The lights were still on in the kitchen, so Rosemary held out hope that her older sister was still in the shop.

"Rosemary?" Lavender's muffled voice broke through the night.

"Yes! Let me in!" Rosemary heard the locks clicking before the door opened and spilled light into the alley. She ducked in and slammed the door behind her.

"What the hell happened to you?" Lavender's eyebrows were halfway up her forehead.

Rosemary looked down at herself. Her shoes were on the wrong feet and her dress was completely twisted. She couldn't imagine what her hair looked like.

"Me? Oh, I'm fine. I need a ride home though. Right this second. Drop everything and take me home." Rosemary nodded quickly. "Please."

Lavender leaned against the counter and crossed her arms.

"Yeah, that's not going to fly. What's going on?"

"Okay! Okay." Rosemary blew out a breath. "I may have done a small spell that backfired in my direction, and I need to do a counter spell as soon as possible or...there will be consequences. That I would rather not face."

"Rosemary." Lavender rolled her eyes and moved to clean up the countertops. "What did you actually do?"

Rosemary scrunched up her nose and shifted on her feet.

"Oh, fine! I tried to do a trust spell on Asher so he would immediately trust me and believe everything I said so I wouldn't have to break a human into the idea of being with a witch and could let him know what actually happened to Morana! And it backfired!"

"How?"

"Ugh! Lavender! I was supposed to give him a blow job to seal the deal but he sneak-attack went down on me, and now I'm worried that I'm going to trust everything he says instead!"

"Oh for fuck's sake, Rosemary. Would it be such a bad thing to actually earn the trust of your soulmate? I have half a mind to let you suffer the consequences. What would you do if I didn't give you a ride?" Lavender let out an exasperated sigh. "Never mind, don't answer that. Get in the car."

After a silent car ride home, Rosemary sprinted out of the car and straight to the attic. She had left the book out on the table and quickly scanned it for a reversal spell.

"Shit!" There wasn't one.

She needed to think fast. There was a general reversal spell and, apparently, that was going to have to do. Rosemary quickly grabbed four black candles and set them in a circle on the floor. She lit each then sat in the middle, palms outstretched.

"The spell I did was not the one, goddesses please, make it undone," she said quickly. She had used that undoing spell before, but never for something this important. And it only had about a fifty percent success rate. She closed her eyes and imagined the lights of the four candles growing stronger and stronger, the spell becoming more powerful, then burning itself out too quickly and turning into ash.

She slowly peeked through one eye. Two candles were extinguished. Good.

She opened her other eye.

One candle was out, the other barely flickering before it darkened.

"Well, what the hell does that mean?" she asked the ether. "I sort of canceled it? Ugh." Rosemary fell down to her back and stared at the ceiling. She would have to be wary of Asher for a while, at least until she figured out whether or not the counter spell worked.

Rosemary stretched her arms above her head and tried to find the overwhelming relaxation she'd felt with Asher less than thirty minutes ago. It would have been nice to lay in bliss for a good hour on his desk and not fly into sheer panic and rush home.

Her soulmate was an alpha in the sack. And he gave amazing head. And was okay with screwing on his work desk.

Things were looking up.

Chapter Eight

"I've got a mule, her name is Sal, fifteen miles on the Erie Canal, she's a good ole worker and a good ole pal, fifteen miles on the Erie Canal, we hauled some barges in our day, filled with lumber, coal, and hay, and we know every inch of the way we go from Albany to Buffalo," Rosemary sang. Her familiar, Verruca, hopped next to her and let out a deafening croak, clearly disapproving of her song choice.

"Well, if you want to hear something else, sing it yourself," Rosemary chided.

She sat crossed-legged in her herb garden, her basket nearly full of fresh cuttings. She took her time and cherished every stem she snipped today, giving thanks for the herb and its contribution to the garden. After the magical debacle she got herself into the night before, some good, old-fashioned garden worship was in order. Things were really starting to explode in the Bay garden in late June. It was time to bring some of that fragrant goodness into the house via bouquets with a hint of magic.

Rosemary ran a sprig of oregano through her fingers, admiring how verdant and healthy each tiny leaf looked. There may be a curse hanging over their heads, an angry hedge witch trapped by Laurel, threatening revenge, and two warlocks coming for them, but at least it would be a good summer for growing.

She couldn't help but feel a pinch of relief. Things with Asher were happening, in whatever messed up way the spell would lead them. But he had admitted attraction to her. And then absolutely destroyed her with his mouth. It was a good start.

"Low bridge, everybody down, low bridge, we're coming to a town, and you'll always know your neighbor, you'll always know your pal, if you've ever navigated on the Erie Canal." Rosemary collected her basket, walked it to the screen porch, and grabbed an empty basket. Now it was time to get some flowers out of the garden.

"You are singing very loudly," Verbena called, coming around the side of the house. "They can probably hear you in Solaris."

"I bet they can!" Rosemary laughed.

Verbena turned the corner, dressed immaculately as always. Today she had on a white sundress and red heels. She looked like an advertisement for New England in the summer.

"I come looking for blooms to help sell a dark condo," Verbena said.

"I have a bunch of lilacs that are looking amazing," Rosemary answered, popping out from between the hedgerows. She had added a wide-brimmed hat to her ensemble, which looked like a mix between hippie-herbalist and athleisure, with her flowing, flowery top and simple black capri leggings on bottom.

"Any blue? They are a good omen of home and peaceful living."

"A couple. They're over here." Rosemary threw her head to the side of the house. "Real estate going well?"

"It is," Verbena answered. "Actually, I got a very interesting call from a potential client."

"Oh yeah?" Rosemary stepped over an errant bunch of thyme that had somehow migrated out of the herb garden and into its own little plot. She never pulled out plants that did that; if the plant wanted to live on the side of the house between the concrete path and the window well, who was she to judge? She loved watching the personalities of her plants; some were little go-getters when it came to scouting out more foreboding living locations. Curious little creatures.

"Yes, it looks like our sheriff is going to put down permanent roots on Star Island in the form of a house."

Rosemary stopped walking. "He is?"

"Yup." Verbena couldn't contain her smile. "And not one of those small one-bedroom, one-bathroom vacation type rentals on the coast. He wants a big yard for a dog or two, at least three bedrooms, something near the woods and away from neighbors." Verbena regarded Rosemary with knowing eyes and raised an eyebrow. "So, is there anything you would like me to add to the wish list?"

"What do you mean?"

"I would prefer to find the perfect house for the two of you to sell to him, rather than find something Asher is looking for, only to have it back on the market next summer when you are knocked up with twins or something. I've watched Laurel. She and Owen went from casually dating to never being apart more than a couple hours in the space of a week. I will not wreak havoc on my career like that."

"Verbena," Rosemary rolled her eyes, "twins do not run in our family. Plus, I think I would know if I were a hyper-ovulator. If I did manage to ovulate two eggs, I would sense it immediately. I am beyond in tune with my body." She paused and looked over her sister. "You're going to get your period tomorrow. And it's going to be a doozy," she added for good measure.

"Thanks for the heads-up. Either way. He didn't say anything about room for a garden..."

"Oh, well definitely it'll need space for a huge garden. Preferably one that can be fenced if he wants dogs. And space for a few fruit trees. You know I love a good screened porch, a south facing window for indoor plants, space for a table big enough to seat twelve...let's see." Rosemary closed her eyes trying to think of her perfect house. She didn't want to live in town, but it sounded like Asher didn't either.

Verbena laughed. "That was a pretty quick turnaround. Three bedrooms enough? Any bathroom specifics?"

"Maybe look for four bedrooms, so we have an extra space. And I want a very big tub or space to put one in. Huge tub. Asher's basically a tree."

"Tub to fit both you and a tree without sloshing the water over because we both know what you are going to do in that tub. Done and done."

Rosemary walked up to the lilacs and pulled her shears out of her pocket. She looked for the prettiest and most fragrant blooms. They were sure to enhance and enchant the feel of the place.

"Any news on your soulmate?" Rosemary asked.

"What do you mean?" Verbena answered quickly, her hands twisting together.

"You ever going to move in with him? Or, you know, talk to him?" she pressed. Rosemary didn't mind her own business. Even with Verbena.

Verbena crossed her arms. "It's complicated, you know that."

"I know it is complicated, but I have no idea *why* it is complicated. None of us do. You don't even talk to Luke anymore. A few years ago, you seemed on the right path, and now suddenly, it's like you are trying to ignore him."

"There are a lot of things you don't know about, and please don't try to figure it out," Verbena snapped.

"If I must keep my nose out of it, I will. But you heard the voice on Beltane. Owen is here, now Asher is here...it's only a matter of time before fate throws the two of you in a room and locks the door."

"I'm aware." Verbena rubbed the bridge of her nose and took a deep breath. She pushed her perfectly straight blonde hair away from her face. "Can we talk about something else? I don't want to get worked up about it right now."

"Worked up? Verbena, are you okay?" Rosemary reached out and cupped her sister's elbow. "Did he do something? Bad? Did Luke do something unforgiveable?" Fear rose from her stomach to her heart. How could that have happened? Rosemary was always in tune with her sisters.

"No! No. He didn't do anything."

"Then what is it? Verbena, I'm worried about you; we're all worried." Rosemary tried to catch her eyes, but Verbena wouldn't look at her.

"It was me!" Verbena shouted. Rosemary jumped back a little. "It was me. I did the shitty thing, okay? Not Luke. Luke is perfect. I fucked up." Verbena ran her hands over her face a few times. "I don't want to talk about it. I need to focus on work, okay?"

Rosemary nodded but internally, she disagreed. The last thing Verbena needed to focus harder on was work. She was a non-stop working machine. Rosemary had always thought that realtors lived very lucky lifestyles, making their own hours, getting large chunks of time off and then making bank over one big sale. But Verbena never seemed to stop working. The market on Star Island had been exploding lately, mostly thanks to her de-ghosting a lot of the land and houses and making it a much more family-friendly vacation spot. She deserved a break.

And what on earth could Verbena have done? Rosemary wanted to know so badly, but she didn't press her. Verbena was like a ball of raw nerves. She didn't need any more contact right now.

"Let me put these in water for you," Rosemary said, heading back to the house.

"Thanks. I'm going to grab some lemon balm and I'll be in."

"For the showing?"

"No, for me," she answered, but was out of earshot before Rosemary could ask a follow-up question.

Rosemary was going to put together a bouquet for Verbena. Something with a bit of forgiveness, a sprig of hope, and definitely a bloom for second chances. If she didn't want to talk about it with Rosemary, she wouldn't press her, but it hurt her heart to see her sister so upset.

Midsummer was Rosemary's favorite holiday. Of the eight main holidays celebrated by modern witches, each Bay sister took the reins of the celebrations for their favorites. Rosemary oversaw both Beltane and Midsummer, but Midsummer really spoke to her. By then, the earth had come into full bloom, and could be celebrated in all its bounty.

After the surprise announcement of a wild six months at the last festival, Rosemary was planning a quieter Midsummer. There would be some gardening, some symbolic cutting of herbs, some tasteful cakes and salads, and a ton of wine. This whole soulmate thing plus the knowledge that a family of evil warlocks and their sorceress sister were after their blood was stressing them all out. They needed a night to relax and unwind.

Normally, Rosemary would have suggested they all take part in the Finnish ritual of collecting seven different flowers to put under their pillows to send dreams of their future spouses. But now Laurel had met Owen, Rosemary knew Asher, and Verbena's soulmate was already on the island as well. Lavender and Sage were both firmly uninterested in finding their soulmates, so it wouldn't go over well. Instead, Rosemary improvised.

"Is Owen invited tonight?" Laurel asked. She was still doing her client readings in their parlor—unless they were home visits—so while she was sleeping in Owen's rental on the beach, she was still a regular fixture around the house.

"That depends."

"On what?"

"Whether or not he is comfortable with a few sky-clad activities." Laurel's soulmate, Owen, was part of the Davies water witch clan, so he was accustomed to the festivals, but Rosemary celebrated a little more feverishly.

"Does my boyfriend want to watch my sisters and I run around our property naked?"

"He would have to participate. You know the rules, you can't stay unless you lose the clothes." Rosemary smirked. "If we get our kit off, so does he."

"I think he'll pass. But since it looks like several of us might be settling down with soulmates in the next few months, can we start toning down the amount of magic we do naked in the summer? Since Owen is magical, I would like to be able to celebrate these days with him in the future. And, you know, I don't really want to run around naked in front of Asher next year."

"Noted. I promise next year we will all have our nipples and our bushes covered." No promises on asses, Rosemary thought.

"Thank you. I appreciate it. What time should I be back?"

"We'll start at seven. Don't forget to wear bug spray. Everywhere."

Rosemary had done a very good job keeping her mind away from Asher the last two days. With work, all her gardening, and Midsummer preparations on top of it, there simply wasn't time. Her hands and mind were far too occupied to think about his mouth on hers, the lovely things his fingers and tongue did to her body, or the sound of his voice roughly demanding her to open her legs.

Rosemary stopped winding twine around the base of a bouquet and got a glass of ice water.

Had she ever wanted someone this badly before? That was easy, of course not. She'd never really wanted anyone before. Sure, she had gotten horny, had sex, or met with warlocks and performed sex magic on many occasions. But she had never wanted anyone like she wanted Asher. She craved him. She needed to see him again, touch him, let him touch her.

Rosemary settled back in her seat and exhaled, picking up the bouquet to finish it. She'd stayed away from town other than her one shift at Therese's since Asher had played her body like an instrument in his office. She needed to figure out what her next step was. She couldn't very well show up at his house, strip naked, and demand he take her to bed for the rest of her life.

Wait, could she do that?

No, she was determined to organize all the thoughts in her brain before talking to him again. And she needed a hair of control if she wanted to talk and not simply drop to her knees and return the delicious favor he'd given her.

"Fill me up. I'm getting hammered tonight." Sage was the last sister to make her way to the backyard. The other four were sitting around the blazing bonfire, enjoying the sparks.

"Oh good, so in a couple hours we can all look forward to you stoically staring into the fire without comment. You turn into a pensive man from the 1840s when you drink too much," Rosemary teased, handing her youngest sister a full glass of wine.

"I won't get comatose. I'll stay fun-Sage."

Rosemary raised an eyebrow. She wasn't sure fun was an adjective she would ever use to describe Sage. Stoic. Sarcastic. A little macabre. Willing to murder for the ones she loved. But never fun.

"Wine, potato salad, herb salad, sausages off the grill, strawberry cake, and brownies. This is a pretty good spread, Rosemary," Verbena said between bites.

"I made lavender lemon cupcakes with cream cheese frosting at work today and had some extras. I'll bring them out for a late-night treat." Lavender took a deep drink from her cup. It was difficult for her to relinquish the reins of food preparation for the holidays that were not hers.

And she only had Yule under her wheelhouse, though she made up for it by inundating the entire family with enough food to last from Yule straight through Imbolc.

"Eat up, sisters," Rosemary chided. "The sun goes down in an hour, and when the moon comes out, we will be busy with our spell work."

"Is this a naked night?" Sage asked.

"It is!"

"Great." She slunk down in her seat. "Someone bring me no less than three sausages with a grainy mustard on the side."

"It's a little chilly," Lavender complained.

"Please, it was fifty-eight degrees on Midsummer two years ago. It's a balmy sixty-three tonight!" Rosemary answered, shrugging out of her dress.

"One of these years, we're all going to get pneumonia and Dr. Flores is going to ask, how on earth did all five of you get pneumonia in June? And I'm going to answer, Rosemary made us run naked in the moonlight," Lavender huffed.

"It's not that bad," Verbena defended, already in her birthday suit. "Nothing like a sharp breeze to really wake you up!"

"What spell are we doing that requires nudity? Or did you make us take our clothes off because you like doing spell work naked?" Sage bemoaned. Sage barely tolerated spell work. And she really hated being cold.

"Little of both, Sage. Stand closer to the fire, it'll warm you up."

Rosemary grabbed the small bouquets she had made that afternoon, each holding oak leaves, bay, and a single thistle flower. She quickly passed them out to her sisters.

"Make a circle around the fire. Raise your bouquet in the air."

"Tell me what we are doing before we do it," Sage said.

"It's a protection spell. We could all use a boost of protection, right?"

"All right, that's fine with me," Sage conceded, the rest of the sisters nodding.

"Perfect, let's begin." Rosemary took a deep breath, raised her bouquet above her head, and looked to the sky to begin.

Lavender shrieked and hit the ground behind the fire. Sage yelped and took off into the woods, Laurel close at her heels.

"Oh, shit!" Verbena cried and raced towards the house.

"What the hell?" Rosemary mumbled and slowly turned around.

There, with the shadows of flames dancing across his face, was Asher.

"Hello, gorgeous."

Chapter Nine

Asher did not come to the Bay house on the pretense of catching all five sisters dancing around a bonfire naked like a bunch of wild heathens.

He came, flowers in hand, to properly ask Rosemary out to dinner. He'd be lying if he said she hadn't occupied his thoughts completely since they hooked up on his desk, and he definitely wanted more with Rosemary.

Specifically, he wanted to finish what they started.

When he had gotten to the front door and knocked, no one came. The lights were on, though, and he could hear voices carrying from the backyard. He had assumed they were sitting outside enjoying the cool summer night.

He was wrong.

Or rather, he was wrong about the manner in which they were enjoying the cool summer night. They were definitely having a lot of fun before he got there and caused mass panic.

Truthfully, Asher didn't see anyone but Rosemary. He saw a blur of skin in the darkness, immediately running for cover, but Rosemary's ass had all his attention. He would have been able to pick it out from a lineup, without ever seeing it before. Once his hands had wrapped around that succulent piece of flesh a few days ago, he would know it anywhere.

Rosemary stood in front of him, her hands on her hips, completely naked and looking him straight in the eye.

"Hello, gorgeous," he breathed.

"What on earth are you doing here?" she asked. She made no move to cover herself up or run away, and he took the opportunity to drink in the sight. Her hair was down and loose, her curls settling on her shoulders, a small smirk kissed the corner of her lips. Asher found himself wishing the bonfire was a little brighter. She was backlit and he'd love a clearer look at all the curves in front of him.

She was beyond captivating, clothed or naked.

"Came to see you."

"Well, you've seen me." She grinned and motioned up and down her body.

"Very much enjoying the view," he confessed.

She pursed her lips, but he could tell she wanted to giggle.

"Aren't you cold?"

"Not really. I run pretty hot."

"Yeah, you do." Asher took a deep breath. This wasn't how he had planned doing it, but here they were. "These are for you." He handed her the flowers. "I came here to say I want to see you again. And not just naked, though I do like seeing you naked."

"Oh, really?" She raised her eyebrow. She took a deep inhale of the flowers and stepped closer to him, her hand finding his in the darkness.

"Really," he growled and pulled her closer. His hands went to her waist, quickly traveling to her lower back and carrying her against him. He wanted her. He'd wanted her like crazy since two nights ago. It had taken all his willpower not to ignore Charlie and flip her over on his desk, then bury himself in her until she screamed in delight. But he was the sheriff. He had a job to do. He really wished that call had come in twenty minutes later, though.

Asher bent his mouth to her neck and pressed his lips against the soft skin behind her ear. Damn, she smelled so good. And her skin was heaven under his hands. She wiggled closer to him, wrapped her hands behind his neck, and breathed the smallest moan.

Asher was undone.

"Rosemary!" a voice from the darkness cried out.

"What?" She glanced over her shoulder but thankfully didn't move away from him.

"I am naked, hiding behind the fire, and Verruca just landed on my back."

"Who's Verruca?" Asher asked.

"My toad." Rosemary turned back to Asher, smoothing her hand over his chest. "I have four naked sisters to go fetch."

"I'm going to ask you about that sometime."

"And I'm going to tell you about it sometime." She paused. "See you soon?"

"Definitely." He bent down and brushed his lips against hers, just for a moment, then released her. "I'm going to stand here for one minute and watch you walk away."

She threw a mischievous smile over her shoulder.

"Enjoy the wiggle," she teased.

"Oh, I am."

Asher couldn't fall asleep.

At first, he couldn't fall asleep because he was painfully hard and more than anything wanted to go back to the Bay house, throw Rosemary over his shoulder, take her to his bed, and do wicked things to her body until the sun came up. And then begin and finish the next day the same way. He took care of that with his hand and a very stimulating visual of Rosemary splayed out on his desk.

But he still couldn't sleep.

He wanted to talk to Rosemary. Or hold her.

What was going on?

Asher never fell hard this fast. He never fell hard ever. He'd had girlfriends over the years, mostly not serious. His entire life he had only been looking for a little fun, never in a hurry to settle down. But now, he simply looked at Rosemary and wondered what her plans were for the next five years.

Around four, he accepted that sleeping would not be happening. He got up and made a breakfast of three eggs, salsa, and two pieces of sourdough toast. He rounded out the meal with a banana and two cups of coffee, then jumped into the shower.

When he got out, he threw on some shorts and a T-shirt, not ready to get dressed for the day yet. His shift didn't start until nine, and he didn't want to sit around in a button-down for three hours. He picked up his phone and opened his email.

Natalie Evans
Did you see this yet? I'm calling you later today.
Buffalonewsfast.com/twoyearslater

Asher grimaced at the link address. He hadn't let his mind turn to it yesterday. He'd done everything in his power to distract himself, and for the most part, Rosemary had done the trick. But he couldn't put it off forever.

He clicked the article and leaned back in his seat.

Two years have passed since gunman Nik Blane opened fire during the annual ScandiFest in Buffalo, killing two police officers and one civilian, and injuring three others, including another police officer, before turning the gun on himself. The event hit the tight knit community hard. His target and former wife, Alison Olsen, survived the shooting and is slowly regaining the ability to walk. "I feel so guilty about all the violence Nik caused. He wanted to kill me, just me. I don't know why he hurt all those innocent people. And my heart breaks for the families (of the deceased)."

Officers James Harris and Walter Robinson were both killed at the scene, while civilian Erik Lederson died two days later from injuries sustained in the shooting. Officer Harris is survived by his wife, Paula, and their two children. Officer Robinson, a twenty-year veteran of the Buffalo police department, is survived by his brother, Paul. Erik Lederson is survived by his wife, Cathy, and their three children.

Asher tossed his phone across the table and swallowed. His hand instinctively went up to his left shoulder. He wasn't sure if it would ever stop hurting, but he'd been so lucky. Alison still couldn't walk, five kids didn't have their dads, and Walter...Walter was gone.

Asher stood up and paced the room, trying to keep thoughts of the day from encroaching. He needed to keep busy. He needed to keep his focus off that day. An active body made for a busy mind. He couldn't take a clonazepam this time, with work starting so soon. Those things really knocked him out. Better to occupy his mind than medicate it.

With that thought, Asher decided to get to work early. There was always something that needed doing.

Evans—

Since I have not heard from you in two days, I'm guessing you've stopped looking into my sister's disappearance. Screw you. She's a defenseless woman and was probably murdered on your little island and you're trying to cover it up. Well I won't stop looking, asshole. I will hire a PI or come there myself. Have you even interviewed Laurel Bay? That woman is pure evil and definitely had something to do with my sister's disappearance.

Who's your boss? The governor? I'll be calling her office today.

Ivan

"What the hell?" Asher mumbled, taking the time to read the email two more times. This man seemed like he was losing his grip on reality. Asher exhaled and opened a new draft to reply.

Mr. Stoch—

I am sorry for your frustration. Missing person cases can be very disheartening. If you could send me a list of her closest friends in Montana, I would be happy to reach out to them and see if any of them have heard anything from her. Sometimes, a person will send a text to a random friend, while forgetting to notify family of a change in plans.

I will not give up the search for her, though I have hit dead ends here. Several people saw your sister over the course of her visit, but no one knows anything about where she was staying or what she was doing on Star Island. I will also reach out to Chatham police and see if they can circulate her picture. If someone has seen her on the mainland since her visit, it will be good to focus the search off Star Island.

You are, of course, welcome to contact the governor of Massachusetts, but

usually their office does not handle this sort of thing. If I find any evidence
that she was taken across state lines against her will, I will hand this over to
the FBI.

Thanks—
Sheriff Evans

The FBI, as if Asher could be so lucky. For once in his life, he would love
to put a bow around this case and hand it to the Feds. He couldn't help but
feel like the person that needed investigating was Ivan Stoch.

He pulled up the National Crime Information Center database to run a
background check on Morana and Ivan. He marked them both as urgent,
pertaining to a missing persons case. It usually took a little while for those to
come back, even when marked as urgent, so he pulled out some random
paperwork to complete while he waited.

An hour later, Asher had both files in his drive. He opened Morana's
first.

"Let's see," he mumbled. "Nice rap sheet, Morana." There were over
fifteen arrests for destruction of public property, graffiti, and disturbing the
peace. Asher wasn't too worried about those; a lot of people went through
phases in their teens and early twenties that included these sorts of offenses,
but quickly grew out of them.

What concerned him were the five arrests for battery, two for resisting
arrest, and one for breaking and entering. How this woman had never
landed in prison, Asher had no idea.

He switched to Ivan's file and was met with a similar list of offenses.
Public drunkenness, breaking and entering, graffiti, but Ivan also had been
convicted of aggravated assault. There was definitely more to this family
than Ivan was letting on.

Asher's cell buzzed on his desk. It was Natalie. He glanced at the clock.
Technically, he wasn't supposed to start working for another thirty minutes.
He picked up the call.

"Hey, Natalie."

"Morning," she began. "You at work already?"

"Yeah, but in the office. Just finishing up some random things. What's
going on?"

She sighed. "You know I have to call and check in on you. You said you didn't want me to make a big deal of yesterday, but that doesn't stop me from calling today."

"Thank you for not calling yesterday. I managed to stay busy."

"Asher, it's okay to grieve and have a dark day. That day was...well it was one of the top three worst days of my life, and I wasn't even there."

"Glad my getting shot broke into your top three," he answered dryly.

"Don't be a dick. You getting shot, Dad's heart attack, and when Mom fell down the stairs last December. Those were all pretty shitty days."

"They were." He let a beat pass. "Did you talk to Mom?"

"I told her not to call until Saturday."

"Thanks."

"I went to the mass for Walter. They had one at Saint Angela's. It was nice, I saw a lot of your cop buddies. I saw Paul. Everyone said they missed you."

"You know I can't go..." He let his voice trail off. He cleared his throat quickly.

"I know. No one expects you to. Maybe in five years, right?"

"Yeah. Look, I should get back to work."

"Yeah, yeah, I know. But Asher, seriously, if you need to talk, I'm here. I know you're done with the whole appointed-therapist time frame, but you went through a trauma. You might be on an island in the middle of the ocean, but I'm sure they have therapists there, too. Don't bury it down too deep."

"I won't. I promise."

"I love you, little brother."

"Love you too, little sister."

Asher hung up and flipped his phone around in his hand a few times, then opened a text to his mom.

> Asher: Hey Mom. Wanted to let you know I'm doing okay. Got through yesterday just fine. Swamped with work but I'd love to talk with you this weekend.

Asher pocketed his phone and turned back to his paperwork.

Another anniversary was over. Little by little, June twenty-first would fade back into being a normal day.

Chapter Ten

Rosemary wanted to send Asher a sext.

But to sext Asher she would need his phone number, which she still didn't have. Technically, she could have called the police station, but since it wasn't a normal place of work, like an insurance company, it felt inappropriate, especially if all she wanted to do was say inappropriate things to him.

She opened her laptop and pulled up the Black Hat Haberdashery. She noticed she had three unread messages and clicked to read them.

Daisy

Hi Rosemary! Here's the spell you asked for—I've only done it three times (once for myself and twice for friends) but we always used over two bushes of thyme. Also, if your soulmate is human, like my adorable but non-magical hubby, they will not come along for the past-life ride! Make sure you have good ventilation if indoors or someone to make sure animals don't crawl on you if outdoors.

Good luck! Daisy

Rosemary chewed on her lip. She had messaged Daisy, a bee witch living in Florida, about a past life spell she had created. While Lavender's spell had a great success rate, it brought your soulmate along. It wasn't that Rosemary wanted to hide the past from Asher, but she wasn't sure she'd be able to get him on board to mind-bound time travel in the next week.

She clicked to her next message, which was a "Happy Midsummer" blast from her garden witchery group, and then opened the next.

TheDarkestNight
You think I don't know where you are, Bay Witch? You think you are safe on that island?
I know what you did.
Bleed the Bays Dry.

"What the fuck?" Rosemary breathed. She clicked on the username, but it was an empty profile.

Bleed the Bays Dry. If there wasn't a blood curse hanging over the Bay witches at this exact moment, Rosemary wouldn't have thought anything of it, just some witch spam.

But this wasn't spam. It was a threat.

A shiver ran down her spine, never a good sign for a witch. Rosemary jumped out of her bed and slammed her laptop shut. She clamored down the stairs, through the kitchen, and into the backyard.

She grabbed fistfuls of marjoram, vervain, and mint, pulling her shirt up to collect them. Rosemary hurried back into the house and snatched the ball of twine and pair of sharp scissors off the kitchen counter.

"As I bind these herbs," Rosemary began, twisting the twine around the leaves in the way of the sun, "keep those that wish me harm far away. Put rough seas, strong storms, and ill winds in their path. May the earth rise up and stop them. Keep the Bay witches from harm." She tied off the end, then walked to each doorway and drew an X across the threshold with her bundle.

She brushed the bundle across the mantle above the fireplace, then settled it in the center. A small pulse of energy ricocheted through the house. She released a shaky breath.

It worked.

Rosemary peeked into the kitchen at the oven clock.

"Five-thirty. Everyone will be home soon," she reassured herself. "Bath time."

"Who's home?" Laurel called from the parlor. Rosemary was still enjoying the water, having spent the last ninety or so minutes turning into an absolute prune. She'd heard Lavender and Sage come in a bit earlier but figured her disturbing email could wait until she had a proper soak.

"What's wrong?" Lavender's voice answered from her downstairs bedroom.

"Family meeting," Laurel replied.

Rosemary could hear chairs around the dining table being shuffled and the kettle filling with water. She could also hear Verbena, so either she showed up without Rosemary noticing or Laurel brought her.

"I'm in the bath," she called down. "I'll be out in three minutes." She dunked her head underwater, bemoaning the fact that she hadn't gotten a full two-hour soak as was the plan. She had even scented the water with rose oil.

She came down in her robe, her hair wrapped in a towel on her head, and took a seat. Laurel had her laptop out, which was not how family meetings usually began in the Bay household.

"Has anyone been on Black Hat Haberdashery lately?" Only Rosemary, Laurel, and Verbena were members of the witch social media platform, but occasionally they fell off checking.

"Not for about a week," Verbena admitted.

"Yes," Rosemary answered slowly, "And about that."

Laurel turned the screen to the center of the table, and everyone crowded around it before Rosemary could finish.

"I was messing around on it this afternoon. Owen went to the mainland to pick up his truck, and I didn't have any clients. Look at this new post."

Rosemary squinted.

What the hell is going on in Montana? By KitchenKate458
I live in Billings and it's like all hell has broken loose north of here. Why is

the sky red? It's not a storm and my human neighbor said she hasn't noticed it. I would think I was hallucinating but my very magical eight-year-old daughter can also see it. Any other Montana witches out there know what's going on?

I'm in Miles City and can see it too! Figured it was something everyone could see—we live on a homestead and are all magical here —SylvieLovesBlackCats

I'm all the way in Calgary and noticed this morning! Can anyone do a read on what kind of magic it is? —EllietheEh

Can someone post a picture? I'm in Chicago and can't see it but I'm very curious. I'm a cloud witch—I'll be able to tell you if someone is messing with the atmosphere in a magical sense— WrenL

I'll grab one on my way home from work and post it in about thirty minutes —KitchenKate458

The next post was of a sky that looked like it was about to give birth to a tornado but instead of green, the clouds swirled bright red, pink, and orange. It looked like the sky was on fire.

Whoa, that is not cloud magic, but definitely is magic. Holy crap. Might be worth the drive to Montana to check it out. Anyone know where it originated? — WrenL

"There are three more pages about where it might be coming from, but no one knows exactly," Laurel explained. "I can guess."

"Morana is from Montana, right?" Rosemary asked.

"Yup. And warned me that if I thought she was scary, her brother was a chaos warlock."

"What the hell does that even mean?" Sage asked. "I've never met a chaos witch. Is it only a warlock thing?"

"Maybe?" Laurel answered. "And she had another brother, too, the metal warlock. I can only imagine they are starting to go a little crazy that she hasn't come back."

"So do we prepare for an attack from the brothers?" Lavender asked.

"I can do protection spells at everyone's place of work tomorrow," Verbena offered. Their house and Owen's rental both already had protection spells around them, but the bakery, the florist, and Verbena's office did not.

"That's probably a good idea. We don't want to take any chances. I would think that if this is chaos magic, the chaos warlock is still in Montana. But he might be sending minions here, metal warlock or otherwise," Lavender warned.

"Damn, we should have hired minions," Sage replied dryly. "Knew I forgot to do something."

"We don't have the budget for minions. If only Laurel could see the lottery numbers," Verbena sighed.

"That's not how hedge magic works," Laurel pointed out. "Okay. Be on the lookout for warlocks or magical minions, stay in protected zones, try to travel in groups, and don't wander around alone. Be aware that random warlocks might try to steal your blood while walking down main street. Good plan."

"Um, I have something to add," Rosemary interjected. "I got a weird message on Black Hat today."

"From who?"

"TheDarkestNight? Probably not their legal name. But I don't know who it is and they have a blank profile."

"What did it say?" Lavender asked.

"The gist was 'bleed the Bays dry.'"

"Shit," Sage said, suddenly paying close attention. "That's intense."

"It is, especially since we only thought the Stochs knew about it."

"It still might only be the Stochs. The Haberdashery is mostly women but not all. Morana has those two brothers, plus just because there aren't cousins listed in the compendium doesn't mean they don't exist."

"True." Rosemary sighed.

"What's your username?" Sage asked.

"ParsleySageRosemaryandBay," she answered.

"Rosemary! That's your real name. And my real name," Sage complained.

"Not really, just a little," she defended.

"Okay," Lavender interrupted. "It's too late to change it, but if I were looking for a Bay witch on the Haberdashery, the first thing I would do was type 'Bay' into the search engine."

"Well, I didn't know that we were going to be the targets of a centuries-old blood curse in 2010 when I made my profile."

"Never mind." Lavender turned to Laurel. "How are you getting home?" Lavender asked, clearly not feeling super protected at the moment.

"Owen's outside in his truck."

"You made him wait outside?" Rosemary was surprised. Laurel and Owen were as good as married; he was welcome at family meetings, especially those of the magical nature.

"No, he wanted to call his mom and figured it would be a good time to do so. We'll head back to his house now. I'll text if I see a chaos warlock. Come on, Verbena. Be safe everyone."

"You too." Rosemary bit the inside of her cheek. Should Verbena create some protection wards around Asher's apartment and the police station? It wasn't like she could ask him about it yet. Plus, the police station might be deterrent enough.

Her heart did an uncomfortable thump against her ribs. How could she protect Asher from something he didn't know existed?

The next morning, Verbena visited the florist, Lavender's bakery, the grocery store, and Luke's bar, The Muse, just to be on the safe side. With a few whispered words and a bundle of herbs in her oversized purse, protection wards were set. Morana had figured out a way to confuse the first set of wards, but they all had high hopes these would be stronger.

Rosemary was up with the sun that morning, rather unusual for her. Most mornings, when she heard Sage moving around the room, getting dressed before the sky shifted from black to pinky blue, Rosemary would simply roll towards the wall and chase dreams for a little while longer. Today, she attempted that but was met with a burst of energy.

After a few pieces of toast slathered in raspberry jam, Rosemary decided some gardening was in order. The morning was perfect: a few wisps of white clouds stretched across the cornflower sky. She went to the rose garden, dragging the hose behind her. After giving the plants a thorough watering, she cut some of her favorite blooms and made a pile for Verbena as well. Rosemary had an abundance of pale peach flowers this season and thought her sister could use a beautiful bouquet for her apartment. There was nothing like a beautiful burst of roses, ranunculus, and dahlias on a dining table in June.

She puttered around the rose garden a little while longer, letting herself admire how beautiful it looked. It was gorgeous enough to put a smile on any English garden enthusiast's face, if she did say so herself.

Rosemary dragged the hose back to the house and checked over her herbs. From the tarragon to the thyme to the chervil, everything was healthy, verdant, and thriving.

She was suddenly hit with a pang of sadness.

She wasn't going to live here anymore. It wasn't like she would move out tomorrow, but sooner or later, her life was going to jump off this path and onto a new one. She wouldn't share a room with Sage, she would start over somewhere else with a new garden, and there wouldn't be a fresh batch of baked goods every morning in the kitchen. Her new life was already pulling her away, and from the sound of it, that new life was going to include a house with three to four bedrooms, a big bathtub, and apparently a dog.

"Oh goddess," Rosemary mumbled. "If I'm going to get weepy about moving out, I should probably talk to Asher again." The last time they'd seen each other, she'd been stark naked, and he'd looked hotter than Arizona in August. Though, it would probably be a good idea for them to have some sort of contact during which Rosemary was not naked. Try as one might, sex was not something soulmates could do twenty-four hours a day. Even Rosemary was going to need a break for more than just sleeping and eating. They would need to converse occasionally. Maybe even with clothes on.

With that in mind, she put away her tools, washed up, and decided to take a little completely clothed field trip.

Chapter Eleven

Asher's door buzzed.

He wasn't expecting anyone. In fact, no one had buzzed his apartment in the three weeks he had lived on Star Island.

It was unsettling.

He got off the couch and hurried to the intercom, which had never been used, and pressed the talk button.

"Hello?" he asked suspiciously.

"It's Rosemary. Are you busy?"

"Um, no." Asher's mind raced. First, he didn't have any condoms. Shit. He should have grabbed some after their night in his office. They could do other stuff, though, right?

"Want to go for a walk with me?" Rosemary asked.

Okay. Not a strictly here-for-sex-visit.

"Sure. Do you want to come up?" he asked, poised to buzz her into his apartment and spend the thirty seconds it took for her to ascend the stairs power-cleaning. His bedroom door was open, revealing an unmade bed, overflowing laundry hamper, and wet towel slung over the dresser. Plus, his breakfast dishes were still in the sink, as well as a pan from last night. At least he was dressed.

"I think if I come up, we won't go for that walk. Why don't you come down?"

He laughed. "I'll be down in a minute."

When he got out of the apartment building, Rosemary was sitting on the curb. She wore a knee-length dark green skirt, white T-shirt, sturdy sandals, and had a backpack on. Her hair was pulled away from her face but still loose in a style his sister referred to as "half-up."

She looked like a freaking goddess.

"I was thinking," she started, coming to her feet, "while you have seen a lot of the island on your patrols, you probably haven't gotten to really enjoy it yet. So what do you say? I'll show you some of the best places to get lost on Star Island. Away from the tourist hotspots. Nothing puts a damper on a peaceful summer morning like a group of bachelorettes handing you eight phones to take the exact same picture over and over. Want to check out some of the quieter places?"

"I'd say that sounds like a perfect way to spend an afternoon." Asher took a step closer to her. Even outside, she smelled amazing. That woman was like a walking bouquet of flowers.

"Well, then let's go! There's a great path that winds through the woods and along the coast that we can hop on not too far from here."

"Oh, I've heard about that path. Apparently, it's a pretty popular place for teenagers to drink in the autumn."

Rosemary giggled. "I forgot you were a cop for a minute. Do you bust a lot of teens drinking?"

"Occasionally, I guess. My last job was a lot different than this one. Honestly, I'm looking forward to sending drunk seventeen-year-olds home." He followed Rosemary down a quiet street and then onto a paved path through a wooded part of the island.

"You weren't a sheriff on a tiny island in the Atlantic known for hosting bachelorette parties and weddings, with a swanky side and a normal side? I thought that was a pre-requisite for the job!" She smirked.

"No, I was a good old-fashioned beat cop in Buffalo. Though from about November until March I'd be in a car. Too cold there."

"You're from Buffalo?"

"Born, raised, and adulted there for a while."

"What made you leave your home for Star Island? I mean, I know it's beautiful here, but it would be hard for anyone to start someplace completely new."

He mulled it over in his mind. Did he like Rosemary? Yes, very much. Did he hope this was going to turn into something, be it short or long? Definitely. But he wasn't quite sure he was ready to tell her about why he left Buffalo.

"It's a really long story but the short version is that I was ready for a new home and a slower pace. Star Island seemed like as good of a place as any."

"That makes sense. I moved here when I was just shy of nineteen. It was a whole upheaval of life as we knew it. Took a while to get used to," she explained nonchalantly.

"Jane mentioned that you lost your parents and then moved here. Must have been hard."

"It was. More so for the younger three. It's never easy to lose a parent. But Lavender, my older sister, she came up with a plan and stuck to it. Our house here had been given to us in our great-aunt's will. We owned it outright, only had to pay the taxes. Our house in Ohio still had a mortgage and none of us had dependable jobs. So Lavender dropped out of college, we sold our childhood home, and now we are five sisters living very happily in an old cottage on Star Island. Or rather four sisters. Verbena has an apartment. Oh, wait. Three now. Laurel is going to move in with her boyfriend."

"Owen Davies, right? I met him the first time I saw you." He grimaced internally. That sounded stalker-ish. He risked a glance in Rosemary's direction. She didn't seem to mind.

"Yeah. They're looking for a place together."

"Isn't he from Maine?"

Rosemary stopped and scrunched her nose in confusion.

"I ran a background check on him," he admitted.

"Why?"

"Because I have a missing person case and he is involved intimately with the only lead I've gotten, who isn't really a lead at all, so don't worry about that."

"Okay." She paused. "Did you run a background check on me?"

"What? Of course not!"

"Well you ran one on Owen, I'm guessing you did one on Laurel, too."

"That was pertaining to a case. I would never run a background check on a woman I was interested in. That's unethical." He paused. "Would I find anything if I did?"

"Eh, I was a wild teenager. But I've calmed down. I threw a beer bottle at a fence when I was seventeen, not knowing there was a cop on the other side. So, yeah, I was arrested once. And then again when I was twenty-one."

"You throw another beer bottle?"

"Nope. I gave Officer Ramirez—he retired a few years ago—a heart attack at the beach on the Vega Peninsula."

"That doesn't seem like an arrestable offense."

"I was naked," she said plainly.

Asher couldn't help but chuckle. Between her naked antics a few nights ago and being arrested for public indecency, it looked like Rosemary had a streaker side.

"You sound like a hardened criminal," he joked. "I got arrested when I was sixteen."

"For what?"

"It's not cool. In Buffalo, you can't drive late at night until you turn seventeen. I got pulled over for failing to use my turn signal at twelve-fifteen a week before my birthday."

"Bad boy for life!" She giggled. "I think you mentioned earlier that you were 'interested' in me. Care to elaborate?" Her lips curved into a smile.

Asher looked behind them to make sure no one was within earshot.

"I'll let you in on a secret." He leaned closer to her. "I don't devour the pussy of a woman I'm not interested in."

Rosemary widened her eyes as her breath fell much faster than it had.

"Don't say that right now," she breathed.

"Why not?" he asked, taking a step closer to her, his hand brushing over her hip. Asher couldn't help it. She was like the moon, and he was the moth. Her mere existence drew him in, to whatever fate waited for him there.

"Look." She threw her head in the direction of the path. "We're at the coast and this is a favorite spot for families. If you're going to talk about devouring my pussy in your baritone voice and look at me with that intense stare, there better be follow through, and this isn't the spot for it. As you know, I can be very loud." She raised her eyebrow, then walked ahead of him towards the water. As Asher's gaze followed her, he could hear the din of children playing nearby.

Fuck.

Asher took a deep breath, thought about jumping in the freezing cold ocean, and followed her.

After walking close to three miles, Rosemary took Asher to a bluff overlooking the water. It wasn't secluded, several people walked by on the path behind them, but it was quiet and peaceful. Asher would have commented that the view was the most beautiful thing he'd ever seen, but that was sitting next to him in a white T-shirt.

"Family?" Rosemary asked.

"Pardon?"

"Who is your family? What is your family?" She laughed. "Who are the people that are important to you?"

"Like most people, I do have a family," he teased. "My sister is my closest family. We're actually sort of the same age."

"Are you a twin?"

"No, we're both adopted. And because of grade cut-offs I was a year ahead of her in school. But our parents kind of raised us like twins. Complementary outfits and all."

"That's adorable. I hope you have at least one picture of you in lederhosen with your sister." She inched a little closer to him until her thigh pressed against his.

Asher grinned. "My mom probably has at least ten. She loved taking pictures of us in ridiculous outfits. My dad passed away about three years ago."

"Oh, I'm sorry."

"It's okay. He had a good life, and I had a good dad. Natalie's married. That's my sister, her name is Natalie. She's married to a woman, Sophie." He paused. "I'm really protective of her. I can't stand when people treat her badly."

Rosemary smiled. "Do they have kids?"

"No, not yet. None of your sisters have kids, right?"

"Nope, none of the Bays have procreated yet. I have a feeling in the next few years that will change though."

"Why?"

She shrugged. "The tide's about to turn. Already started. Our lives have seasons, and this season is ending and we're heading into the next."

"So what's the agenda for the next season of your life?" he asked, genuinely curious.

"I imagine my list is pretty similar to yours." She flashed a grin.

"What's on your list?" He laughed.

"A house in the woods with a man I can't wait to fuck when I get home from the florist, a garden overflowing with herbs and flowers in the summer, and two to three children running barefoot in the backyard. Maybe a dog."

Asher nearly choked.

First, that was very similar to his current hopes for the next five years. Secondly, listening to Rosemary saying the phrase "can't wait to fuck" followed by the look she gave him...he wanted to be the man she couldn't wait to fuck.

"That's a very good list."

"Thank you. I take pride in it. Oh, and I also want to open my own company designing flowers for weddings. I do all the weddings for Therese right now, and I think I could strike out on my own."

"Really? That's amazing."

"Let's hear your list." She nudged his shoulder with her own and let their touch linger a moment.

"I've been holding back getting a dog since I moved here, so that's definitely on the list. Definitely want kids. And I like the idea of coming home after a long day and seeing a beautiful woman working in the garden."

"If she needs help in the garden, I'm available, but I ain't cheap." Rosemary winked.

"I don't think she'll need help in the garden." Asher wasn't sure what possessed him to say that. He wasn't looking to settle down. He barely knew Rosemary. Natalie and Sophie had dated for nearly five years before they got married, and while that seemed a little long, Asher definitely needed to know a woman for longer than a week before throwing himself in heart first.

But Asher was smitten. This woman was quickly capturing his heart. She had wrapped her hand around his soul and there was no turning back.

"I used to do something with my mom at the end of every day called the happy and the hard. We would tell each other the happiest moment of our day and the hardest moment. It was great. It gave us both a chance to talk about something that had been difficult, but also share in the joy of the good. My sisters and I don't do it anymore, but I miss it." She exhaled. "I don't know why I told you that. I haven't thought about it in years."

"Well, let's hear it. Hardest part of today?"

Rosemary looked out over the water, like she was really contemplating the hardest thing to happen so far.

"They are intertwined today. The happy and the hard." She turned to him and licked her lips, the simple movement like warm honey over his heart. "Hardest thing was working up the courage to buzz you. Happiest thing is right now. Being here with you."

"You had to build up the courage? You're the most confident person I've met in years," he admitted.

"I am confident, I won't deny it. But that doesn't mean I don't get nervous if something is important."

"I'm important?" Asher asked.

"Course you are." She leaned against his shoulder, snuggling towards him. "I don't let just anyone go down on me in a police station." She smiled wide, biting her lip.

"I'd hope not." Asher risked setting his hand on her leg, palm up. She immediately wove her fingers through his as if she'd taken his hand a thousand times before.

"Your turn. Hardest and happiest."

"Okay. Happiest is easy, sitting here with you looking at the ocean. Hardest..." He searched his brain for the answer. "It's not really today specific. But that missing woman, her brother is really worried about her. And I hate that I can't help him. I feel like when someone's missing it's so much worse than knowing what happened. Maybe she wanted to start a new life, or maybe she drowned herself when she was here and her body's already halfway to Europe. I just hate not being able to give him an answer."

He looked over to her to gauge her reaction, but she wasn't looking at him. Her eyes were firmly attached to the sea and seemed faraway.

"Sorry, I shouldn't have brought it up. Sometimes my line of work can be a real downer."

"No," she held up her hand, "don't censor what you do for me. You're being a good cop. The world needs good cops."

"That it does."

Asher let a few beats pass, his mind muddling in its own mess.

"I don't really like being a cop," he confessed.

Rosemary's attention snapped away from the ocean and squarely at his face. "Are you serious?"

"Yeah. I sort of fell into it. In the neighborhood I grew up in, like fifty percent of the guys become cops. It was just the way of it. Then I graduated college without a real career path and decided to apply to the police academy. I like protecting people, but that's not what a lot of it is." He smiled grimly. "Should have been a bodyguard. More straight forward."

Rosemary looked at him, really looked at him. She didn't stare or gawk or lower her eyes, but she did keep her eyes stuck on his face through the silence.

"What did you study in college?"

"History. I know, not a great idea. But my parents were gung-ho that we study something we loved, and I'm not going to lie, I love history. Give me a documentary on the tsars of Russia or the Haitian Revolution or the Boxer Rebellion any day of the week and I'll be a happy man."

"So you still keep up with history, in your own way."

"Yeah. It's hobby now, but I still love it."

Rosemary nodded. "I didn't go to college. I took a few botany classes at the community college on the mainland when I was nineteen. For a bit I thought if I really wanted to make something of myself in the flower world, I needed a degree in botany and to breed some new kind of rose, or something like that. But botany was really freaking hard for me. I was a solid B student in high school and suddenly majoring in a science wasn't in the cards. I dropped out, built my own garden, and started working at Therese's part-time. It turned out my love of flowers was enough. I'm really good at designing bouquets and centerpieces, and even if I never create a plum-colored hydrangea, I still do important work." She paused and furrowed her brow. "That was a really convoluted example that I basically told you to say you don't have to be a cop. If you love history, make it work for you. Just because the job you have is important and lots of people are fulfilled by it, doesn't mean you are. Or that you should feel guilty because you aren't."

Asher let her wisdom sink in and felt a weight lift off his chest. Being a cop was such a huge part of his identity, but not by choice. It was like he'd been stuffed into the box and couldn't figure a way out.

"You'd be a good career counselor."

"Me? No way. I'm all about following your heart's desire. I'd be telling brilliant pre-med kids to become sculptors. Their parents would hate me." She giggled.

They sat there a while longer, talking a little less but inching close together until Asher had his arm firmly around Rosemary's shoulders and she rested her back against his chest.

"Should we walk back?" Asher asked. It had to be close to dinner, and they were a good three miles away from food.

"Mmmhmmm," Rosemary answered. He pulled her to stand, but instead of turning to the path, Rosemary stood close to him. She wrapped her arms around his waist and laid her head against his chest.

"That's better," she sighed. "I like it here."

Asher took a steadying breath, then let himself hold her. He slipped his hand around the curve of her waist, and the other snuck beneath her hair. His fingers teased the bare skin of her neck for a moment.

She hummed in approval, the smallest noise, barely audible over the surf, but it set Asher on fire. He wildly looked both ways down the path.

No one.

"Rosemary," he began, his hand moving to cup her chin and turn her face to look up at him. "I—"

"Follow me," she said quietly, grabbing her backpack with one hand, and him with the other. She dragged him away from the water, off the path, and into the forest. They stepped over the wild growth, toppled trees, and a few bursts of bright purple flowers.

"There," she said with satisfaction once they were out of view from the path. She put both hands on his chest and backed him against a tree and pulled her shirt over her head.

"Kiss me, Asher," she commanded.

He didn't need another direction, dragging her against him, his hands immediately on her butt and pulling her up to meet his mouth. Their lips met in an immediate hot tangle. He loved that about kissing Rosemary. She didn't play coy; she knew what she wanted and went for it.

She gasped and moaned and dug her hands in his hair, against his shoulders, down his biceps. She was like a wildfire, burning bright and blazing out of control. And he wanted to be razed to the ground.

She wiggled out of his arms and turned her back to him, holding her hair out of the way.

"Undo it," she said, her bra waiting in front of him. Asher made quick work of it, glad he hadn't had to fumble with it while kissing her at the same time. She shrugged it off and turned around.

"Fuck," he said. Asher was sure he had a goofy grin on his face, but he couldn't hide it. Rosemary naked made him very happy.

"Thank you," she answered, then grabbed both of his hands and put them on her chest. "Play with these," she commanded, then got down on her knees and unzipped his pants.

"Oh, shit." Asher searched the forest wildly for any passersby. He could not be caught getting head in the woods. He'd get fired, probably shamed, and maybe need to move off the island.

"No one's coming," she insisted, reaching into his shorts and pulling out his cock. She looked up at him and flicked her tongue across her lips. "Pay attention to my tits," she reminded, then slid her mouth over him.

Asher groaned. He trained his gaze on her, watching her work him with her mouth and loving every minute of it. He rolled his thumbs over her nipples, smoothed the skin around them, and then pinched her lightly.

She moaned against his cock, and he almost came.

"God, you're gorgeous," he growled. Against her orders, he let one hand move to her hair and buried his fist in it but kept one hand teasing her nipples.

She didn't stop moaning, and Asher had never experienced such ungodly ecstasy from a simple noise. It was like the world was waking up all around him, and he never noticed the joy of sound before.

He pushed her away, then turned and came hard, his fist around his own cock. Asher leaned his head against the tree, his lungs still trying to find air in the middle of the woods.

"You know, I would have swallowed."

Asher turned back. Rosemary was standing in front of him, sly smile on her mouth.

"Come here," he growled, and grabbed her. He flipped her so her back was against his chest, her sweet ass pressing against his still sensitive cock. He nipped her neck then said, "Watch for people."

"No one is coming," she began but melted into a moan when he shoved her legs apart. He put his hand up her skirt, found her panties, and pulled them halfway down her thighs.

"You want this, right? You want me to touch you?"

"Goddess, yes. Go fucking nuts." Rosemary raised her arms above her head and hooked her hands on his biceps.

"Good." Asher trailed one hand to her breast, kneading and swirling and pinching. The other walked up her thigh, a solitary finger parting her lips, and found her clit swollen, wet, and welcoming. He dipped into her, gathering even more of her delicious moisture, then slid back to her clit.

"You feel amazing," he said, his mouth muffled against her hair. "So hot and wet. I can't wait to fuck you."

"Yes," she breathed, grabbing him. He stuck his thigh between hers, widening her stance, and slipped a finger inside of her.

"You are fucking amazing. If you hadn't just sucked me off so spectacularly, I'd lay on the ground and fuck you until you came all over my cock and begged me for more."

"I want that," she panted. "We'll do that. But right now, don't stop. Because, because, I'm..." Her voice trailed off, her moans turning frantic until she clenched around his finger and he had to hold her up from falling.

"Fuck," she finally breathed. "Kiss me."

Asher slid his hand from between her legs and gathered her against his chest, their mouths meeting again. Her lips were swollen and soft, and his cock twitched against her belly.

God, what was this woman doing to him?

"I'm definitely going to make you follow through on that forest floor fucking this summer." Rosemary giggled drowsily. She nuzzled her head against his chest.

"You better," he answered, and kissed the top of her head.

When they finally decided to make the walk home, Asher felt like he'd just lived through one of the most important days of his life. This woman was exceptional. Astounding. Otherwordly. She was magic.

"Do you want to come up now?" he asked when they were a block away from his apartment. He definitely had plans to fuck her on the forest floor, but he'd also really like to fuck her on his bed. Or couch. Or floor. Or kitchen counter.

"I do, I really do, but I'm not going to," Rosemary answered.

"All right." He was more than a little confused. He was pretty sure they'd just connected beyond a normal afternoon spent between two interested adults.

"This afternoon was pretty perfect. Let's leave it like that." She took her phone out of her pocket and handed it to him. "Text yourself from me. And then text me tonight and tomorrow and the day after. And call me. Talk to me all night. Tell me stuff about when you were a kid and all your hopes and dreams and shit. And then ask me out on a date. Okay?"

"Definitely." He punched a quick text in her phone. "Do you want a ride home?"

"My bike is right down the block." She went to her tiptoes and kissed his cheek, lingering just a moment. "See you soon."

"Goodbye, Rosemary."

Chapter Twelve

Rosemary Bay was falling in love with Sheriff Asher Evans.

He was her soulmate. She knew she was going to fall in love with him, she knew she already sort of loved him. But now, going through the process of falling in love with him felt odd.

She didn't know if he snored, how he took his coffee, what he looked like when he just woke up, or his favorite food. She had never met any of his friends, his family, or been to his hometown. She did know that he had a dirty mouth, she loved it, and he could hold her entire weight up while she broke apart from an insanely earth-shattering orgasm.

But she needed to get to know him better, his mind at least. And she wanted to do it fast.

Rosemary: You up?

Asher: Yes, is this a traditional you up text because I start work in an hour, but I can make it work.

Rosemary: LOL, it is not. I have some questions for you.

Asher: Begin.

Rosemary: What is your favorite food?

Asher: Everyday food, pizza. Special treat food, crème brûlée.

Rosemary: Ooh, that's a good one. What's your favorite color?

Asher: Orange

Rosemary: Animal?

Asher: Dog for a pet, but I really love polar bears.

Rosemary: What side of the bed do you sleep on?

Asher: Whichever is closer to the door. Anything else?

Rosemary: How do you take your coffee?

Asher: Usually in a to-go cup from Dunkin Donuts but your sister's Americano is pretty good. So is a straight cup of black coffee from the diner.

Rosemary: All good answers.

Asher: Your turn. Same questions.

Rosemary: All forms of potatoes, green, toads, don't have a side of the bed, and I prefer tea, but I've been known to enjoy seasonal monstrosities. Lavender has a great gingerbread latte in December that has like two-thousand calories in it.

Asher: One more question.

Rosemary: Go ahead

Asher: What do you sleep in?

Rosemary: Most nights, a T-shirt.

Asher: Just a T-shirt?

Rosemary: I usually have some sort of panties on too, though not always. What do you sleep in?

Asher: I live alone. It depends on the weather and ranges from flannel pants and a long sleeve to nothing.

Rosemary: Best answer yet. I feel bad you are heading to work and I'm already in bed and about to fall asleep. Listening to my sister snore.

Asher: Who snores loud enough that you can hear them in your room?

Rosemary: LOL, I share a room with Sage. I know, very weird that I am thirty-one and share a room with my twenty-three-year-old sister, but it works for us.

Asher: If it works, it works. Have a good sleep, Rosemary. I'll talk to you tomorrow.

Rosemary: What time is your shift over?

Asher: 8. I usually get home around 9 and then pass out for a few hours.

Rosemary: Hope it's uneventful.

Asher: Knowing Star Island, it will be.

Rosemary: Good night, Asher. Text me in the morning if you want.

Asher: Night, Rosemary. I will.

Yup, that settled it. Rosemary was definitely falling in love with Asher Evans.

"Rosemary! Lavender! Sage! Get in here!" Laurel shouted from the kitchen. The three sisters currently residing in the Bay cottage were enjoying a nice night outside with wine, but Rosemary had a feeling that was all going to change.

"Look." Laurel pointed to a stack of paper on the dining room table. Owen was at her side, his arm around her waist and brow more furrowed than usual.

"What are they?" Rosemary asked, picking up the first few sheets.

"They're letters."

"I'm coming for you, Bay witch. I'll have your blood and your sisters', too. I know what you did to Morana," Lavender read.

"Yikes. I assume this is from one of the brothers." Rosemary flipped an envelope around. "Where did you get these?" There was no return address visible. She rolled her eyes. The post office needed to get stricter on that.

"My PO box. It's on my website as a way to contact me."

"So they definitely know about the curse," Lavender said, taking a seat at the table and stacking up the papers. "And we can guess they have connections to other witches and warlocks who they may have told about the curse. So the person on the Haberdashery was either one of these guys or someone they told."

"We need to break that curse," Sage said.

"The ghosts said it wasn't breakable," Laurel reminded.

"It wasn't breakable in the early 1700s. Magic has evolved in the last three-hundred or so years. Witches and warlocks are doing spells no one thought were possible," Sage pointed out. "Has anyone even tried to break the curse? We're a long line of hearth and home witches; we're not exactly known for our curse-breaking abilities. Are there witches or warlocks who specialize in breaking curses?"

"Not that I've ever heard. It's more about being good at casting them than breaking them." Lavender straightened the pile of letters in front of her.

Rosemary had been tossing an idea around in her head the last couple days, and now seemed the best time to bring it up.

"I'm going to look into my past life or lives," she stated. Her eyes immediately met Lavender's, who looked like she had lost all fight in her.

"Asher's a human, Rosemary. It will be really hard to explain to him what's going to happen," Lavender began.

"I'm not going to use your spell. I contacted Daisy through the message boards. She's the witch who said to burn a shit ton of thyme. She said as long as my soulmate is human, I will be the only one who goes back. Her human husband saw nothing."

"You're going to burn all your thyme?" Laurel sounded horrified.

"Yes. It's my thyme, and I can grow more. I'll go to the mainland and get some seedlings when I get back from the past. It's not too late in the season for them to take root. My supply will take a hit, but it won't be depleted."

No one said anything for a few beats.

"Are you sure he won't see anything?" Owen asked. Owen had traveled to his past life with Laurel a few weeks earlier. Laurel had been burned for witchcraft and Owen beaten to death by guards for trying to save her. Rosemary knew whatever was in the past was probably very grim.

"He won't. You're a sonofawitch. I could tell you were magical in some sense the moment I saw you. I don't get that from Asher," Rosemary said convincingly.

"When are you going to do it?" Lavender asked.

"Tomorrow night. Since I'll be burning a significant amount of thyme, I'll need to be outside, and it's supposed to be warm and dry for a while. I hope you all won't mind trading off watching over me. I don't think anything will happen, but it would be nice not to wake up covered in owl pellets."

"Nyx would never!" Laurel defended.

"Maybe not Nyx, but she's got some sketchy friends." Rosemary took a deep breath. "I'm going to go to bed. I've heard traveling to a past life can take a lot of a witch. I should get a good sleep."

When the three Bay witches who had first been cursed visited, they mentioned the past had answers for all of them. Laurel found out why Morana was coming after her. Maybe Rosemary's past held the key to breaking the curse. She had to try.

Rosemary picked up her phone and opened the conversation with Asher. They'd been texting throughout the past two days, just about stupid stuff. Rosemary sent him a picture of a cool bouquet she had made, he sent her a picture of a black lab puppy that had tried to attack his car. They'd been flirty, but neither of them had made the move to make another set of plans yet. Rosemary knew the next time she saw Asher, the floodgates would open. She needed the time to be right.

> Rosemary: I'm going to Boston for the night tomorrow. I'll be back the next afternoon.

> Asher: Sounds fun.

> Rosemary: I might be hard to reach, so don't panic if you don't get a text back from me right away.

> Asher: In Boston?

> Rosemary: When I get back, let's hang out, just the two of us, OK?

> Asher: Yeah, I'd love to.

> Asher: Are you all right?

> Rosemary: Yes. I will text you as soon as I get back, OK?

> Asher: Sounds great. Have a good time.

Rosemary exhaled audibly and set her phone on her bedside table. She turned several times until the covers on her bed wound through her legs like restraints and she could hardly move.

"What is wrong with you?" Sage's whisper echoed off the walls.

"You're awake?"

"Yes. You are moving around like an animal and furiously poking your phone." Sage propped her head up on one elbow. "What's wrong?"

"I'm nervous."

"About?"

"Looking into the past, of course. Wouldn't that worry you?"

Sage switched on the light on her bedside table and shrugged. "I don't know. It already happened. I don't think any huge secrets are lurking in the past."

"You mean a secret like Laurel cursing an evil witch over lifetimes and reaping the consequences now?"

"Laurel's so dramatic. Let me rephrase it. I can't see you having anything in your past that's going to haunt you in this life. Laurel? Yes. Me? Most likely I have an army of pissed off witches and warlocks set on hunting me down this time around because I buried them alive in retribution for their desecrating the sacred woods of my patron goddess."

Rosemary giggled.

"Rosemary, you're basically a rainbows and sunshine witch, if there was such a thing. Are garden witches ever evil? My first instinct is to say no."

Rosemary did pride herself on making a good first impression and always trying her hardest to be kind and go so far as to attempt to make friends with everyone she came across.

"Go to sleep, Rosemary. You probably have a really boring past life, and we will gain no new information from it. Or you were, like, a royal concubine of Charlemagne."

"Oh! That would be fun. Or terrible. I don't know much about Charlemagne." Rosemary snuggled under her covers, feeling better. If constantly pessimistic Sage wasn't the least bit worried about Rosemary's foray into her past life, she shouldn't be either.

"But if Asher was Charlemagne, I'm definitely going to have a serious conversation with him about all the wives and women. Even in a past life, I know I am more than enough to satisfy him both sexually and emotionally."

Sage snorted a laugh. "Go to bed, royal concubine."

"Good night, you little dark protector of forests."

Chapter Thirteen

Asher fidgeted in his seat. He needed a new desk chair. This one was too short on the tallest setting, and he felt like his legs were jammed beneath the desk.

The chair was only exasperating his mood. Something had been off with Rosemary when they texted last night, and he couldn't quite pinpoint what. She was going to Boston for the night, but would be unreachable? That was odd. He could see if she was going to be on a boat in the middle of the Atlantic, but one of the biggest cities on the eastern seaboard? Unlikely.

Asher had the bad habit of jumping to worse-case scenarios. When Natalie told him they needed to talk when they were twenty, he had worried for a week that she was dying. When he showed up at Penn State where she went to college and she told him she was gay, he had laughed out of relief, and inadvertently offended her. After apologizing and telling her he thought she was dying, he hugged her and said he'd had a feeling for the past six years.

Right now, he thought Rosemary was in trouble. He had half a mind to show up at her house and ask why she was going to Boston and if he should accompany her.

He would not do that. He wouldn't do that because while he was a needless worrier and he jumped at every opportunity to protect people, he wasn't crazy. If Rosemary needed him, she would say so. He decided to repeat that every hour on the hour until she got back from Boston.

He really hoped she wasn't going to see another man. They had just started this mutual attraction, and he had no say over whether she would be faithful to him, especially since they hadn't discussed it. But all the same, he could not help the jealousy that seized his heart if his mind turned to her with someone else.

He did not like this feeling.

Around noon, Asher was knee deep in paperwork. He had no idea being sheriff of a small town would involve more paperwork than being a beat cop in Buffalo, but somehow it did. These Celestials sure did get into a lot of property line disputes that ended in the police being called over stupid things like a shovel being left on the wrong side of a fence.

"You have a visitor," Jane's voice rang out over the intercom.

"Is it Rosemary?" Asher asked automatically, then grimaced. He wasn't sure if he was supposed to be so overtly open when it came to Rosemary. Did people in small towns mind when their sheriff dated? Were they dating? Yes, Asher concluded. He could say that he was dating Rosemary Bay.

If anyone bothered to ask.

"No, it's Morana Stoch's brother. Ivan. From Montana. He is physically on Star Island and in the department. He wants to see you." Jane did not sound happy with the development.

"Oh, shit," Asher mumbled. "Can you keep him out there for two minutes, and then send him in?" He had tons of paperwork spread out over his desk that was not for the eyes of the public.

"I'll let him know."

Asher quickly organized the paperwork into something resembling a pile, shoved it into his drawer, and did a once over of the rest of his office.

A loud rap on the door and jiggling of the handle let Asher know that Ivan had arrived. Asher didn't make it a habit to lock his office, but he did if he really didn't want to be interrupted.

He stood up and crossed the room, clearing his throat before opening the door.

"Ivan, nice to meet you. I'm Sheriff Evans." Asher stuck his hand out to shake the man's hand.

He gawked at him.

"You? Oh, you've got to be kidding me. Of course it's you." Ivan rolled his eyes and pushed past him, shaking his head. "It figures. I've had a shit month and a shit week and now a shit day. Do you know how long it took to get to this miserable spit of land from Montana? Forever. Longer than walking from Ynglings' land to yours, and that's without a cart. I had two layovers plus a terrible bus ride to get to Chatham. Why on earth would anyone live here?"

Asher furrowed his brow. What on earth was this man talking about?

"I'm sorry?"

Ivan looked back at him and narrowed his eyes. His expression slowly changed from confusion to acceptance.

"Oh, all right," he said slowly. "Where do we start, Sheriff Evans?"

"Why don't you have a seat and I'll go over everything again." He motioned to the chair.

Ivan took a seat and began inspecting Asher's desk.

"No pictures of your wife?"

"I'm not married," Asher answered, walking around to the other side of the desk.

"Girlfriend then? You must have a shot of her somewhere around here." His eyes searched the room.

"Are you here to talk about your sister or is this a social visit?" Asher was getting pissed. He never talked about his personal life with citizens at work. Was this guy high right now? His eyes weren't dilated.

"Look, I know the Bay family had something to do with it. Morana was in contact with Laurel, and she lied about it. I don't know what your connections are to this family, but I can start my own investigation now that I'm here."

"No, you can't. You don't have a PI license in the state."

"No harm in asking a few questions, right? A few of those sisters work in town. Nothing stopping me from patronizing their shops."

"Are you threatening the Bay family?" Asher could feel anger rising just beneath the surface of his skin. He fought to keep it in control.

"Threatening? I'm not an idiot. It's clear that this island has some sort of weird code against turning on their own." He smirked. "I'm staying at the Williams Motel. Try not to lose track of me while I'm here. And if I do go missing, know that the Bay sisters most definitely had something to do with it."

Ivan stood up from his seat, pushing it back so forcefully that it clattered to the ground. He then turned and left, slamming the door so hard, it bounced back open.

Asher stood up and rounded the desk, moving to replace the chair.

"He's a gem," Jane said, walking through his door. "Should I have someone follow him?"

"No, he's staying at the motel. And he'll stand out like a sore thumb." Ivan Stoch had the same ice hair as his sister, as well as a permanent scowl and shifting eyes. He couldn't imagine anyone forgetting his presence. While striking women were noticed, their presence usually didn't threaten anyone. One look at Ivan would have more than half the population keeping an eye on him.

Still, Asher would personally keep tabs on Ivan. He planned on checking in at the motel at least once a day, as well as swinging by the Bay sisters' places of employment to make sure he wasn't hassling them. Rosemary wouldn't be at work today or tomorrow, so at least he didn't have to worry about him going after her. But Lavender and Verbena both worked in town. He'd make sure neither of them had any unwanted questions.

Asher couldn't shake the feeling that Ivan had thought he was someone else. The way he dove into conversation with him, almost as if they knew each other well...it was unsettling. Seeing him in person, Asher was surprised he didn't have the telltale signs of a drug addict. But his eye movements were normal, his skin clear, and he looked like he showered regularly and ate a good amount. It didn't rule out drugs addling his mind, but it made the case harder for Asher to use as an excuse.

Maybe Ivan was simply a strange person. Either way, Asher had paperwork to finish, and a quick round to do of the Centauri Peninsula before he went home. He sat down and got back to work.

Chapter Fourteen

Rosemary held a bundle of thyme in her hand and inhaled deeply.

"I will be able to grow more," she whispered, bending down to cut another huge handful. She was piling up thyme in the bonfire pit where it was sure not to spread to other parts of the yard. She would have to do the beginning of the spell alone, so none of her sisters were affected by the burning thyme, but Lavender was going to watch from the window and make sure the flames stayed under control. The last thing they needed was all of them to fall under a past life spell and spend hours passed out on their grass.

Within ten minutes, all her beautiful thyme had been cut away and formed a large, fragrant, green mound. Rosemary spread a flannel blanket on the ground for her to sit or lie on. She wasn't sure if her body would be frozen sitting up once the spell took hold or if she would fall over. Either way, the idea of centipedes crawling through her hair and over her face gave her the creeps. She might be a garden witch, but she didn't need bugs all over her body while she took a trip down memory lane.

When Rosemary reached out to Daisy for more information, she didn't get much. The spell didn't affect human soulmates, but Daisy had no idea how long Rosemary would be out for. She was prepared for a full twenty-four-hour event, like the spell Laurel and Lavender had performed, but maybe she would be lucky and only be out for five hours. Either way, she would hopefully leave with the information she needed. The Bay ghosts said they needed to look to their pasts for information on the Stochs and the curse. Laurel found out why Morana was so obsessed with getting Laurel's blood. Maybe Rosemary's would turn something up.

Unlike Laurel, Rosemary had no idea what sort of past life or lives might be waiting for her on the other side of this spell. Laurel's hedge witchery gave her some psychic abilities, so she had dreamt of her time in medieval France before actually going there. Rosemary was going in blind. She could be going back one hundred years or three thousand. It was anyone's guess.

Rosemary took a deep breath. She really hoped she didn't end up in the Ice Age freezing to death.

Rosemary did one last look around. Her toad, Verruca, was sitting calmly on the log beside her, staring up at her.

"Hop along to the garden, V. It's going to get weird here and I don't want you dreaming about when you used to be a dinosaur." Rosemary shooed the toad away who, of course, listened and hopped contentedly towards the flowers.

Rosemary drew in a shaky breath.

"I can do this," she affirmed. She lit a piece of kindling, then nestled it beneath the thyme. She took her seat on the flannel and waited.

Daisy said it might take a few minutes for the fumes to get going and her to fall into a trance. Rosemary breathed deeply, letting the smoke from the thyme fill her lungs. Her anxiety heightened with each breath. Was this a mistake? What if it was truly horrible?

"It'll be over before I know it," she mumbled, then fell over.

Asher felt awful. His body ached and he could barely keep his eyes open. In the last fifteen minutes, he'd gone from feeling completely healthy and normal to feeling like absolute shit.

He turned his patrol car down his own street and quickly radioed that he was sick and going home. Charlie said he would swing by his patrol area in a few minutes. Asher was only supposed to work another hour, but he felt like he needed to get out of the car.

He ambled up the stairs of his apartment, gripping the railing as he went. He was so dizzy. He needed a glass of water and Tylenol. He felt like he was on fire.

Asher pushed through his apartment door and dropped his keys on the floor. He stumbled to the kitchen and grabbed a Gatorade, trying to take a drink, but it tasted like soot in his mouth.

Asher shuffled to the bathroom, flung open the medicine cabinet, and got out his thermometer. His mom had bought it for him when he got his first apartment. He hoped it still worked.

He stuck it under his arm and reached for the Tylenol. He wasn't going to wait for the results. He swallowed two pills without any liquid and slid to the bathroom floor.

The thermometer beeped and he pulled it out to see the results.

"105.1. Holy shit," he panted. Where was his phone? He needed to call 911. He groped his pockets, feeling it but unable to use his hands. His head slid down to the floor, the cold tile giving him a little relief.

He closed his eyes and passed out.

Chapter Fifteen

In a dark and icy world, there is nothing quite like the arrival of spring.

Gundrun sat cradled in her mother's lap, her arms encircling the little girl's waist, marveling at the beginning of the sweetest season.

"Idun comes, no matter what. No matter how dark and terrible the winter is, she always comes and awakens the earth with her greens and pale yellows." Her mother pointed out slivers of verdant beneath the melting snow. Gundrun reached out her hands, running blades of grass between her small fingertips.

"Idun will watch over you," she said, pressing a small kiss to her daughter's hair. "Long after I am gone, she will be here, and she will never abandon you." Her mother smothered a cough with her hand and quickly smiled. "You are blessed by spring, just as I am. People will try to take advantage of it. Even those you think love you. Keep your blessing close to your heart."

Gundrun nodded solemnly. Even at seven years old, she felt the gravity of her mother's words.

"Do not tell your father. Do you understand? He will not be kind if he knows of this."

"I won't," she promised, laying her head against her mother's chest. She didn't really understand why she shouldn't tell her father when she heard the flowers calling to her, or the seeds beginning to burst forth beneath the hard ground. But she would never betray a promise made to her mother. Her mother was like warm sunlight and soft rain—she sustained Gundrun and brought her all the joy of the world.

Before the summer overtook the spring, the life of Gundrun's mother had gone out. She'd slowly withered away under the gaining light. Gundrun was confused; her mother grew stronger with the sun every year. Why should her life be taken during *her* time? Idun walked among them these days. It was a time meant for joy.

She sat beside her mother on that terrible morning, eyes wide and afraid, watching as the breath in her chest grew rapid and then finally ceased.

"That's it," her father said gruffly, standing and moving from his position next to his wife. "It's over." He walked towards the door of their house, blocking out the light with his form until he exited.

Gundrun looked to him, but then beyond. Towards the door, she saw her mother. She was well again, a glowing version of the woman who had just left her body. Her hair was alight with rays of the warm sun, the dress on her body one made of shimmering raindrops and white clouds. Beside her, a woman made of flowers beckoned her with apples.

Her mother looked back to Gundrun, smiled, and turned to follow the flower woman.

Gundrun cried out but her mother didn't stop. She walked on into a blinding light until nothing remained but the dappled sunlight of the day.

The woman of the flowers glanced at her.

"Gundrun. You are one of mine." Her voice boomed in her ears, but she knew her father could not hear it. The woman turned and disappeared into the light.

"Come now. We need to eat." Her father's voice broke the spell. She wanted to cry out, do you not see? Idun was here, my mother in her care. But she would not betray the promise. Gundrun simply dipped her head and followed her father out of the house without another glance at her mother's body. They would burn the body once her kinsfolk said goodbye. It was an empty vessel now. The magic of spring within her had disappeared.

Gundrun walked out into the warm day, quietly toeing off her slippers to feel the earth beneath her soles. The power of spring coursed through her veins, stronger now than it had been moments before.

She was blessed by Idun, great goddess of spring and youth.

Skáldi walked behind the cart. His father and youngest brother, Hakon, sat behind the horses, his mother and sisters, Kenna and Nessa, behind them. He and Eitri walked for now. It wasn't far, less than a day on foot, and he would not dare complain. They were going to see an old friend of his father's. Word had come to their clan that his wife had died in the spring, and his father would pay his respects. There had been murmurings of the man falling on hard times after the death of his wife.

"How much further?" Skáldi whispered to Eitri. They'd been before, a few years earlier, but Skáldi didn't remember the way.

"We're nearly there," his brother whispered back. He raised his hand to point over the hill in front of them. "See the smoke there? That's where they live."

They picked up their pace with the destination so close in view. Skáldi couldn't wait to take a piss and then sit for a moment. His bladder felt near to explosion.

His father steered the horses towards the house, finding a place to tie them up and help the small children out of the cart. Skáldi looked at the house in confusion. It was little more than a shack. His village was large; there were more than ten houses in total. His father's sister and her family lived there, as well as some more distant cousins. This house stood alone in the woods. There were no boisterous animals outside, only a handful of chickens that looked close to death, too weak to peck for food.

"Stay here for now," his father muttered to his mother. "Let me find him and alert him to our arrival before we barrel down the door." He handed Hakon to his mother, who propped him on her hip.

"Kenna, fetch water for the horses. Eitri, go with her," she added. Skáldi shuddered at the feel of the place. In high summer, it felt off, nearly dead. Where were their fields? What did they eat?

Skáldi slunk off towards the woods, looking for a place to relieve himself where his mother wouldn't scold him for being too close to the house. He ducked behind a few trees until he felt relatively covered. He quickly undid his belt and sighed with relief. It had been hours since they stopped.

He finished, replaced his belt, then turned to walk back to the house.

"Who are you?"

Skáldi nearly yelped. Standing not an arm's reach in front of him was a little girl, face and arms covered in mud, her hair a wild tangle surrounding her head.

"Thor's balls!" he shouted. "You scared me!"

"Who are you?" she asked again, her eyes narrowing.

"Skáldi. My father is here to see your father. I think. You live in that house?" He pointed beyond the tree.

"Yes."

"We're here to see if you are starving after your mother died."

"Not yet."

"What's your name?"

"Gundrun." She stuck her hand out towards him. He didn't move, unsure what her intent was. Her dirty fingers reached his face and cupped his cheek.

The world around them stopped. Nothing moved or chirped or croaked in the woods. All was silent.

Skáldi blinked hard. The dirt covering Gundrun melted away, replaced with sunlight and bursts of flowers behind her. Her cheeks were red as apples and her eyes locked on his, glowing with delight.

Skáldi fell to his knees, his legs slamming into wet mud, breaking her hand away from his face.

"Are you all right?" she asked, crouching beside him.

He looked up. The dirt was back, and the beautiful light faded away.

"Yes." He quickly got to his feet. "Fine."

"Why did you fall over?"

"I don't know," he grumbled, stepping around her towards the house. "My mother brought honeycake. I think it's for you."

Gundrun pushed past him, scampering towards the house at full sprint. She may have told him they weren't starving, but the speed of her feet told him otherwise.

"Eck! Don't grab at the cake!" The woman bearing food held it high out of Gundrun's reach. "I'll feed you plenty soon enough." She handed the food to one of the girls and snatched Gundrun's wrist.

"Men and boys, fill the tub with water and then make yourselves scarce. Go hunt some rabbits or the like for our meal tonight." She turned to Gundrun. "We'll get you cleaned up and then I'll feed you until your sides ache."

Gundrun didn't remember the last true bath she'd taken. Her father had told her to swim in the sea a few times, but she hadn't seen soap since her mother died many months earlier. Once the bath was filled, the woman, who introduced herself as Sivi, stripped Gundrun of her clothes and dunked her over and over, scrubbing every bit of grime off her body. She lathered up her hair as well, then meticulously picked through every tangle with a comb that had sat unused since her mother's death.

"You need to bathe and brush out your hair. Otherwise little things will come and live in your tangles and on your skin," Sivi explained, pulling out the last knots. "You are very beautiful, just like your mother. You need to take care of your beauty. Poor Freya would weep seeing it covered in such muck."

Sivi plaited her hair tightly, telling her she could keep her plaits in for one week, but then must unweave them and wash her hair before plaiting it again. She gave her one of her daughter's dresses they'd brought, the girl called Kenna, and declared all Gundrun's clothes needed a good washing before she could wear them again.

Sivi didn't make her wait any longer, though, and gave her a plate piled high with honey cake and berries. She promised a big meal once the men returned with something more to cook. Gundrun devoured her plate, licking each one of her fingers clean. She couldn't remember the last time she tasted food so delicious.

Gundrun spent the remainder of the day listening to Sivi tell her how to live. She watched Sivi scrub her clothes and hang them to dry in the wind, she practiced plaiting Kenna's hair so she would be able to deftly do her own, and Sivi showed her how to mend a tear in her skirt with a needle.

"Your father..." Sivi paused, looking for the right choice of words. "He is grieving your mother. He may not remember to care for you, so you must do it yourself. When you are hungry, look for berries. Ask him to show you how to catch a rabbit. Learn to fish. But keep yourself clean and your hair pulled back. If you live like an animal, people will fear you when you come of age." She lowered her voice. "When you are older, a good, strong husband can take you away from this." She nodded once.

Gundrun listened intently. She wanted to get away from this, the hunger, the dirt. She wanted to live in a family like Sivi's, full of people and life. She would do it all, bathe, plait her hair, wash her clothes. Anything for a chance of escape.

Skáldi hung back from Gundrun the rest of the trip. He didn't understand what he had seen, that burst of flowers and light, and certainly didn't want to tell anyone about it. After his mother had cleaned her up, she didn't look nearly so frightening, but he was still wary.

They stayed for four nights, then packed up to walk home. Gundrun cried and hugged his mother tightly when they left until her father dragged her away and yelled at her to get into the house. Skáldi didn't understand why that man was so cruel to his daughter. His own father only raised his voice once, and that was when Eitri accidentally set the barn on fire. Even then, his father was only angry for a moment, before clearing the damage and repairing the building, hand in hand with Eitri.

"Why didn't we bring her with us?" Skáldi asked once they were far enough away. His mother walked beside him now, Eitri riding in the cart.

"It wasn't my place to steal a child away from her father."

"He doesn't like her very much."

"That may be true, but she is still his. And one day he might find he needs her."

Sivi and her family came to see Gundrun every year. Sivi would praise Gundrun's accomplishments, teach her something new, like how to draw healing marrow from the bone of an otter or to use the feathers of a dead bird to read the signs of the season.

Sometimes she came with only her husband and daughters, but twice more she brought her sons. One of them, Skáldi, was always kind to her now. He chopped wood for their pile, caught fish and gave them directly to her, even gave her a flower when he left once.

She found his attention odd, but she was more beautiful now, or so Sivi told her. Perhaps Skáldi only wished to help a pretty face.

Skáldi grew into a strong young man. He tended his families' fields, coaxing oats and greens out of the earth whenever the sun warmed it. The earth was nourished with the rain, his sweat and blood. He cared for it as a man did a loved one.

He needed a prolific and successful harvest, this year especially. This was the summer he would go to fetch Gundrun.

It had been ten long years since he saw her surrounded by flowers and light, and he knew what it meant now.

He was meant to marry her.

She was grown now, too, a woman. He'd seen her a few times since their first encounter, and with each time, she grew more beautiful. He saw her in his dreams often, a woman with hair like the pale sun and cheeks like red apples. He needed to go to her. He knew he was meant to protect her.

Five years earlier, he begged his mother to let him go back to her, bring her to them. His mother refused, reminding him she was still a girl, not yet a woman ready for marriage. And he was still a boy, mostly at least. He had no house of his own, no land that he tended alone. He then spent five years preparing for Gundrun.

He talked often of her around the fire in the cold winter months, as travelers and traders gathered in their longhouse. She was the girl he knew would be his wife, the woman who came to him in his dreams. He praised her light and her serenity.

Skáldi had a house now, simple but enough for a family just beginning. He had his own plot of land outside the village. He grew oats and barley and could keep a wife well fed through the winter months.

Once the spring thaw was complete, he would go to her, offer her marriage, and bring her home, away from her father. He needed to be at her side to protect her. He needed to give her a good life.

Life went on. Gundrun learned how to take care of herself, without any help from her father. She could snare a rabbit and catch, gut, and clean a fish. She found all the best places in the woods for berries, hid the crusts of bread and jars of honey so that when her father disappeared for nearly a month in the winter, she wouldn't starve. Gundrun raised herself into a capable young woman under Sivi's guidance when she visited.

Once she had started the slow transformation of girl into woman, her father began to make comments about finding her a husband. Gundrun didn't mind; she wanted to leave this sad home, find a place with a bright fire and cheer, babes of her own to adore and raise.

But none of these men her father spoke of ever came to see her. It was always him returning from trading with tales of men as tall as trees and richer than kings interested in her hand. She doubted very much that a king would bid for a bride unseen. In reality, these were probably poor, pock-faced farmers looking for a woman to work hard beside him.

She didn't fear a life like that, though. Any man that helped place food in front of her was better than her father.

"Fáfnir Yellowbeard will marry you," her father announced upon returning from a trading expedition in late winter. He handed her a bag of oats, which she quickly snatched and hurried to the fire. She hadn't eaten in two days. There was still some dried fish left, but she hadn't known when more food would come and wanted to stretch it. A bowl of oats was much more interesting than her prospective husband.

"He's a raider, very rich. I told him of your great beauty and he agreed to marry you."

"And what will you be getting in return?" she asked, stirring the oats until they mingled with the water. "I'm sure you are not giving me away."

Her father guffawed. "My precious daughter? He's offered a great many jewels from his last raid. He went to a place called Angleland. Have you heard of it?"

"Of course not. The birds do not sing of Angleland." She sighed. Gundrun did not remember the last time she saw someone other than her father. It had been at least a year since someone came looking to trade with them, and usually her father forbade her from speaking to strangers. She hadn't seen Sivi in three summers.

"Well, he is rich, and you will be fat."

"When am I to be married?"

"Autumn. He'll be raiding from now through summer. He will come for you once he returns."

If he returns, Gundrun thought glumly. She hoped her father had another plan if a storm sunk Fáfnir's boat to the bottom of the sea. Or someone in Angleland ran him through with a blade.

She wouldn't despair, though. Here was her chance of leaving, of beginning a home of her own, with a family of her own.

A month later, Fáfnir Yellowbeard came to meet his bride-to-be, with blood on his blade and wolfish-eyes. Gundrun had a terrible pit in her stomach, warning her that she was trading her father for a much worse man. He snarled like a lynx in the night when he spoke, and his eyes held no joy, only evil and death.

Her father stayed close by while he was there, which was only for a few hours. She was sure he'd only come to make certain she wasn't an ugly cow. Gundrun had the distinct feeling her father knew that if he were to leave them alone, she might to try kill him if he touched her.

"Your father did not lie," he growled, taking the risk to twist her plait between his fingers.

"About what?" she snapped, whipping her head away from him. He smelled like rotten fish and piss. Had he come straight from a sea voyage?

"You certainly are a pretty girl. One I wouldn't mind keeping my eyes open for." He barked a laugh and slammed his shoulder against hers.

She stood up and walked towards the fields.

"I need to harvest the greens. If you would like to help, you may join me. Otherwise, go speak with my father. I am sure the two of you have more to discuss."

"I will not do women's work, no," he laughed again, "but I look forward to our wedding, Gundrun." His voice dripped like spoiled fruit, but he walked away and left her in peace.

Gundrun did not like anything about him. But as he was a raider, she doubted they would spend much time together. He would give her babies to dote over, and hopefully be more interested in seafaring and terrorizing the Anglos than spending any real time home with her.

Her father was so proud that night, constantly barraging her with facts about Fáfnir's wealth or his prowess on the battlefield. She cared little for anything he had to say and began to wonder if she was better off to run into the wilderness and live off the land alone.

"Skáldi!" someone shouted to him as he tilled the fields. He raised a hand, blocking out the low early spring sun.

"Fáfnir," he replied but went back to his work. He had no patience for the raiders, always coming to his village to trade. As if they had need for jeweled cups and crosses. No one could eat gold.

"I have news!" he called again.

Skáldi set his hoe down. Fáfnir was walking closer, a wide smile on his face.

"Yes?" he answered impatiently.

"I am to be married!"

"Congratulations," he responded, but could not help pity the poor woman to be saddled with this beast. A year earlier, Fáfnir had grabbed the backside of his sister, Kenna, and was promptly throttled by her husband, Ríg. Kenna had been about to burst with child at the time. Skáldi was surprised she didn't knock him out herself.

"It's someone you know," he continued. "A pretty girl you've known forever."

Skáldi felt his stomach drop. Eitri would never consent their younger sister, Nessa, to marry this man. He couldn't.

"Who?" he demanded, suddenly anxious.

"Gundrun, with hair like the sun and a backside I can't wait to have my hands on."

Skáldi felt his blood rush up his body and settle behind his eyes.

His Gundrun. It couldn't be. He was her protector, and to have this horrible man as her husband...it couldn't be. He could not allow it. He wouldn't.

"You've met her, then?" he asked, trying to remain calm.

"I have. I met her father first. He was a simple man to bribe. Skinny, too. A few more treasures thrown his way and I probably could have had her as my slave." He burst into hysterical laughter.

"When will you be marrying her then?" Skáldi glanced down at his hoe, wondering if he should bash the man's skull in now.

"After the next raid. Need to bring back some impressive wares for my new bride."

Skáldi nodded and turned back to his work, grabbing for his hoe.

"I wish you luck on your raid then. May you return with great treasure." He smiled and nodded at the raider. The treasure would help soften the blow of Gundrun being married already when he returned.

"Skáldi!" Fáfnir clapped him on the shoulder. "You are an enigma. I tell you I will marry and, honestly, fuck the woman of your dreams, hold her down and fuck her at least once every night, yet you do nothing but till your field." He laughed. "We are very different."

Skáldi could feel his heart beating rapidly throughout his entire body. He shook off Fáfnir's grip and turned back to the ground.

"Yes, we are. Be off, Fáfnir."

He did leave, still laughing and shaking his head as he went. Skáldi finished his work in the fields. He would have a bountiful harvest this summer, plenty of food to last the family through winter.

He returned home, bathed himself and combed out his hair before tying it back. Then he went to the longhouse, ate well, and returned to his home to sleep.

He would leave in the morning to fetch Gundrun.

Gundrun pulled out yarrow by the handful. She'd found a patch growing a moon earlier, and it was helpful in nearly all wounds. She could harvest it now or use it later when she had the need. After all, she would be expected to save the life of her husband if he ever returned from raiding with a festering injury.

Gundrun had begun to stockpile certain things she might find a need for once she was married. She had no idea what her new home would be like, nor how long it would take her to learn the rhythms of the earth there. She may have been glad to see this home firmly in her past, but at least she was familiar with the land.

Fáfnir didn't live nearby. She wouldn't see the house until he came to fetch her after his voyage, but he lived further south, a better spot for leaving on raids. It wasn't too far, a few days by horse and cart which, apparently, he had.

She wondered if she would come to visit her father after she was married. She doubted he would come see her. Maybe after he sold the jewels and pissed through his food.

She turned her attention back to the woods, looking for her favorite herbs and berries to bring home. Soon. Soon she would have her own home, hopefully with an often-absent husband.

Gundrun finished in the woods and sauntered back to her small garden. She grew greens, potatoes, and a few herbs she managed to transplant there. She loved to tinker in the garden, to feel close to Idun and her mother, even if her father complained that it dirtied her hands. She reminded him that it was a good skill for a wife to grow things. She wouldn't depend on her husband for everything. Those potatoes had fed them through long winters.

"Gundrun?"

She whipped her head around. A few paces from her stood a man, tall and dark-haired, his hands on his hips. She lifted her hand to block the sun from her eyes.

"Skáldi?" she asked. She hadn't seen him in years. "Skáldi! What are you doing here? Is your mother all right?"

"She's fine." He offered his hand and helped bring her to her feet. She glanced up at the giant that stood in front of her. Last time they'd seen each other, he'd barely been a blade of grass taller than her. He had new tattoos also, a pattern along the side of his neck, traveling until it was lost in his beard.

"Would you like to come in? Have something to eat?" She brushed her hands against her skirt. Her father was gone, she didn't know where. Probably trying to trick someone out of their mead. She turned towards the house.

"I came to fetch you."

"Fetch me? What does that mean?" She laughed, continuing through the door as he followed.

"I came to marry you," he explained.

Gundrun spun on her heels to look at him.

"Marry me? Are you insane?" It had been nearly five years since she'd lain eyes on the man, and now he expected her to run off with him. "You've never spoken a word of this before. Unless you've talked to my father and he hasn't told me."

"I haven't spoken with your father."

"Your mother never said anything either," she began.

"She knows I'm here. She'd be glad to call you daughter."

"I'm promised to another," she insisted. She pulled out a small jug of mead she'd hidden from her father. If it was up to him, Gundrun would never have a drop of it to herself. She poured a splash of mead into a mug and handed it to Skáldi.

"I know. I know him, Fáfnir." His brow furrowed and he downed the liquid she offered. "No, you can't marry him. Let me protect you." He paused. "You shouldn't marry him. He's...he's not good to women. You wouldn't be safe with him. Please."

"I can take care of myself." Gundrun raised her eyebrows and took the cup from Skáldi's hand and drank.

"I don't doubt you think you can," Skáldi answered, "but he's a raider. He isn't kind or gentle. He will break your heart and your body. I've seen what he's done. Lathi, his last wife, she was nothing but a shell by the time she died. Never without a blackened eye."

Gundrun shuddered. She knew her father had no care as to whether a husband treated her well.

"How did you even know I was promised to him?" she pressed.

Skáldi shifted uncomfortably. "I've been talking about marrying you for years. I always thought I'd come back here, make you fall in love with me. He knew this." Skáldi's fists balled at his sides. "When he struck the deal with your father, he found me, told me all the things he was planning on doing to you." He set his jaw. "He won't be good to you."

"Skáldi," she began.

"Please, Gundrun. Let me protect you. I've known, since the first time we met, I've known I was meant to marry you."

"How?" she asked. True, Gundrun had always found him handsome. Her stomach even did a pleasant flip when she looked at him. And he was kind and strong and came from a good family. A family that would accept her. Perhaps even love her.

"When we first met," he began.

"When I was starving and you fell over?" she interrupted.

"Yes. I saw you...surrounded by flowers. And I dream about you the same way. As if you are always walking through the woods mid-spring."

Gundrun felt the color fall out of her cheeks. He could see that? She wasn't supposed to tell anyone about the blessing of Idun, but Skáldi could see it?

"Gundrun," he took a step towards her, his hands finding hers. "I can promise you these things. I will protect you with my life. I will keep your belly full through the coldest winters. I will cherish you as my wife. It will be my life's work to make you happy."

"Skáldi." Her voice caught in her throat. She didn't know what to do with that sort of declaration. Her father never spoke to her with kindness, or even respect. To hear a man say those words to her...Gundrun was overwhelmed.

"Yes," she whispered.

And with that, the decision was made. She would not suffer through her marriage with Fáfnir while Skáldi offered her such wonderful things.

She let her head lean against his chest. "Take me away from this place."

Four years later, and Skáldi still couldn't quite believe how dear Gundrun was to him. Their life was filled with hard work; they tilled the fields together, coaxed enough food out of the unforgiving earth to survive the winter, and spent the cold, dark days in each other arms, or cuddled in front of the fire. A year after their hasty wedding, their oldest, Knutr, was born. Skáldi thought his heart would burst with happiness at the sight of his child. Two years later, Leifr joined their family. With the love of his life by his side and two healthy sons to raise, Skáldi felt more blessed than any man alive.

The family grew, and not just with children of his own. His brothers and sisters added child after to child to their clan, their small village becoming more prosperous over time. They stuck with farming, it was their truest skill, and left raiding to the greedier towns and individuals.

There was one family member that never shared a cup of mead by the fire, nor worked alongside in the fields. Gundrun's father stayed away. He came once, seeking her months after she had left, to force her back to Fáfnir, but by that point, Knutr already grew in her belly. There were some threats and shouting, but in the end, he left and never returned.

"You have been tinkering over there for hours. Come to bed. It is cold and lonely without you," Skáldi complained. He walked from the bed to the spot where she sat, tirelessly crushing dried herbs into powders. She had her blessing from Idun, and as she grew older, it became something new. She could whisper over plants and make them grow and create powders and potions to help cure ailments. She quickly became their village's Völva, tending to the sick and elderly.

"Both our boys are in there with you," she laughed quietly. "There is no chance you are either cold or lonely."

"Ah yes. Without you I am not the right kind of warm, nor the right kind of crowded." He snuck his hands around her waist. "I would like this warm body next to mine. Not the cold feet of my son on my neck."

She giggled and dropped her work, leaning back into his embrace. His hands wandered over her body, finding his favorite places and lingering. She pushed away her work, snaking her hands over his.

"The fire is still warm. We could go beside it, try to make a daughter." He hummed against her shoulder, biting playfully.

"A daughter sounds wonderful," Gundrun mused.

It truly did. Her sons were rambunctious balls of energy and adoration, but she wanted a girl to keep her company. In a few short years, the boys would join the men in hunting, fishing, trading. Gundrun did not want to be left alone without any children by her side. She wanted to pass along Idun's blessing, as her mother had to her, and have a partner in her herbal work.

They snuck away to the fireside, careful to stifle their moans, and quietly made love without waking the children, an accomplishment for any parent.

"Boys! Go help your mother!" Skáldi commanded. He wasn't sure how much help Knútr and Leifr would be, but he needed a moment talk to his brother without little ears listening.

"Eitri," he called, motioning his brother come closer. "We need more animals."

"We have many strong cows, a few sheep. What more could we need?" His brother brushed off his concerns.

"Pigs. All the signs of a terrible winter on the horizon are here. Do you see the seed coverings? They are thicker than ever before." It wasn't yet Haustblot, but the air was chilled every morning, and frost had already visited more than once.

"Why don't you have Gundrun talk to the earth? Until then," he clapped his shoulder, "try not to worry, little brother. We've survived harsh winters before. Your sons are strong and no longer little babes." Eitri's children were all grown now. He had two daughters nearing the age they would leave to begin their own families, and a son old enough to accompany his father to hunt. The fears of long winters no longer bothered his brother.

But Skáldi's boys were still small, and Gundrun still at childbearing age. A harsh winter could spell disaster for their family.

Skáldi tried to turn his mind from his worries, but it was no use. Eitri was right; he would see if Idun spoke to Gundrun.

Gundrun sat in the field, her legs and hands against the bare earth. She was silent but listening. Skáldi had taken the boys to fish. Before long, the ice would freeze the sea and fish would be a memory of autumn.

Gundrun listened for signs of the seasons.

"Idun, when will you return? With the light? Earlier? Later? Will our children be hungry this winter, will our crops die beneath the earth?" She tried to picture the goddess, a burst of sunlight and raindrops and flowers, hoping she was listening. She wondered if her mother might hear her, if she served their goddess now.

The earth was silent for a great while, with nothing but the sounds of the last birds chirping in the distance, the great loll of the sea against the shore, the rustle of some animal running through the wood.

But then, a voice. A voice as clear as water broke through.

I will not arrive until the Midsummer sun is in the sky.

Gundrun's eyes snapped open. Spring not come until Midsummer? Howling winter for moons on end? Even now, it was not yet Haustblot and the birds were leaving. Gundrun clambered to her feet. They needed to prepare or their family would not see another year.

She went to Kenna and Nessa first, alerting them that they needed to prepare. They would pry all they could from the earth this autumn. Gundrun prayed the onions and carrots would be fruitful. The barley would need to last much longer than normal.

When the men returned from fishing, their bounty was not as great as Gundrun had hoped. She met Skáldi with a heavy heart and told the children to run and play.

"The winter will be far more than half a year long. It will begin soon and end at Midsummer. There will be no spring this year."

A hush fell over the adults. The couples drew to each other, exchanging glances of fear and apprehension.

"We will need at least one more pig to slaughter to get us through the winter." Eitri was quick to react. "The men will hunt every day and bring back rabbit and deer. Praise Idun for giving Gundrun this message. We will find a way to survive."

A full moon before Midwinter, they saw snows higher than Skáldi's knees. Hunting was near impossible in these depths, but they still had vegetables and barley and a few rabbits from the autumn.

The children were still fat, but they would grow thin this year. It broke Skáldi's heart that he could not keep his promise to Gundrun. Even now, he saw that she took little food for herself, giving larger servings to both him and the boys.

He poured a cup of mead and brought it to his wife. The children were sleeping. They spent much of the day sleeping now, when the earth was growing dark and food growing scarce.

"May I tell you a story?" he asked, sliding beside her.

"I would love to hear one," she answered, her head finding his shoulder.

"The day I first saw you, I knew I would marry you. I saw flowers and light all around you, a blessing from the gods. Initially I had thought you must be blessed by Freya with your beauty, but Idun is your patron. It makes sense truly."

"And why is that?" She sounded sleepy as she spoke.

"For you are spring, flowers and rain, black dirt and green leaves and the hope of all the days to come. You are my spring. And I can get through the darkest winter. All I need is you."

"That is a very good story." She reached up to his jaw and tugged on his beard. "Kiss me, husband. And then take off all your clothes."

"All of them? It's very cold," he teased, his mouth moving up her neck.

"Get a blanket for your backside and I'll warm your front."

By Midwinter, the snow was so high, they couldn't leave their home for ten days. Gundrun worried terribly for their kin; Kenna was due with a child in the next moon. She hadn't heard the screams of childbirth yet, but Gundrun still wanted to be with her when the time came. Her girls were not equipped to help their mother alone, and Kenna wasn't young anymore. A difficult birth could lay ahead.

When shouts for help did rise above the howling wind one night, Skáldi wrapped himself in furs and kicked a path to Kenna's house. Gundrun collected her dried herbs, hoping she wouldn't arrive too late. The snow was heavy that night, and the wind continued to drift over the path that Skáldi dug over and over. It was as if the gods did not want Gundrun to leave her house.

By the time the path was clear enough for Gundrun to crawl over the snow, it was too late. Both Kenna and the baby were gone. Kenna's husband, Ríg cursed the gods and shouted to the sky that night. Their daughters wailed into the frigid air at the sorrow of losing their mother. They were still young, none of them old enough to take the place of such a woman. The family was grief-stricken.

Gundrun held her sons close that night, one on either side of her, gripping their backs in panic and sadness. She prayed to Idun, begging for her to come earlier, but the goddess was silent that night.

The snows didn't stop or slow. They became stronger, so strong that Thor's mighty hammer clanged in the sky alongside them. The wind screeched as they did the night they lost Kenna. The fires barely survived the night now.

They killed their pigs first, the two that hadn't sickened and died. They were scrawny things after so many months of little food, but still gave them warm bellies for a few days. The sheep were next, skinny with more wool than meat at that point. They kept the horses. It became clear that come Midsummer, they would need them to offer as trade for other animals.

When the sun was halfway to Midsummer, the snow still fell, and the sky was gray with anger. Gundrun walked out of the village and to the woods on a particularly calm day, trying to find something green beneath the snows. By this time, she could usually find some borage or fennel, even if the snow still fell. It wouldn't be much to add to a stew, but they had been out of carrots for two moons now, and only a handful of onions remained. If Gundrun could find anything to add to bone soup, it would be helpful.

She went to her favorite spots for foraging, dug deep in the snow until her fingers were cracked and bleeding from the cold, and found nothing. The earth was as hard as it usually was in Midwinter.

She collected pine needles in her basket, so she didn't come home empty handed. They would have tea tonight and hope it helped settle the hunger in their bellies. Maybe they would even spare a few drops of honey for the children.

"I need to hunt," Skáldi said, pulling on his boots.

"It is too icy," Gundrun complained. "You'll fall and hurt yourself." She could only imagine trying to nurse Skáldi back to health with little to build up his strength.

"I have to risk it. We need a deer. Or a rabbit at least." He drew his hood tightly around his face. "We will not lose anymore members of our family this winter. We're a moon away from the fire festival. We should be basking in the spring light and enjoying rabbit stew with herbs every day. I cannot let my family go hungry."

"Do not go alone," Gundrun warned.

"I will bring Ríg, Ari, and Eitri. Hakon will stay here just in case."

"In case of what? All four of you dying in the woods?" Gundrun felt like a stone had taken up residence in her stomach.

"No, in case someone comes looking to trade with us. Maybe the homes further south were not hit by incessant snow. Maybe they have a plethora of food to trade."

"And what would we give them? Our children? We have nothing."

"We have two horses. He will trade those."

"I wish you would stay." Gundrun wrapped her hands around his. He quickly pressed a kiss to her knuckles.

"I promised you would never be hungry. You are starving. Our children are starving. I will return soon. Maybe a few days. But I will not return empty-handed."

The four men walked into the wilderness, each mad with hunger and terror. How many more of their family would die in this awful winter? Had the gods forsaken them? They should have sacrificed more when their bounty was plentiful. They would not make that mistake again.

Three days passed. Gundrun awoke each morning with a start, believing she heard footsteps at her door. She jumped out of bed, clamoring to the fire, poking it alive in case Skáldi was home and needed to be warmed by its side. But each morning, she was disappointed. When she gazed out the door, she was met with nothing but white blankets of snow.

On the third day, after the noon hour, she built the fire up and left the boys with cups of pine tea and went to see Nessa.

She trudged through the mounds of snow between the two houses. As she got closer, she could hear Nessa's children, Siv and Tófa, singing quietly but happily. Good, no one here was ill.

"Good morning, sister," Nessa greeted, carefully opening the door so as not to allow too much snow in. "Have you heard any rumblings of the earth? Will we be blessed with spring soon?"

"I have not. I believe Midsummer is when our thaw will arrive."

Nessa looked over her children, both as thin as Gundrun's boys.

"Let us pray to Ullr, our great god of the hunt, that the men are successful. At this point, a single rabbit would be something."

"I pray they can fell a deer at least. We could stretch that for a full moon if we needed to."

Nessa turned into the house to sit by the fire, motioning for Gundrun to come with her.

"I cannot wait to feel the warm sun on my face, to strip off these clothes and wash them in the river. That will be a day, won't it? When we can watch our children splash in the sea, when the men can fish again. How I long for a full belly."

Gundrun put her hand up to silence Nessa and turned her ear to the door. She could hear something. She scrambled to her feet and dashed outside, not even taking care to wrap her shawl tightly around her.

The men had returned.

"Skáldi!" she cried, taking off in a sprint towards her husband. She squinted to see his face, trying to read whether they had been successful or not.

"Gundrun!" he shouted, then raised a pile in his hands. "A boar and rabbits galore! We've each gotten three! And some birds, too!"

A wild boar, twelve rabbits, and a pile of birds! Thank all the gods and goddesses. They were saved.

Winter did last until Midsummer, but when the midnight sun finally came, the snow melted, and the earth came alive. Many of their crops were stunted that year, but the family made provisions. They traded their horses for a cow and a pair of pigs, who they fattened immediately. Skáldi took advantage of the long days and summer sun and hunted constantly. He brought Knútr with him but left Leifr to help his mother with the fields. They would not be so ill-prepared for another winter such as the last.

Everyone became healthier. They were hardly fat and rosy as they had once been, but they all lost the gaunt pallor of the winter before.

The children were older—hardier, too—after a winter like that. They worked alongside their parents, the girls and young boys in the fields, the older boys felling trees for fires or hunting with their fathers. Kenna's oldest daughter, Torvi, became an expert fisherwoman and pulled fish after fish out of the sea, keeping them both well fed and creating a huge store of dried fish for the winter.

"Hello, beautiful woman," Skáldi called to Gundrun on his return from hunting. She was still in the fields, planting, harvesting, speaking to the earth in both gratitude and prayer. He turned to Knútr. "Run inside and hang these to be cleaned." He handed him the pair of rabbits they brought home.

"Do I have to, Móna?" Knútr bemoaned.

"Do as your father tells you," Gundrun chided, then turned to Skáldi. "Good evening, husband." All these years, and he still could not believe his luck at this woman marrying him. He crossed the field to stand beside her, but quickly wrapped his arms around her.

"You look beautiful." He let his hands wander over her waist and down her backside.

"You are virile this evening."

"I am." He glanced around them for any passersby but saw none. He fell to the ground, pulling her on top of him. His hands found her legs under her skirt, moving them apart, until his hand found his most favorite part of her body. "And you are ready for me, I see," he mused, caressing her slowly.

"All this hard work has left little time for us," she complained, then arched into his touch. "I miss your hands on me," she dipped down until her lips nearly touched his ear, "and your cock inside me."

"Ah, woman, you drive me mad with desire," he breathed, quickly untying the laces of his trousers. He shrugged them down, then guided her hips until she covered him.

"Making love to my wife in the middle of a field...it's Midsummer for certain."

The warm days may have been short that year, but when autumn came, they were ready for another winter. The game and fish were dried, the pigs were fat, just in case, and what onions and barley they managed to grow were wisely rationed to last until spring. Gundrun had no warning from Idun that this winter would be terrible like the last, and they entered it with hope.

The loss of Kenna hit the family hard. Torvi was taking over her mother's jobs well, but she'd been forced out a childhood a few years too young. It would be at least four more summers before Ríg found a man to wed her, yet she was running a house on her own.

"Hrøth is having a Midwinter feast this year. He hopes it might please the gods to have a big sacrifice and steer us away from another terrible winter. We should attend," Skáldi told Gundrun one day while she made stew.

"Is it wise to leave our village in winter? We could get stuck in a storm on the road. Would it not be better to wait until spring?"

"I think we should praise the gods as many of us survived as did. Plus, it will give us a good idea how trade will be in the spring. We need to acquire more animals. The pigs are a good start, but eventually we will need sheep and horses again. We have not seen most of our neighbors in over a full year."

"Perhaps you are right," Gundrun conceded, rubbing her temples with her fingers. "Will the entire clan go?"

"There are no new babies to keep home, or women with child," he said, his face grim. "But if you want to stay home, you may," he said slowly.

"Not me. I will go and see if I can trade some of my healing skills for eggs or even chickens. But I don't want the children to come. They are still so young. They have years ahead of them of these feasts."

"I'll talk to my brothers. See if anyone else feels this way."

Most of the families felt the same way. They needed to see what was available for trade, or would be in the spring, but no one wanted to bring their children on the road. It was decided the Eitri and his wife, Auda, would stay home with everyone's children. Ríg also mentioned he wanted to stay home, but Skáldi convinced him to come. His eyes had been dark since Kenna was lost. He needed to leave the village for a little while. And he needed to start looking at some of the young neighbors as prospective husbands for Torvi.

A moon later, Skáldi and Gundrun, Hakon and Liffa, Nessa and Ari, and Ríg walked to Hrøth's long house. The winter had been hard for everyone, but Hrøth's great wealth had seen him through the frigid season. His stores were hit, but no one in their village died of cold or starvation.

The mood of this feast was somber. Many families that came were smaller than they had been the spring before the great winter. Skáldi greeted men he'd known his entire life with heavy hearts. Many were sad to hear of the loss of Kenna and her baby, but Ríg was welcomed by all.

A somber blanket laid over this gathering. They were meant to be celebrating surviving the winter, but truly, they came together in grief. Gundrun found herself talking to other women about the hardships they had faced, the children and loved ones lost, babes that never saw the summer sun. But the women were eager to share their knowledge and she swapped her wisdom of herbs and planting tricks she had learned, and picked up a few new ones.

When the shared grief became too much for her to take, Gundrun walked out into the cold air for some reprieve. She didn't expect to find much, only a few moments of silence and solace in the wind with the fires crackling in the distance over the din of the feast.

"Gundrun."

A face from her past stood a few paces away.

"Hello," she answered slowly, crossing her arms in front of her body. She eyed over his shoulder, hoping someone would join them in the winter wind.

"You survived the winter," he said, walking towards her. "Still beautiful, I see." Fáfnir's grin turned predatory as he continued his stalk.

"I did. My husband did as well." She nodded towards the longhouse, as if to remind him there were many folk within earshot.

"My wife did not."

"I am sorry to hear that," Gundrun answered, her guard slightly dropped. That was two dead wives Fáfnir had now survived.

"She was weak, built like a blade of grass blowing in the wind." He shrugged. "You don't look weak. You look strong."

Gundrun kept her breathing steady. She didn't want this leech to know he made her skin crawl and her soul cower.

"There are many strong women here who lost their husbands last winter. Perhaps you should pursue one of them." She moved to walk past him, but he caught her arm and brought her face to his.

"Your father promised you to me and you ran off with Skáldi in the night like a thief. I had already announced our marriage. You embarrassed me."

"It was broad daylight when I went with Skáldi," she answered, her chin high. "He promised me a better life than you did. And he has delivered."

Fáfnir raised his hand to strike her but held back.

"I am my own woman, Fáfnir. It was not for my father to choose who I spend my life with," she spat, pulling her arm out of his grasp. "I made no promises to you." She stomped away until she was engulfed by other visitors, surrounded by people on all sides.

Gundrun scanned the crowd, looking for Skáldi. She found him, sitting and laughing with Hrøth beside one of the great fires.

"Skáldi," she interrupted, grabbing his hand. "We should leave."

"Leave?" he laughed. "Gundrun, the sun has set on the darkest night of the year. Leaving now would not be prudent. Come, sit with me. I'll get you a cup of mead."

She squeezed his forearm and pulled her toward him.

"What happened?" he murmured, bringing their heads close together. "Did someone lay a hand on you?" His eyes searched the room wildly, looking for a mark.

"No. I saw Fáfnir. He was rude to me. I do not like that he is here."

Skáldi kissed her forehead. "I do not like him either, but Hrøth welcomes all his neighbors. We will stay away from him."

Gundrun nodded, but she couldn't ignore the pit in her stomach. Seeing Fáfnir was a bad omen.

The feast concluded without issue and their family returned home. There was still a great portion of winter left, but the Midwinter feast had been good for the family. Skáldi, Hakon, and Ari were able to secure some trading deals for the spring that would help build their livestock up once again; some farmers were not hit as hard and had breeding cows and pigs due to give birth in the next months. They would trade grain for livestock once the trees budded.

Their hope was renewed.

When the time of year that the ewes began to lactate arrived, Skáldi hunted again with fervor. The snows were not as violent this year, and catching rabbits and the occasional deer was not impossible any longer. He often went out to the woods with one of his brothers and brought back food for several days.

On a clear afternoon, Skáldi was out hunting with Ríg, looking for game larger than rabbits. Quickly, they noticed tracks that were not animal, but human, and made the decision to return to the village. It looked as if a traveler or trader was coming to see them.

They talked as they approached the village. Ríg told a story about Torvi coming into adulthood, and how he wished Kenna was there to see it.

"She is an example of womanhood to her sisters, my strong girl. A beauty, too. I will hold out for a great man for her. She deserves to be cherished in marriage." Ríg smiled fondly.

A figure burst forth from the woods, immediately burying his ax into Ríg's chest. Skáldi shouted in alarm and pushed the man away from Ríg. He scrambled for his knife, trying to find the person who had attacked them without reason when he was hit in the shoulder.

Skáldi looked down at his chest, an ax protruding between his collarbone and arm. Blood flowed freely from the wound, and he immediately felt very cold.

He fought to stay conscious. His eyes searched the perimeter of the woods, but he saw no one. He glanced down at Ríg; he was dead, there was no question.

"Eitri! Hakon! Ari!" he shouted, keeping his back against a tree and his knife raised with his good arm. Who the hell was that? And where did he go?

His chest ached where the ax was buried, but he was afraid to pull it out.

"Skáldi?" Hakon called from the village.

"Over here!" he shouted back. As soon as the words left his lips, he heard someone scamper further into the woods.

Hakon and Ari ran up the hillside towards the sound of Skáldi's voice.

"Holy hell," Hakon breathed. "What happened?" He rushed to Skáldi while Ari ran to Ríg's side.

"He's dead!" Ari gasped.

"We were attacked. Couldn't see his face," Skáldi explained. Hakon eased his good arm over his shoulders and started to walk down the hill.

"Ari, cover us from behind," he commanded.

"What about Ríg?"

"We'll come back for him. Nothing we can do but pray he is chosen by Odin or Freya."

The three men slowly made their way down the hillside, leaving a track of blood in their wake. Skáldi couldn't feel the ax buried in his body any longer, but he didn't think that was good. He was in shock from the injury.

Hakon led him to his house, but Skáldi could hardly keep his eyes open.

"Gundrun!" Hakon yelled, kicking open the door.

Skáldi watched his wife's face turn white, then glanced at his boys on the verge of tears, and lost consciousness.

"What happened?" Gundrun exclaimed, dropping the mending she was working on and running to her husband's side. His clothing was soaked in blood surrounding an ax buried deep inside his flesh.

"He and Ríg were attacked. Ríg is dead."

"Gods forbid it!" she shrieked. Gundrun felt her head turn light and the room swirl.

She took a deep breath and tried to steady herself. She would be no help if she fainted. She needed to stay alert to help Skáldi. If she could.

"Knútr and Leifer, go to Aunt Nessa, tell her I need her. Then go to Auda and Liffa and tell them to stay in their homes, their children, too. You stay with Uncle Eitri. Stay right by his side. No leaving the village, no going outside, do you understand me?" The boys nodded their heads in fear and ran out of the house. She turned to Ari and Hakon.

"Help me get him by the fire," Gundrun commanded. They eased Skáldi towards the flames where she could work. "Do you have your ax?"

Hakon nodded. She grabbed it and placed the cheek of the ax into the fire. Gundrun looked over the wound. He might lose his arm, she lamented, if he managed to survive. Why on earth would someone attack Skáldi? He was a peace-loving man who never swindled anyone. He traded fairly, treated everyone with respect. Gundrun had never heard him even slight another man...her eye caught on a detail of the ax. A serpent twisted around an aspen on the hilt.

Fáfnir. It was his ax. She'd know it anywhere.

Gundrun felt like she couldn't breathe. Her throat constricted and she clawed at her chest, trying to find some relief. That villain had killed Ríg and tried to do the same to her husband. The side of her vision went red with flames and fury.

She would kill him. She would drain the life from him no matter the consequences. She threw her head back and wailed.

Hakon slapped her across the face.

"Thank you," she said, coming back to her senses. She needed to work quickly. She could grieve later.

Nessa burst through the door.

"Good. Ari and Hakon, hold him down. Nessa, wrap a cloth around the ax hilt and be ready with it." They did as they were told, and Gundrun positioned herself over her husband, her hands on the hilt of Fáfnir's ax and her knees on his chest.

"I'm sorry, love," she whispered and quickly kissed his forehead. "Hold him tight," she commanded and ripped the ax out of the wound. Skáldi howled in response, his body flailing wildly.

"Hold him still!" she shouted, grabbing the hot blade from Nessa's hands and applying it to the wound. His cry turned to a gale, something wild and untamed until again he lost consciousness.

"Stay by him in case he awakens. Don't let him touch the wound," Gundrun said to Ari and Hakon. She began to work quickly. She had some herbs that might help him heal, if he would drink a brew made of them. She ran across the room, rummaging through her dried herbs. Oh, what she would give for summer and fresh plants, but she would do what she could. She found the yarrow and crushed it between her fingers before adding it to the water on the pot. She kept her mind focused on the task at hand. She needed to save her husband. She couldn't panic.

She managed to trickle a bit of the brew down his throat before he started coughing it up. She could try again once he was calmer. For now, she soaked cloths with cool water and mopped his brow. She did not know when the fever would come, but it would.

Hours passed, but Skáldi did not wake. Hakon and Ari moved him to the bed, then left to retrieve Ríg's body before the wolves got to it. They would burn him in the coming days. Ari and Nessa would move Ríg's girls into their home. It wasn't safe for them to be alone now. Gundrun's boys stayed with Eitri and Auda for the night, and Nessa stayed with her. She didn't want the boys at home, in case Skáldi woke with a panic. They would come tomorrow to see him. Hopefully, he would be awake.

Gundrun may have been their village's Völva, but she didn't deal with battle wounds. She helped babies into the world, mended bones children broke when they were foolish, soothed fevers. She had only cauterized small accidental knife wounds before.

Nessa nodded off in the corner, now that midnight had come. But Gundrun couldn't sleep. She sat by the fire, listening to Skáldi's labored breath, hoping he would call out for her, wishing he would open his eyes.

Morning came without sleep, and Skáldi twisted and turned in his state now. The fever was here, and Gundrun bathed him with cool water and kissed his cheeks to soothe him.

"I love you," she whispered to him, over and over, hoping her voice might bring him back to her.

"Would you like me to fetch the boys? So they can wish him farewell?" Nessa asked gently.

"No!" Gundrun shouted, her voice a shrill, fiery rage. "He is not going yet." She stilled herself. "I am sorry, I am not angry. You may bring them to say hello, not goodbye."

Nessa nodded and went to collect them. Gundrun turned back to her husband, clutching his hand.

"Skáldi, please wake up. I don't want to live this life without you. And the boys, you have so much left to teach them. They can barely fish, Knútr is still afraid of skinning a rabbit, and you know Leifr loves you more than me. We need you."

He mumbled and shifted, but his eyes remained closed and his voice silent.

Knútr and Leifr came to his side with tears in their eyes and stilled tongues. She told them to kiss his forehead, tell him they loved him, but to run along and stay with Uncle Eitri. She didn't want them here if it turned ugly, and she was beginning to accept that it would.

"Idun," she asked quietly, "if you...if you can save this man, he is very dear to me." She had no response though.

The goddess of spring had little to do with the wounds of men.

The world was on fire.

Skáldi was alive. He could only be alive with such pain coursing through his body, such an unbearable heat across his skin and deep in his muscles, a never-ending, pounding agony in the forefront of his thoughts. He could hear Gundrun calling out to him, to come back to her, but he couldn't reach her. Waves and rows of flames and darkness stood between them, and he was unable to do anything but live in this torture.

He remembered bits of things, the ax wound, Ríg's dead eyes facing the sky, Gundrun's panicked look when she saw him, a blur of his boys in his peripheral vision. He chased after visions of his family, finding them sometimes and with them a few moments of reprieve from the fire. He tried to live in memories of the past summer, hard work alongside his wife, teaching his boys to fish and hunt, cups of mead by the fire with his brothers. He dug into his mind, finding visions of Gundrun in the spring, her hands in the earth, the days she wound flowers in her hair, the moments they were alone and she whispered words of love to him between pants of passion. He did have flashes of the first time he saw her, that child of spring, surrounded by all the good of this hard earth.

He could sense she was near him. Even if he couldn't see or hear her, he felt her presence. She was with him always. His love, his dear wife, his breath of spring.

Gundrun.

Time passed, and he felt his body growing weaker and less able to withstand the fire. He struggled with it, knowing he would die and leave his family behind. The man in the woods...he was still out there, lingering. Would his brothers be able to protect his family?

He had failed them. He was their protector, and he would leave them vulnerable in this harsh world.

He stirred. For the first time, Skáldi could feel the world around him. He struggled with all his strength and opened his eyes.

"Gundrun," he managed to mumble.

"Skáldi? Oh, Skáldi, I'm right here." She grasped his hands, her nails scratching at his skin. "Can you drink some water? Or mead? You've been very ill," she rambled. He felt her moving behind him, reaching, pressing a cup to his lips.

"Gundrun, shh," he choked out. "I love you."

She stopped moving. She stared at him, her eyes full of grief. She raised her hand to his face.

"I love you." She paused. "You gave me a wonderful life. And beautiful boys. You saved me."

"Oh, Gundrun, my life would have been nothing without you in it." He tried to raise his hand to her face, but the weight of it was too great. "Beautiful woman, with light and flowers around her."

She leaned down and kissed his mouth, soft and surrendering. He wished he had more time with her, more time with their children. He wanted so much more. His poor heart hurt with wishing.

But he would be thankful for the time they had together. He would rejoice in having known the love of an astonishing woman and seeing two of his children born and grow to childhood.

"Goodbye, my dearest love."

"We will meet again," she whispered, her face buried against his neck.

The sun had risen ten times since they burned Skáldi. It had set as well, and the animals were fed, and seeds planted, early berries of the coming spring picked. Meals were eaten and children cuddled, but all that turned to ash under the haze of losing Skáldi.

Gundrun was adrift without him.

She held her children closely, grasping at them in fear. She could not lose anything else. They worked beside her in the woods, searching for the first herbs of spring. She was too fearful to let them hunt with their uncles. Fáfnir could still be out there, waiting and watching. He could destroy her completely.

The gods would not punish her so. She would not believe it. She was blessed by Idun—her children had to have some protection. But this world was cruel, she remembered. Her mother had been blessed by Idun, yet married an uncaring man and left a young daughter in her death. She wouldn't expect anything.

There had been no sight of Fáfnir since his ax killed her husband and Ríg. But Gundrun did not think he was gone. Why would he kill her husband and then disappear? Surely there was more vengeance on the horizon.

She wished they had never gone to Hrøth's Midwinter gathering.

When the snows had melted to nothing but persistent puddles, he came.

He came with fifteen men, all dressed for battle with their axes and spears in front of their bodies, their shields at their sides. They marched into the village, demanding an audience with Eitri, for he was the eldest brother and their leader.

"Word of your brothers' deaths reached our village," Fáfnir began. "How unfortunate that such evil befell your family."

Gundrun bit her lips to keep from screaming, "Murderer!" in his face. She wrung her hands together rather than around his throat. She wished she had the strength to cleave his head from his body.

"Thank you for your condolences. Now why have you brought these men so armed into my family home?" Eitri remained calm.

"Only to show the protection I can offer. I have a proposition for you."

Eitri nodded.

"Your lands were hit badly by last year's winter. We were not. We were raiding in the south and brought many of our women and children. We have great riches, more slaves, and good stores of food. You need animals, you need protection. I would be willing to trade with you."

"We have nothing to trade. As you said, our winter was harsh. We do not have the funds to make such an advantageous agreement."

"Oh, but you do. I want something simple." He raised his hand and pointed at Gundrun. "I would like Gundrun for a wife. I will give you two cows, three pigs, a slave, and my protection should you be so horribly attacked again."

"You, monster," she breathed. She couldn't control her rage. "You murder my husband and then come to my house demanding I marry you! You are a snake whose head needs to be cut off!" she shrieked. "May the gods rain curses upon your head!"

"Gundrun!" Eitri shouted. "Nessa, take her out of here. The children, too."

Nessa wrapped her hand around Gundrun's arm and pulled her away from Fáfnir. "Come on," she muttered. "Children follow me."

Once they were outside, Nessa turned to Gundrun.

"Do not attack him and spite us all."

"He murdered Skáldi and Ríg. We should slit his throat right now," she spat back.

"So his men murder all of us? Make slaves of our children? Gundrun, think of the entire family. Skáldi would not want you to put your children at risk."

Gundrun walked away from Nessa and the children until she was out of the village and among the trees. She wandered between the trees, her mind not straying from the villain welcomed into her village. She hoped Eitri turned him out.

She foraged while she was walking, finding early berries, wild herbs, even some mushrooms. She carefully picked through those that were poisonous and those that could be consumed without fear. She could not wait until Eitri threw Fáfnir and his men out of the village and she could hold her boys close to her. She hoped he drowned on his next raid, his body slowly sinking to the depths of the sea while he flailed helplessly.

Gundrun sat in Eitri's hall that evening after the children were asleep. The other women were not there, it was only herself, Ari, Hakon, and Eitri watching the flames of the fire crackle.

"We will accept Fáfnir's offer."

Eitri's words stung her like a thousand wasps.

"I am part of your family, and you would sell me to that terrible man," she answered plainly. "For what? He will take whatever he wants from you."

"We need the animals. And the guarantee that he will not attack us again."

"Guarantee? Fáfnir has no honor. If you give him me, he will take your fields, and your harvest, and your daughters when they are older. What if he tires of me and decides he wants Auda instead? Or Torvi? He is a raider.

They have no patience for watching things grow and building something with their own hands. They only steal what they want. He will murder you all if he wants to."

"It has been decided. He will return for you when the moon is full in the sky." Eitri paused. "I did not tell him you have children. I leave up to you their fate. You can bring them if you like or leave them with us."

"Do I want to bring my children to live with the man that murdered their father? No, I do not," she spat, trying to still her chin from shaking.

Gundrun felt her eyes begin to burn.

She would leave them. Her sweet boys. She had to. She didn't trust Fáfnir to care for them like a father would. She did not trust him to care for anyone. Her children would be farmers, like their father before them. Not cutthroat raiders who stole what didn't belong to them and killed without conscience.

"Hakon," she turned to her brother. "Will you and Liffa take them in? Skáldi has taught them much, but they are not yet grown. They will need the guidance of a father."

"Of course," Hakon answered quietly, his eyes not meeting hers.

"And be kind to them. They will lose both their parents, like Kenna's girls, but they are much younger." She glanced around the room at the faces of the men she thought loved her like a sister. Perhaps they did. But they were not brave enough to stand up to Fáfnir.

"I hope Skáldi cannot see how ill you've treated me. It would break his heart." She turned on her heels and walked away.

Saying goodbye to Leifr and Knútr destroyed what little heart Gundrun had left. The only reason she could go through with it was her faith that Fáfnir would never know they existed and leave them alone. He wouldn't have a reason to hurt them, once he had her.

She said goodbye to them the night before and bid them not wish her farewell in front of Fáfnir. She didn't think she could keep her nerve if they were there. She held onto their bodies, still those of small children who needed their mother. She took deep breaths of them, memorizing their scent and feel, hoping the memory of them would sustain her through the days to come.

Most of all, she prayed Fáfnir would be dead soon and she would come for them.

She didn't say that to them, though. Gundrun couldn't bear her children cling to false hope for years only to have Fáfnir live well into old age.

The next morning, she wore her hair loose and wild and her dirtiest dress. Her face was smudged with mud from her work in the woods the day before. She would not be presented as a prize to Fáfnir. He would have the shell of herself, but no more. She packed little, a few of her herbs and medicines. She left most of it with directions for Nessa.

Fáfnir arrived, with his men and the animals promised. He shook hands with Eitri and Gundrun fought not to spit at him. He could still burn their village to the ground, taking her children with it.

"Come along, bride," he said quietly to her, taking her by the arm. "Let's get you home and looking like a wife fit for a man such as myself. Not a grief-stricken widow."

She said nothing but followed him. She didn't look back. She didn't take one last gaze at the beautiful home she had with Skáldi, at the fields they tilled together, the place they raised their sons, the village that was the first true home she'd ever had. She knew if she looked back, she'd lose her nerve, try to run away, find her boys and hold them to her heart, refusing to let go.

So she only looked forward. And in her mind, she began to devise how she would live in this new life.

It took four days to reach Fáfnir's huge village. There were so many people, and it was loud and stank like urine. There was no charm like her home had, no sense of kinship. When Fáfnir paraded her past the other men, they didn't look at him with congratulations or kinship. They looked like they wanted to murder him.

She followed him to the longhouse and eventually to his bedroom. She eyed the bed with suspicion. Did he want to fuck her already?

"Not tonight." He laughed and smacked her bottom as he walked by.

"No, I will be waiting until after you bleed. I'm not raising another man's brat. Go to sleep, you look awful. Tonight, I will present you to the village and I want you to look beautiful. You must be beautiful, especially in front of my brother." Gundrun noticed the way Fáfnir seethed at the mention of his kin. "He brought home a new bride a few months ago. She is not as lovely as you but is already fat with a child. You will be soon. I need heirs. Lots of sons." He smirked. "I will send a slave to help."

That evening went on, and she was made to look the beautiful new bride. And every night after, she sat by his side at dinner, saying nothing, speaking to no one, alone in her thoughts. But she listened. She knew that everyone hated him. Everyone hated everyone here. There was no love between families, no kinship. This village of raiders was full of cutthroats and thieves and liars and usurpers.

Fáfnir's brother, Varg, was the leader, not him. Gundrun could feel the jealousy rippling off Fáfnir's body when Varg spoke. They were short with each other, competing on who told better stories of raiding, who brought back better riches. Fáfnir visited Angleland while his brother went someplace to terrorize the Franks.

Varg was no better than him and had grabbed Gundrun's backside every time she walked past. One night, he'd even grabbed her arm and whispered disgusting things in her ear before releasing her. He promised to take her on as a concubine once his brother went raiding again.

A moon passed and Gundrun's bleeding still had not come. She was not certain if she was with child or not, but she was certain of two things. She would never lie with Fáfnir and she would not give birth to Skáldi's child in this awful place.

When another moon passed, Fáfnir became irritated with waiting. He came to her one night, with rage in his eyes, his fists balled at his sides, yelling to the gods.

"Are you with child?" he demanded. "Tell me. Did that farmer put a baby in you after all these years?" He pushed her to the bed, holding her wrists down as she squirmed. "Did he?" he shouted now, his voice ringing in her ear.

She held his gaze, refusing to cower to him.

"Let me get you something to drink," she said quietly. "My bleeding will come. It always does." Her voice was even and steady and he released her arms and allowed her to stand. She walked to the table in the corner of the room and poured two glasses of mead, one for each of them. The pitcher had been set there earlier in the day, and she had been waiting for the chance to pour her new husband a drink.

She gave him his glass, drinking from hers. He drank his in one gulp, liquid streaming down the side of his cheeks. When he finished, he threw the cup to the side.

"Why do you do this to me? Why didn't you marry me before? It was settled." He pulled her towards him and wrapped his hands around the backs of her thighs, resting his forehead against her belly. Her arms hung limply at her sides, her gaze at the wall in front of her.

"I wanted to marry a man who loved me, and who I loved. Skáldi was kind and adoring. I had no interest in being your broodmare. I still do not."

"You are the prize beside me," he continued. "There is no greater honor than to be married to a raider as successful as I am!" His voice boomed, then faltered. He choked on a cough.

"I am not a prize, and I will never be your wife," she answered plainly. She tipped her cup and finished it.

"You *are* my wife," he snarled and grabbed her around the waist, throwing her to the bed. He moved to crawl over her, but his elbows buckled, and a cough overtook his speech.

"No, I am not. You will die here and so will I." She rolled away from him, sitting on the edge of the bed.

His eyes went wild, looking at the discarded cup on the ground, errant drops pooling on the ground.

"What did you do? You witch!" Fáfnir clutched at his throat.

She smiled and put her hand against her heart.

"I poisoned us both. Every single person here wants you dead. Your brother has been trying to murder you and fuck me since I came. There will be no question as to who killed you and your new wife. Why would I kill you and also take my own life? No, no. I begged the gods to rain curses down upon you and your kin, and I am the deliverance."

"Why would you?" He coughed again, this time choking, trying to clear his throat.

"I needed to protect my children."

He pushed her out of the way and tried to run out of the room but collapsed to his knees. Gundrun sunk onto the bed, taking delight in watching him attempt to crawl for help.

There was no help. She made sure of that. She chose the most lethal mushrooms she could find to soak in the ale all day. They'd be gone before anyone heard them.

She leaned back onto the bed, curling around herself, and closed her eyes. It wouldn't be long now. She let her mind wander away from this room.

Gundrun felt Skáldi beside her, his arms circling her waist. And now here was Knutr, smelling like grass and water, wiggling beside her belly. Leifr joined them, finding a spot between his parents, his cheek pressed against her shoulder, their family together in an embrace. There. This was peace.

Her breathing came quickly now, and a sharp pain in her chest kept her from drifting away with her family. The poison would work soon, but the waiting was hell.

"Gundrun," a voice as sweet as rainwater called to her.

She opened her eyes and sat, suddenly not feeling any of the effects of the mushrooms. She glanced towards Fáfnir, he was dead on the floor.

"Gundrun."

She lifted her gaze.

Idun was there, in the room, light and flowers bursting forth from her. She smiled at Gundrun and held out her hand.

"Come, my sweet daughter. Come and find peace."

Gundrun stood, all the pain of life melting away from her, and stepped towards the goddess.

Chapter Sixteen

Asher breathed.

His cheek was stuck to the bathroom floor. He needed to get up. He needed to get his phone and get to the hospital.

He snuck his arms beneath his body and pushed up. His entire body hurt, but his wound was on fire. It felt like he'd been shot yesterday, not a full year earlier.

He crawled to the living room, pawing the floor until he found his phone where it had tumbled from his pocket. He rolled to his back and quickly dialed 911.

"I need an ambulance."

As the Sheriff of Star Island, Asher was very impressed how quickly paramedics got into his apartment and him into an ambulance. He didn't remember much of what they were saying, only that they were taking him to the small hospital on the island. There was a water ambulance and helicopter pad to take patients to the mainland, but they thought his needs could be met at the local hospital.

Once they arrived at the hospital, his vitals were taken, and someone came in and was taking down his symptoms.

"You took your temperature and it was 105, you tried to call 911 but passed out, correct?"

"Yes."

"And what time did this happen?"

"I got home from work around six, so around then."

"Six in the morning?"

"No, six at night." Asher furrowed his brow. He glanced out the small window and noticed it wasn't dark out yet. It was summer, but what time was it?

"Last night?"

"I don't know," he said slowly. His head hurt.

"And you said you were hallucinating?"

"I think so. Or dreaming, I don't know." A nurse came in and hooked an IV up to his arm. The cool burst of fluids in his veins settled his mind a little but not much.

"Your temperature is only one-hundred and one now, but it's likely your fever partially broke when you were asleep. And I imagine you are very dehydrated with such a high fever and no fluids for nearly twenty-four hours." The doctor paused and turned to the nurse. "Let's try to get three bags in him in the next six hours. And bring some apple juice in." She turned back to Asher. "No vomiting, right?"

"No, just the fever and hallucinations."

"Apple juice it is. Once you keep that down, we'll move onto crackers, see if we can get you eating a meal." She nodded and left, the nurse following behind.

Asher leaned back onto the hospital bed, which was surprisingly comfortable, and rubbed his eyes.

He had hallucinated. That was the only logical explanation. Being transported into another life in ancient Norway where Rosemary was his wife but had a different name, and he took an ax to the same shoulder he was shot in, was insane. Speaking another language in his dreams but understanding all of it was insane. Seeing children he had with Rosemary that looked like perfect little mixes of the two of them was insane.

He fought a chill and pulled the blanket over his body. He must have hallucinated. He was sick, his temperature and dehydration showed that. Hallucinations must have been just another symptom.

Either that or he was losing his mind.

Chapter Seventeen

"My babies," Rosemary moaned, rolling over. "My beautiful boys." She could feel her throat closing with grief. The pain was insurmountable. She tucked her knees towards her belly, curling around herself.

"Rosemary!" Lavender's voice cried out, and a moment later her hands were on her.

She opened her eyes to the reassuring sight of her sister.

"Oh, Lavender." She tried to talk but her tears came furiously and choked her words away. Lavender pulled her to sitting, wrapped her arms around her, and cradled her head.

"I was a mom," she wailed. "They were so beautiful. Oh! Those sweet faces. Knutr and Leifr. Lavender, they were perfect." Her heart was on fire. This grief was too much, too sharp. She needed something to take the edge off it. Those little faces, those perfect children, she couldn't get them out of her head.

"Please, give me something. A valium, whiskey, a joint, something to make me feel better," Rosemary begged, clutching at her sister.

"Shh," she soothed in response. She pulled Rosemary to her feet and threw her arm around her shoulders. "You need to give it time. You've just come back. In a few hours, it will start to be less intense. By next week, the pleasant memories will stick, the others will start to fade."

Rosemary nodded miserably and leaned her head against Lavender. They walked into the house where Lavender had set up the parlor. The couch was made up like a bed with a tray pulled alongside it.

"You need to eat. Your body has been starved for the last twenty-four hours."

"Twenty-four hours? I was out for that long?" Rosemary gasped.

Lavender looked at her watch. "Technically, twenty-two hours. It's four in the afternoon."

"Shit, that's a long time. I guess it wasn't a faster option than the bread you make." Rosemary crawled onto the couch, pulling the blanket over her. She was hot, yet shivering uncontrollably. She couldn't stop shaking.

"I don't think one can rush past life memories." Lavender rummaged through the kitchen, putting together a plate of food. "So do you want to talk about it?"

"My past life?"

"Yeah. If you don't want to, you don't have to. Trust me, I get it. Sometimes those things are just too raw."

Tears stung the corners of Rosemary's eyes, but she blinked them away. Skáldi's hands around her waist, her first glance at Knutr's face when he was born, Leifr working beside her in the fields. Saying goodbye to Kenna. Leaving her boys behind. Killing Fáfnir.

"How about vague details instead of particulars?" she said, then cleared her throat. She could get through this.

"Norway. Viking but I don't remember using that word. Raiders was what we called them. It was so fucking cold there. The definition of cold as hell. I complain about winter here, but we have heat. And down comforters and durable waterproof boots. I do not know how I didn't lose any of my toes."

"Maybe that body was made of sterner stuff than this one," Lavender said and offered her a chocolate frosted cupcake.

"Thank you. And probably. Um, I still had a connection to the earth, but it was different." Rosemary's eyes flickered, remembering. "Crap, I was blessed by Idun!"

"Idun as in the Norse goddess of spring?"

"Yes! We talked...a few times. And she came for me when I died." Rosemary paused. "I wonder if that connection still works."

"Do me a favor and take down a bunch of calories before you attempt to contact a deity."

"Will do," she promised, taking a huge bite of the cupcake. Ah, sugar. It really was divine. She didn't mind that strict diet of berries, game, fish, barley, oats, and honey, but there really was nothing like butter, flour, and sugar.

"Interesting turn of events, I poisoned myself," Rosemary announced. "So not burned alive by an angry mob. Kind of a step up."

"On purpose?" Lavender was horrified.

"You know that saying, a fate worse than death? I was on my way to it. Don't worry, I took an asshole down with me." She grimaced, remembering the pure terror on Fáfnir's face when he realized she'd killed him.

That murderer deserved it.

Her heart thudded, remembering when Skáldi slipped away from her. She squeezed her eyes shut. She wasn't going to concentrate on the horrible parts right now.

She finished the cupcake, and Lavender handed her a slice of pizza.

"This is not what I was expecting next, but I appreciate it," she said, stuffing it into her mouth.

"Hold on, my phone's ringing." Lavender walked back to the kitchen to get it and Sage walked in from the yard. She was covered in dirt and dust and looked like she had rolled around outside.

"Oh, you're up," she said nonchalantly, as if Rosemary had simply nodded off on the couch for a few hours. "See anything cool?"

"You know, a twenty-something year life, the birth of two children, marrying my soulmate, murdering the man that murdered my husband, normal stuff."

"Yes!" Sage thrust her fist in the air. "Were you like a dark angel of vengeance?"

"Not really. More like I was sold to a murderer to keep him from wiping out our entire family."

"Grim." Sage grimaced.

Lavender walked back in the room, the phone still pressed against her ear. She looked to Rosemary.

"It's Verbena. She just saw Asher get into an ambulance."

"What?" Rosemary panicked. The feeling of losing him, holding onto him as the life slipped from his body, all rushed back into at that moment. "What happened? Is he okay?"

"She doesn't know what happened. He was awake, though. Looked like shit but wasn't bleeding."

Rosemary sprung from the couch and made it all of five steps before getting dizzy and falling to her knees.

"Slow down. You've basically been high as a kite and sleeping for a day. You can't just start running." Lavender still had the phone cradled against her cheek but came to Rosemary's side and helped her to a chair.

"I need to see him. I need to make sure he's all right." She was beginning to panic. Rosemary tried to get up, but her legs felt like jelly. She just needed to get to the car. Sure, her body was basically useless, but she felt like her arms still worked. She could drive slowly and get there.

"I'll take you," Sage offered. "But I'm going to jump in the shower first."

"Sage, please, take me right now." She had to get to him. What if...what if he was dying again? He needed her.

"No. He needs to get checked in and you are not his wife. Or related to him. Or even his girlfriend. You don't have immediate access. Drink some water and eat some more while I get changed. I promise I'll be quick."

Rosemary collapsed back in the chair and closed her eyes. She brought her hands up to her forehead.

This wasn't happening. Asher was a cop. Sure, Star Island was hardly a warzone, but still. Murderers lived everywhere. What happened to him? Did someone attack him in his apartment?

"Rosemary, get out of your head." Lavender's stern voice broke in. "Have a muffin."

"No more cupcakes?" she tried to joke. It failed as her brow crumpled the moment she made eye contact with her sister.

"This is a protein muffin. If you're going to go to the hospital for goddess knows how long, you'll need more than just pure sugar." Lavender thrust it into her hand, then walked into the kitchen. "I'm going to pack you a bag. I want you to eat in the car and when you are waiting there."

"Lavender, I'm fine. If I'm hungry, I'll eat."

"You've been bouncing between the depths of despair and joking. I don't really trust you to take care of yourself right now, and you're not a plant, so Sage won't remember to water you. Just eat." She walked out of the room.

"Whatever you say," Rosemary called softly, feeling another wave of anguish.

After the longest fifteen minutes of her life, Sage emerged from upstairs with her hair piled in a wet bun and wearing a clean T-shirt and jean shorts.

"Okay, let's go."

Rosemary pressed her forehead against her window, trying to stay calm. Her head felt horrible, her stomach churned, and the erratic beating of her heart was doing nothing to calm her nerves.

"Eat something that Lavender packed," Sage said.

"I think I'll throw up if I do."

"Then don't. Do not throw up in the car. How about a sip of water?" she said, handing her a water bottle. Rosemary took a small sip and forced it down.

She needed to see Asher. She needed to confirm that he was all right. Once she saw him, could put her hands on him and feel that he was breathing, his heart was beating, she would eat.

She wanted to run to him, wrap herself in his arms and bury her face against his chest. She wanted to reminisce, and grieve, and feel all of this with him.

But she couldn't. She needed to remember that he was mortal, a non-magical being. He may have lived multiple lives, but she didn't do a spell that allowed him to see Norway or Knútr and Leifr.

She let a whimper escape and screwed her eyes shut.

"Are you all right?"

"I just need to see him," Rosemary answered, swallowing her pain.

Lavender said it would get better. She only needed to wait for the gut-wrenching reaction to remembering her sons to fade.

Sage helped Rosemary to the front desk of the hospital. Being a small community hospital, they didn't have a traditional ER. Everyone entered through the same door, and there was a small waiting room for those with less severe symptoms.

"Evening, Rosemary, Sage, what can I help you with tonight?" Josh, a kid Sage went to high school with, worked the desk at the ER. One of the downfalls of living in such a small place was basically no privacy. Josh was bound to keep to himself whoever he saw at the hospital, but he still knew.

"I need to see Asher Evans. He was brought in by ambulance."

"Oh." Josh paused. "Does he know you are coming?"

"No, but I need to see him," Rosemary pressed.

Josh's eyes flickered to Sage. "We usually only allow family."

"They're dating," Sage cut in. "Seriously. Been keeping it quiet because of him being the new sheriff and Rosemary being, well, Rosemary. But she's been a worried wreck since he texted her to tell her he was here, and she could really use the reassurance that he's okay."

"You and the sheriff are dating?"

"Josh!" Sage snapped her fingers. "This is included under HIPPA or whatever. Don't go telling everyone."

"Of course not. Uh, let me get a nurse to walk you back." Josh picked up the phone and called back and within a few minutes Shelly, one of the nurses who frequented the florist, was walking Rosemary to Asher's room. Sage opted to stay in the waiting room with directions that Rosemary would let her know if she was going to be longer than thirty minutes.

"Sheriff Evans?" Shelly knocked on the door, opening it slowly, "You have a visitor."

Rosemary slowly walked into the room. Asher was in bed, propped up with pillows, hooked up to an IV. He was pale, but he looked relatively unharmed.

"Hi, Asher," she said, slowly coming to his side.

"Hi." He was staring at her. Not just looking, boring holes into her soul with his eyes.

"I'll leave you two," Shelly said. "You've got a call button right there if you need me. I'll be back to do vitals in about forty minutes. Make sure he rests," she said to Rosemary and then left the room.

Rosemary closed the distance between herself and the bed. She tried to stay calm, but it was no use. She raised her hand to his face, stroking his cheek. His stubble had grown out since the last time she saw him, and it was soft.

Skáldi had a beard. She never knew him as an adult without facial hair. It was warmer, he said, than a bare face. She remembered him nuzzling that beard against her neck on the cold nights.

Rosemary suppressed a shiver.

"You're okay?" she asked tentatively.

"I am. They think I got a really bad virus. Hit me like a ton of bricks last night." He didn't take his eyes off her.

"What happened?"

"I was working and started to feel really sick. Headed home, had a fever of 105—"

"A hundred and five! Isn't that dangerous?" Rosemary had never heard of someone burning hotter than 104.

"I guess. I passed out for close to twenty-four hours. Had some pretty intense hallucinations."

Rosemary felt her stomach drop. Hallucinations? For twenty-four hours?

"When? When did it start?"

"Around six last night."

"What did you see?" she half whispered. She grasped both his hands. She wanted to crawl into the bed and lay against him. She needed to feel his skin against hers, to be cradled in his arms. How was this happening?

His eyes flashed in fear.

"You."

Tears sprang from her eyes before she could stop them.

"Gundrun?" Asher whispered.

Rosemary nodded. "And you were Skáldi." She couldn't slow her tears now. They streamed down her face in fat wet drops. Her nose ran and her chest heaved.

"That...couldn't have been real. It was a dream. I was sick and I dreamt of a different world and put you in it," Asher tried to convince himself.

"No," she breathed. How could she have done this to him? With no warning? Her spell had dragged Asher along with her, but unlike Laurel and Owen, there was no finding comfort in each other afterwards because he had no idea what it was. The spell, she must have done the spell wrong somehow.

"I have to tell you something, and I don't want you to panic." She took a deep breath. There was no point in hiding anything any longer. He'd seen too much. "I am a witch. And I did a spell to see into my past life. I thought I took care that you wouldn't come with me, but I failed." She bit the inside of her lip trying to still it. "I'm so sorry," she mumbled.

"Rosemary, that doesn't make sense. Real witches...they don't exist."

"You had two sisters, Kenna and Nessa. Kenna died in childbirth. Your brothers were Eitri and Hakon. We had two children, Knútr and Leifr. Such sweet boys, with your face and my hair. You told me I was made of light and flowers. I was a witch then, speaking with Idun, and I'm a witch now." She tried to grasp his hand, but it was slack beneath hers.

"Asher, please," she begged, grasping for his shoulder.

He shrugged her off.

"No." He looked away from her. "No. It can't be real. It can't be true, because if it was..." His voice trailed off.

"I'm sorry," she whispered one last time, and fell to the floor.

Rosemary woke up a little while later in a hospital bed of her own, with Sage sleeping in a recliner next to her. She was hooked up to an IV and another machine beeped incessantly. She carefully rolled onto her side to face Sage.

"Sage!" she hissed.

"What?" her sister mumbled without opening her eyes.

"Why am I in a hospital bed and hooked up to all this stuff?"

"Because you fainted in Asher's room, and he called his nurse to help you. And then she got you to your feet and you fainted again. And then you tried to crawl out of the room yelling, 'I just need a cupcake,' so they put you on a gurney. They took your vitals, which were shit, and you had a fever of one hundred and two, so they put you in your own bed. They are convinced you and your boyfriend have the same bad bug."

"How long ago?"

"I don't know, three hours?" Sage shifted and opened her eyes. "I am going to need you to help me one day next week to make up for how tired I am going to be tomorrow."

Rosemary grimaced. "If you want to go home, you can."

"I'm not going to leave you in the hospital alone. I'm not an asshole." Sage sighed. "How are you feeling?"

"Okay. Like, my body feels amazing. IVs are incredible. Whoever invented IVs should win an award or something. My heart still hurts though. Less intensely, but it still hurts."

"You want to tell me about your past life yet? I doubt the doctor is going to let you go home for at least a few hours." Sage scooched the recliner closer to the hospital bed and stuck her feet under the covers. "It's cold in here. I never understand why hospitals are always freezing."

"This isn't cold." Rosemary smiled. "Midwinter in Norway with only a fire to warm you is cold."

Chapter Eighteen

Asher called in sick. He didn't want to, but he'd spent twenty-four hours unconscious and another twelve in the hospital. His body needed a day in his apartment recuperating.

He still couldn't wrap his head around it. Past lives? It seemed like something out of a book. But how else could Rosemary know those details? He hadn't told anyone anything about what he'd seen. She knew names... hell, she knew the names of their children.

His heart leapt, an uncomfortable panic gripping it. Were his children okay?

No, he told himself. Even if they both lived to be eighty, they'd lived over one thousand years ago. They were gone.

Guilt washed over him.

If it was real, if that life in the dark world of snow and ice and pain was truly his own, then he had failed them. Failed Gundrun, failed Knútr and Leifr, failed his entire family.

A searing heat flooded his shoulder. His fingers explored his scar, as they often did when he was overcome with emotion. The ax hit him in the same spot. The ax had killed him though. But then again, the bullet would have killed him if not for modern medicine. And antibiotics. There'd been multiple surgeries, weeks in the hospital. Skáldi had crushed herbs and mead dosed by a grieving wife preparing for her widowhood.

Asher lay back on his bed and let his eyes close, trying to focus the good parts of whatever life he now remembered. Seeing Rosemary, or rather Gundrun, for the first time and the unearthly way she was surrounded by flowers and light. Those cold nights when they piled the blankets high on the bed and the boys slept between them, but he would still kiss her over them until she giggled and swatted him away. Hunting. He had loved hunting. The thrill of bringing down a deer and then cleaning it and presenting it to his family. Asher had never hunted before, but now he felt a strong interest in going out into the woods and providing food with his own actions. Tilling the earth with Gundrun by his side. The sense of accomplishment he felt watching the land provide nourishment for his family.

Beautiful Gundrun.

She was Rosemary, but not entirely. Gundrun's hair was blonde instead of brown, her body lean and rough from years of labor, but her smile, her eyes, the lyrical nature of her voice, her mouth on his, they were all the same.

Asher felt like his soul had been pulled from his body and left to wilt in the snowy woods a thousand years ago.

He needed to talk to Natalie. He didn't think he could call her and say, "Hey, this woman I'm dating is a witch, and it turns out that we were married in a past life and someone murdered me in that life and I'm stressed about it," but he could tell her he was upset. She would understand that. He grabbed his phone off the nightstand.

"My little brother! How are you?" Natalie answered the phone extremely chipper.

"Ah, I just got out of the hospital," he confessed.

"What? What happened? Should I come? Sophie," she called away from the phone. "Bring me my laptop so I can look for flights to Boston!"

"No, no, no you do not need to come here. I'm fine and home now. I was really dehydrated."

"Dehydrated? What did you do, forget to drink water?"

"No, I got a really high fever, and the doctors think it was just an intense virus." Repeating the hospital diagnoses was probably as close to the truth as he felt comfortable sharing at this time.

"Were you puking up a storm?" She sounded considerably less worried now.

"No, just really sweating."

"Yuck. But I'm glad you are okay. Are you sure you don't want me to come? Just to hang out, make sure you don't relapse. Or I can call Mom, have her swing by Star Island and nurse her baby back to health?"

"Do *not* call Mom." After he got shot, Asher's mom had been a complete wreck, and he didn't want to worry her over something like this. She was so anxious that he didn't like to bother her with anything except happy news now.

"Okay. What else is going on?" Natalie asked.

What else, Asher thought. Only that he had spent twenty-four hours reliving a past life with the neighborhood florist who he found himself thoroughly intoxicated with in this life.

"Actually," Asher began. He paused for a moment. Once he did this, he couldn't go back. But after the day he'd had, Asher didn't want any more secrets.

"Usually people follow up the phrase 'actually' with more words," Natalie prompted.

"Do you have the letter from my biological father?"

"Of course."

"Can you take a picture of it and send it to me? But don't read it. Please. At least not until I've had a chance to."

"I would never. Are you sure? You've had a rough day already. Biological parents aren't always what you build them up to be in your head, as I know from experience."

"I'm sure. And I have no expectations. Your mom was seventeen and alone. This adult man made a strong choice to give me up."

Natalie blew a breath out. "Shit, Asher. Are you sure I shouldn't come? It might be a good time for us to hang out, pretend we're teenagers again and listen to angsty emo music."

"I'm sure. But send me the letter. I'm lying in bed drinking fluids and only getting up to pee. Perfect time to peruse a letter from my DNA donor."

"Okay. Call me if you're sad or sick or just want to talk. Wait, call the doctor if you're sick, not me. But for the other stuff, call me."

"Goodbye. I'll call if I need you. I promise."

Asher fidgeted with his phone, waiting for the text to come through.

He didn't like to think about his biological family. The little he did know was pretty bleak. His biological mom died when he was three months old, and then his biological dad raised him until he was two. When he brought him to the state, he claimed he didn't have the mental capabilities to care for a child alone. Asher didn't remember his biological dad at all, but he was mad at him for years. He might not have memories, but that two-year-old was abandoned by the only family he had. Asher let his mind flick to Knutr and Leifr for a moment. He would have died for those boys.

He lucked out with his parents and Natalie though. They were more family than he ever could have hoped for. He had a childhood full of love and support and still had that with Natalie and his mom.

His phone buzzed and Asher flipped it over quickly, tapping on the picture to zoom in. He took a deep breath and started reading.

Ash—

I don't know how to start this letter, but it needs to be written. I hope the people that adopted you are good people. They seemed nice and smart and kind when I met them. The guy, your dad I guess, he looked like he would really take care of you. I hope they gave you the life I couldn't. I used to drive by their house to check on you once a week. They gave me the address in case I wanted to send you birthday cards and stuff. You looked happy, playing in the yard or sitting on the front porch blowing bubbles with your new mom. She caught me once, so I stopped. I didn't want her to think I was going to try to kidnap you or anything. I knew that you'd have a better life with them.

I'm sorry I've never sent you any birthday cards. That day is a hard one for me. I promise I'll try to send one this year, even if it's a little early or a little late.

I don't know how old you are now, when your parents decided to give you this letter. I told your mom to wait a while, that it wasn't something for a little kid to read. You're probably in high school now. I bet you're real tall. You don't remember me, or your mom, but I used to call her my Amazon and she called me Sasquatch.

I want you to know that I think about you all the time. How much I wish things were different. If your mom hadn't died. She was a good woman. So strong, so beautiful. She could have figured it out, how to live the way we live and still have you.

I'm sorry to write this to you in a letter. There's something you need to know about me, and you. I would tell this to you in person, but I don't think I'm going to be around much longer. And you need to hear this as someone old enough to handle it and understand what it means.

The world we live in isn't what most people think it is. There are things that go bump in the night, all sorts of magical beings that live beside us. I hope you believe me and don't think I'm on drugs or something. I'm not a druggie. I've done a lot of bad things, but my mind is clear.

I'm not telling you this because you are something weird, like an elf or whatever. But you are important. You're from a line of Guardians. I'm one, my dad was one, same with his dad. We protect the magical beings that need it. I know you're probably reading this, shaking your head, but you'll believe me one day when you meet the person you are supposed to protect. Mine was your mom. I don't know if you'll fall in love with your charge or just protect them, but it will be the greatest calling of your life.

When you find your charge, you'll know. There will be a draw to keep that person safe no matter what the consequences. I know this sounds like a load of bullshit, but if you need help navigating, there's a Guardian safe house in Skinnyatlas, NY. I'll put the address at the bottom. I'll add the numbers of a couple of my buddies, but we're getting old. I don't know if any of them will still be around by the time you read this. I hope I am. I really do. If I am, please call me. The adoption agency has all my information for you. I keep it up to date.

If you don't want to talk to me, but still need to talk to someone, call one of these guys. They're all good people.

I'm so sorry I couldn't keep you. I made a lot of enemies guarding your mom. She was the stronger one, between the two of us. Stronger in every way. And without her, we were vulnerable.

I love you more than I could ever explain, my dear baby boy. My sweet Ash.

Your Father

Asher carefully set his phone on his bedside table and laid his head back against his pillow.

That was not what he expected.

Hearing from his father, technically from beyond the grave, he didn't expect an invitation into a new life. A magical life.

Asher's life was a mess. He'd gone from a normal summer—one with a new girlfriend in a new place—to hallucinating a past life, his girlfriend admitting to being a witch, and now a letter from his biological father claiming he was part of this other life that didn't make any sense to him.

A Guardian? What the hell did that mean? He was a cop, sure. He'd been born wanting to protect people without ever really understanding why. He thought it was a calling like others had toward a vocation like teaching. But now that was supposed to mean he was something else? At the biological level?

He didn't think that man cared an inch for him. Asher had gotten over the abandonment, the sheer pain of being given up by the person who was supposed to care most about him in the world, by painting a portrait of a terrible human. He told himself his biological father was a drug addict or a criminal. That if he'd kept him, Asher would have ended up dead in an alley like the abandoned kids that made the news. Asher believed that he was a bad person for giving him away.

But he wasn't.

He was a good man trying to keep his son safe. Hell, was this the truth? Was Rosemary a witch? Was he a Guardian? Did he live another life hundreds of years ago filled with a great love and two perfect children?

Asher rolled onto his side, wishing he could make all this hurt and revelation go away for a moment so he could think. His mind bombarded him with visions of his life in Norway, all the what-ifs that could have been with his biological parents, questions about what it meant to be a Guardian, and what on earth his mother had been to need one.

He needed someone to tell him what to do, tell him how to get through this.

He needed Rosemary.

Chapter Nineteen

Rosemary was released at ten a.m., two hours after Asher had been allowed to go home. He hadn't come say goodbye or texted her or left a message with her nurse. Sage watched him walk out the front door through the window.

He simply left the hospital, and with it, her.

Her heart ached. She wanted Asher, to put her arms around him and know that he was there and alive and going to be with her. Lavender had said that soulmates could still leave each other and break each other's hearts. Rosemary was praying to every goddess of love she could think of that it wouldn't come to that. She'd barely had the chance to fall in love with him in this life; she couldn't lose him already.

She shuffled to the car with Sage by her side, fighting exhaustion. They'd both gotten fitful sleeps in the hospital. Around three in the morning, Sage had insisted she scooch over so they could share the small twin. It was hardly comfortable, but having her sister next to her did lessen the pain in her chest a little.

"I need something pre-made for breakfast, what about you?"

"I guess," Rosemary answered glumly.

"Perk up, R. He'll come back to you. Just give him time." They both slid into their seats. "How about the full breakfast from the diner? I'll get two to go."

"Sure." Rosemary was hungry. It was like her stomach was betraying her heart. She should be too sick to eat, but thinking about a mess of eggs and hash browns and sausage made her stomach growl. She could at least force down a few bites.

Town was quiet. There were a few cars parked on the street, but nothing like a usual late June morning. Next week, when the Fourth of July hit, the island would be crawling with tourists. Maybe everyone was saving up their days to vacation over the holiday.

"Do you want to come in?" Sage asked as she pulled into a parking spot.

"Absolutely not. I'm going to sit here and wallow. Maybe put on some sad music."

"Wallow away. But if you're still like this in a few days, I'm going to start hassling you about it."

"Deal." Rosemary slunk back in her seat and rubbed her eyes.

Rosemary couldn't shake Norway from her thoughts, so instead of wallowing, as she had planned, she started to think about all the interesting skills she had. Gundrun could catch and skin a rabbit and cook it into a pretty tasty stew. She could also build a fire from basically nothing, even in damp weather. She could make clothes, distinguish safe mushrooms from poisonous ones, have a baby without an epidural or prenatal care or even clean sheets. Ugh. If she had a child in this life, she was going with an epidural all the way. Maybe even full-knocked-out anesthesia, like they did it in the nineteen-fifties. Modern medicine was miraculous.

She could cauterize a wound, which was horribly disgusting, but if she ever found herself in the middle of a battlefield with no access to a hospital, that could come in handy.

What else...she spoke a completely different language. Maybe Old Norse? She didn't even know what it was called. Could she still speak it?

"Minn nam en Gundrun." She laughed. "Guess I can still speak it. That will be useful, well, never." Guess there wasn't a chance she would suddenly understand and speak a language like Spanish or Mandarin that could help her in any way in this life. Maybe her soul would be looking back at knowing American English a few lives from now and think of how useless it was.

She glanced outside the car, her mood a little lighter. There were parts of her past life she could think about without getting overly depressed. She would simply focus on those.

Across the street, she saw a man with hair like ice suddenly turn towards her, his face pinching. He stomped across the street and pointed at her.

"You!" she heard him yell, even with her windows rolled up.

"Oh, shit," she breathed.

It was Fáfnir.

Why the hell was Fáfnir on Star Island? She quickly locked the doors and looked around the floor of the car for something to defend herself but came up short. She scrambled towards the middle of the car, trying to steer clear of the windows.

"You, bitch," he said, smashing his fist against her window. "You little murderer. I ought to pull you out of the car by your hair and drown you after what you did to me."

"You killed Skáldi," she shot back, surprised by her bravery. "Get the fuck away from my car."

"I should have known you'd be around here. You probably killed Morana, too."

Morana? Was this one of her brothers?

"I'm going to call the police if you don't walk away, Fáfnir."

"It's Ivan Stoch. And I'm guessing you're one of Bay witches."

She didn't answer but held his gaze.

"Get. Away. From. Me. I'm not kidding," she said sternly.

"Or what? You'll come out here and fight me? I'll knock you into the street."

"What the fuck did you just say to my sister?" Sage appeared behind him and immediately had her hands around the collar of his shirt, dragging him away from the car.

"Get off me!" he shouted. Sage complied, pushing him back a few steps. A couple of other people stepped out of the diner to see what all the shouting was about.

"I'd walk away," Sage lowered her voice. "No one is going to take kindly to a man putting his hands on a woman. Even though I could probably beat you into a bloody mess." Sage stood her ground. She wasn't particularly tall, but no amount of clothing could hide the fact that she could carry a barrel of apples without breaking a sweat. Ivan, on the other hand, looked like he'd been strung out on heroin in the last two weeks.

He sneered and jogged down the street, quickly turning the corner.

"You all right, Sage?" Luke called from across the street in the doorway of his bar.

"Fine. Weird tourist," she called back before getting into the car. She slammed the door quickly, then turned to Rosemary while she shifted into drive.

"Who the hell was that?" Sage asked.

"Fáfnir or Ivan. Morana's brother. I killed him." Rosemary sunk down in her seat.

"You did what now?"

"He's the one I killed. In Norway. Oh fuck. I killed a Stoch in another life. He knows about the blood curse. And he's here. Shit!" Rosemary rubbed her hands over her face. "He's going to kill me. And probably all of us. Steal our blood and all that nonsense. Why the fuck did I tell him I poisoned him? I could have pretended someone else did. He could have showed up all 'sorry someone killed the two of us, can't believe that happened.' I'm such an idiot."

"Well, it was hundreds of years before we were cursed, and you weren't even a Bay then. Plus, I don't think any ancient humans were known for their sharp intellect. Weren't you more of a smash and grab people?"

"First of all, I was a farmer, so screw you. Secondly, that's exactly how Ivan acted in the last life." She took a deep breath. "What are we going to do?"

"Go home and get behind the protection wards Verbena put up. Text her and Laurel that there's another Stoch on the island and figure out what's next. You've got four magical sisters this time around. No one is going to sell you to that asshole for animals."

"So, Ivan Stoch." Lavender sat at the head of the dining table with *A Compendium of North American Magical Families* in front of her. It was one of the rare times they brought a book down from the attic, but this meeting needed a lot of light, and an eye on the front door in case Ivan decided to stop by. "Metal warlock. He's not the chaos one Morana warned would come after us."

"Perfect, so there is still a damn chaos warlock that might be on his way. That's ideal."

"Sage, positive attitude please. No one likes a Debbie Downer in a time of crisis." Lavender turned back to the book. "There isn't a ton of information about him in here, but they had two magical parents, mother deceased, father...missing?"

"That doesn't bode well," Verbena muttered. She was taking notes on her laptop while looking at all the message boards on Black Hat Haberdashery that mentioned metal magic and particularly metal warlocks.

"Couple of uncles, no cousins listed. Lives in Montana, same address as Morana," Verbena added.

"Regular Google search has lots of arrests and no job that I can find." Laurel was busy punching away at her phone.

"Great. He's probably a career criminal," Rosemary moaned.

"Not necessarily. For example, you don't really have a cyber footprint," Laurel pointed out.

"I don't?" Rosemary questioned. Was that bad?

"Nope. If someone from high school was looking for you, it'd be nearly impossible. You don't have non-magical social media. You didn't go to college, so there's no alumni board or anything with your information. If you want to start your own flower arranging business, you'll definitely have to change that."

"Back to the matter at hand, please." Lavender steered the conversation back to the metal warlock currently on Star Island and very angry at Rosemary. "Rosemary, you have work tomorrow, right?"

"Yeah, I'm doing the noon to six shift alone, then have to arrange a couple centerpieces for a luncheon. I can probably finish most of them during the day though."

"I can stop by tonight and amp up the protection spell there, if you like," Verbena offered.

"Please do."

"I'll pop my head in a few times to check on you. I've got help in the bakery this afternoon. At this point, I think we should be prepared for Ivan or the other one...Miloslav to show up at any of our places of work or here.

We have basic protection up, but we need to brush up on our battle magic."

"Brush up?" Rosemary asked. "I'm sorry, have you ever studied battle magic? I sure as hell have not." While Rosemary was extremely capable when it came to both garden and sex magic, she'd never even looked at a spell book that detailed battle magic.

"I know a little," Lavender admitted. "Nothing that I would feel comfortable relying on, but just enough to last me until the police got there."

"I know absolutely zero battle spells," Laurel added. "But I can always jump into their minds and fuck things up from the inside." She smirked at Owen, who pressed a kiss to her forehead.

"No real magic, but large man who can handle himself in a fight," Owen said, raising his hand.

"I can do some weird shit if I'm near my plants," Sage said cryptically.

"Weird shit? Care to elaborate?" The entire table turned towards Sage.

She shrugged. "My plants listen to me. Not much when you're talking about a bell pepper, but an apple tree can do some damage."

"Unless someone attacks Sage in her orchard, that won't be overly helpful. I'll go through the library tonight, get some simple battle spells under my belt, and pass them along. The fact that Ivan didn't immediately attack Rosemary with battle magic is good. He threatened to punch her, not, you know, throw her down the block. Maybe he doesn't know any." Rosemary could tell Lavender was creating a multi-stepped plan in her head. She was always the most prepared of the sisters.

"What on earth can metal warlocks do?" Sage asked. "I've never met one."

"Metal warlocks," Verbena began, "can bend metal to their will. Some have the power to telepathically lift things containing metals, others have what appears to be superhuman strength when it comes to bending it. Technically, metal warlocks fall under the umbrella of earthen magic, but they are rarely seen as allies with other practitioners of earth magic, such as your more traditional rock, wood, and mud witches and warlocks. That's what's on the Black Hat Haberdashery under the general definitions page."

"Are there any comments?" Rosemary asked, getting up to stand behind her.

"Tons. Most of them say things like, I met a metal warlock once and he was an asshole."

"Oh good. An approachable bunch." Sage rolled her neck and popped it.

"Let's divide and conquer. Verbena, you take Black Hat Haberdashery, put together a list of strengths and weaknesses, also known metal warlocks that might be active on the boards. See if any seem friendly. Or at the very least, not aligned with Ivan Stoch. Laurel, if you wouldn't mind popping into the Hedge World and checking on Morana. I'd be curious if her brother has any idea she's trapped there."

"On it. And I also heard back from the witch's council in France. They said they would not meddle in American affairs, that we need a council that does more than complete a census every five years. I have emails out to members of the Russian council as well as the Egyptian council. I'll let you know when I hear back."

"Perfect. And Sage—"

"Go sit in my apple orchard and hope Ivan attacks me so I can kill him with trees?"

"Sure. I was going to say go with Verbena when she amps up the protection spell in case Ivan happens by."

"I can do that. I'll bring a purse full of fruit to throw at him."

"You do you, Sage. Rosemary,"

"Yes?" She was itchy for a direction.

"You should go to sleep. You've had a rough couple of days."

"I'm not going to sleep. I am going to help." She strummed her fingers against her chin. "Gardening and herbs are my things. I'm going to make some potions."

Chapter Twenty

Asher drove to Rosemary's house like the island was on fire. He was the sheriff, so no one was going to pull him over, and at that particular moment, he couldn't take the distance between them. He needed to see her, if only the make certain she was okay.

He'd spent the day staring at his ceiling, trying to come to terms with everything he'd learned in the last few days. This new world, one with past lives and magic and destinies he didn't understand—it all felt real. Because when he looked at Rosemary, or Gundrun, he knew that he was supposed to be with her forever. He'd never felt so certain of anything in his life.

He was her Guardian. He had to be. His entire life, he'd felt an innate calling to protect. Being a cop hadn't fulfilled the need, but now he knew what it meant. At least, he had a vague idea what it meant.

As more of the memories of Norway flooded back and pieces from the past fit into the present, he was more and more worried for her safety. He'd failed her in the last life, left her and their children without their protector in a world far more dangerous than this one. He couldn't fail her again.

He'd left the hospital without a word to her. He was hurt and confused, but there was no reason for him to be so cold. He had abandoned her again.

He needed to make it right.

Asher pulled into the Bay cottage driveway and parked his car to the side. He would be staying for quite a while and wanted to make sure a car could back out past him if needed. Asher was in this for the long haul, beginning today.

He jogged to the front door, taking the steps two at a time, and rapped twice. The curtain covering the large front window fluttered, and a moment later, the door opened.

"Sheriff Evans." It was one of Rosemary's sisters. He searched his mind trying to remember which one. This wasn't Laurel, or the realtor...

"Sage?"

"Yup." She opened the door wider. The interior of the house was a flurry of activity. Laurel and Owen Davies were in the front parlor, though Laurel appeared to be asleep on a yoga mat while Owen sat beside her. The oldest sister, Lavender, was at the large dining table, poring over a book that looked like it was one-hundred-years old. She even had on white gloves. Verbena, his realtor, was typing away on a laptop, while a cup of tea steamed beside her.

He refocused on the Bay sister in front of him.

"Is Rosemary here?"

Sage smiled and stepped aside. "She's on the porch. Walk straight back through the kitchen and out the door. You'll hear her before you see her."

Asher walked through the house, looking at it through new eyes. This was Rosemary's home, and suddenly everything seemed more magical. The first time he visited, he had thought their décor a little quirky and bohemian, but now it was like a veil had been lifted. There were crescent moons and stars on the floor, bundles of dried herbs in every corner, and small stone statues of what looked like nature spirits. A table in one corner had a velvet cloth over it and a stack of cards in the middle.

The kitchen was bursting with scents; whatever was on the stove was woody and potent, and simmering over a low flame. He glanced in the pot as he passed it. Something in there was bubbling and appeared to be stirring on its own. It didn't look edible, but somehow still managed to smell enticing.

Rosemary was on the porch, chanting softly. He peeked through the door but didn't interrupt her. The afternoon light dappled through the screens, casting spots of brightness and shadows over her face.

His heart panged. She was still light and flowers, just as she had been when he was Skáldi and she was Gundrun. His breath of spring, his sunny mornings and rainy afternoons, his rich soil, his one love.

"Idun, the ever-young goddess, my patroness of lives past and lives forward, I bid you speak to me and renew our connection. I dedicate these apples to you and praise you for the bounty you have given our lands. I thank you for the beauty of spring and green buds and gentle breezes you provide. I give you my faith and put myself in your care." She pushed a basket of apples forward, in offering, then rested back on her heels. Her eyes were peaceful, staring off into the distance.

He tried not to move. Normally, he would feel awkward observing a private moment like this, but with Rosemary, it felt natural. He felt included.

"Asher?"

"Rosemary," he answered, his voice barely more than a sigh. Something about being in her presence completely loosened any tension he held.

She didn't look at him, but her shoulders relaxed and she smiled.

"I'm going to deliver these to the garden. Come meet me in two minutes." She picked up the basket and walked out the door, all the while not looking at him.

He waited, giving her the space she needed to complete whatever ritual he had interrupted, then walked outside.

His mood instantly elevated upon seeing her. She was in between rows of wild herbs, the summer sun speckling across her form. She looked to him slowly and smiled. It was not a grin or sly, but simply happy. She wasn't cross or upset at him, or if she was, seeing him melted it all away.

"I'm glad you came," she began, "I missed you."

He crossed the space between them, jumping over the rows of herbs and grabbed her around the waist, dragging her up his body to rest in his arms.

This. This was right and good and meant to be. She was like a puzzle piece against his body, every hard edge of him merged with the soft curves of her, and together they were whole.

He snuck his hands to grasp her bottom, pulling her up until she wrapped her legs around his waist. She felt so good. She smelled so good. Even the sound of her sighing in relief was so *good*. He wasn't certain he'd ever be able to let go of her again.

"Rosemary," he started, pressing his forehead against hers. "This is insane. It's all insane. How do I have memories from a time over a thousand years ago? And why were we both there? And..." His voice trailed off.

"I have a lot to explain," she answered and kissed him quickly. She moved to talk again, but his mouth seized hers, enticing it back to his. They'd shared a thousand kisses as Skáldi and Gundrun, but now that they were Asher and Rosemary, it seemed like there would never be enough time for all the kisses he hoped to give her.

He teased her lips apart, needing more from her, as much as she could give. She moaned softly, yielding to him, her arms wrapping more tightly around his neck. He wanted this woman.

He needed this woman.

"Asher," she panted, pulling away from him. "Put me down for a second so I can think clearly."

He complied but kept his hands firmly around her waist, their bodies pressed together.

"I need to tell you three things and then you can decide what we do next." She brushed her hair away from her face and shook her head a little like she was clearing her focus.

"Okay." He smiled down at her, and unable to keep his mouth away from her, kissed the top of her head quickly.

"I'm a witch."

"I know." He smiled and tried to kiss her mouth, but she evaded him and raised an eyebrow.

"Let me tell you what that entails. I'm a garden witch. My magic is mostly plant based, though a little bit involved with the earth as well. I did a past life spell that was supposed to only take me for the ride but brought you along. I am so sorry. If I knew you were coming, I never would have made you go through that alone. And lastly, Morana Stoch's brother is Fáfnir. And he's coming after me."

Asher's jaw set, and he immediately felt a burst of need to protect her at all costs. Fáfnir. The villain of the past. Yes. Now when he pictured Ivan Stoch, he saw the face of the raider who had wanted his wife. His Gundrun.

He would not let anything happen to Rosemary.

"Why would he come after you?" he asked. She had never done anything to him, other than marrying Skáldi rather than him. Could he really be angry about that? It was, after all, hundreds of years ago and surely Fáfnir had married someone else.

"Okay. Don't react rashly. This is a new life, and things are a little different this time around."

"Tell me," he pressed.

She took a deep breath and pressed the palms of her hands against his chest. "Fáfnir killed you. He was the one that attacked you in the forest. And then a month later he showed up offering to trade a bunch of animals for me."

"That son of a bitch," he muttered, his eyes drifting towards the gate. How quickly could he find Ivan? It's not like he was going to kill him or anything, but he was definitely going to have words with a man that murdered him in another life. And then insulted his wife by comparing her worth to animals.

"Hold on," she said and grabbed his chin, forcing him to meet her eyes. "I sort of murdered him."

"Excuse me?" Asher couldn't hide the look of shock on his face.

Gundrun didn't have an evil bone in her body. He couldn't imagine her murdering Fáfnir. If anyone killed him, it should have been one of his brothers, in vengeance. They should have stepped up and defended his family.

"Look, after you died, our family decided to cut their losses. They traded me for the animals and a promise of protection. Hakon told me he would raise Leifr and Knútr for me, so I didn't bring them. Fáfnir didn't know we had children. But when I got there, he insisted he wouldn't...well, basically rape me until I got my period, proving he wasn't going to end up raising one of your kids." She rushed through the last bit.

"I am going to kill this man with my bare hands." Asher had never said a sentence with more conviction in his life, nor had his mind ever been changed so swiftly.

"Asher! Let me finish. There was a pretty good chance I was pregnant already, so I poisoned both of us and hopefully did a good job blaming his brother, who was also an asshole."

"You were pregnant?" His heart stabbed. He was trying to keep to his feet, but every fiber of his being wanted to fall to his knees in grief.

"Maybe? But I looked at it really practically. If I was, I didn't want to see what he was going to do to that baby. If I wasn't, I was weeks away from being his wife for real. Neither were futures I could live with. His brother was also terrible. He had mentioned more than once that if anything happened to Fáfnir he would take me on as a concubine. So I really only saw poisoning as a way out."

"Holy shit." He pressed his forehead against hers. "This is my fault. I didn't protect you. I promised I would protect you. You and the boys. And I failed you all."

"Asher, you were hit with an ax in the woods by a murder-crazy raider. It was not your fault. You gave me an amazing life full of love and beautiful children. You were the love of my life." She paused. "More than one, as it turns out."

She buried her face against his chest and tightened her grip around his waist. "We did the best we could. Truthfully, it's shocking we survived as long as we did." She looked back up at him. "No one is going to trade me to Ivan for a couple of farm animals. We can be together this time around, with a lot less fear. And central heating."

He kissed the top of her head, wondering if he would ever be able to let her go again.

"Asher?" she asked.

"My real name is Ash," he said, needing to tell her immediately. This was Rosemary, his love of many lives. "My parents changed it when they adopted me. My biological father..." He wasn't really sure what to tell her about him. He wasn't even sure what the whole Guardian thing meant. He took a deep breath. "My parents who raised me didn't want to me be known as an insignificant speck of dust. An ash to be swept away."

"What?" She furrowed her brow at him. "Oh, goddess, that's not what Ash means." Rosemary wound her hand around his. "Come here." She pulled him away from the garden, deeper into the property. They walked down a path of white stones, following it until they were deep enough that they couldn't see the house anymore.

"There," she said, pointing.

"What am I supposed to be looking at?" He was staring at a bunch of random trees.

She pulled his hand again until they stood beneath a particular tree, and she put both of their hands on the trunk.

"This is an ash. This is what you were named for, not dust. You're strong and offer protection from the elements and are a spectacular work of nature. Ashes are known for endurance and power. You are an ash tree." She smiled. "Makes sense. Ash falling for Rosemary. We're both of the earth." She rested her head against his chest. "Ash," she whispered, his name like a prayer on her tongue.

He looked at this woman, who he had just met but his soul had known forever. She was extraordinary.

"Call me Ash again."

"Ash. My Ash."

He grabbed her around the waist and threw her over his shoulder, then turned on his heels and followed the path back towards the house.

"Where are we going?" She laughed, bouncing against him.

"My apartment. Too many people live with you, and I need to show you exactly how much I missed you and how much I want you. And I'd like to do it with your clothes off, if you're willing."

"Oh, thank every goddess in the ether. About time."

He smacked her ass once, then jogged to his car.

Chapter Twenty-One

Rosemary and Asher didn't talk much in the car. She bounced between eyeing him and looking out the window, at times feeling the nervous excitement the moment demanded, and other times feeling like this was the most normal thing in the world, driving down the road with him, on her way to get naked in his apartment. He pulled into one of the open street spots in front of his building, walked around to her side, opened her car door, and took her by the hand.

Keeping silent, they walked into the building and up one flight of stairs before coming to his door. He unlocked it, pulled her inside, slammed it shut and locked the bolt.

Rosemary caught her bottom lip between her teeth, more out of anticipation than nerves. She'd wanted to be alone with Asher since the first time she saw him, but the want had transformed into an ache since she saw their past. She needed to be with him, really with him, emotionally and physically, and now she had the chance.

Asher leaned against the door, his eyes drinking in every inch of her. She nearly blushed, but she wasn't embarrassed or nervous. She was excited. She couldn't wait to spend the rest of her life being looked at like the most delicious thing in sight.

"I'm bossy and I'll tell you what I want and how I want it. Will that bother you?" he asked. He took two steps in her direction, taking his time closing the space between them.

"No." Goddess, she loved listening to him order her around.

"Good." He walked past her, his fingers grazing her forearm slightly, and continued until he was in his bedroom. He sat on the end of the bed, framed by the doorway, his elbows on his knees. He motioned for her to come to him.

She turned and walked towards him, her lips curling into a wicked smiled.

"Stop," he commanded. "Take your shirt off." He rubbed his hand over his jaw.

Rosemary slowly peeled her T-shirt over her head, taking care not to get her hair tangled along the way. Once her shirt hit the floor, she pulled out the rubber band keeping her hair in a bun and let her hair fall loose.

"Take your skirt off."

She kicked her shoes off and stepped out of her skirt in one fluid motion. It had an elastic waistband, so there wasn't a zipper or buttons to mess around with. Rosemary stood a few feet in front of Asher in nothing but her pale pink bra and panties, her hands on her hips. She knew she looked good, but if she'd had any doubts, Asher's reaction would have silenced them. His eyes did a long sweep of her, from head to toes, lingering at her face and curves. She shivered with anticipation. She wanted his hands on her, and hers on him. She wanted to pull his shirt off him and get those jeans off and...

"Come here," he asked this time, his voice pleading. She walked forward. "You are the most beautiful woman I've ever seen." His hands found her waist and pulled her until she stood right in front of him, a leg on either side of his. He pressed his cheek against her chest and hugged her hard. "Your skin," he groaned, running his palms up her sides and to her back. "I could touch nothing else for the rest of my life and be happy."

Her fingers dug into his hair, keeping him close. She didn't want to ever let him get further than a few feet away from her, now that she had him back. She needed more, every fiber of her being was screaming at her for more. They were together, finally, the past clear to both of them. They needed to make the most of this life and the second chance they had together. They couldn't waste a moment.

His fingers found the clasp of her bra and made quick work of it. She shrugged out of the burdensome garment and exhaled. She was aching for him, and Asher's hands were there in moments, squeezing her, brushing his thumbs over her nipples, teasing her until she couldn't help but moan.

"Be as loud as you want," he mumbled. "No one will hear you here." He guided her closer, closing his mouth around her nipple, his tongue flowing over her until his teeth gently nipped the tender flesh.

"Ash," she panted. Her hands went to his shoulders, giving her enough balance so she didn't fall over. She leaned into his mouth, wanting even more. He teased her using his tongue and teeth, moving between her breasts, kissing everywhere but her nipples, before finally taking the time to suck and adore them. Rosemary was dizzy with lust, a ball of frayed nerves. Every moment of contact between their two bodies burned with the most delightful heat.

He found her panties and ripped them away from her body. Rosemary could hear the fabric tear and for a moment thought *that's never happened before*. But she didn't dwell on it because he pulled her even closer so she could straddle him on her knees.

"Kiss me," she finally managed to say. "Ash, I need you to kiss me."

He pulled his face away from her chest and gazed at her with hungry eyes.

"Where?" he asked devilishly.

"My mouth for now. I'll take every inch of me over the next hour, though."

He grabbed the nape of her neck and pulled her down until their lips met. He immediately teased her lips apart, using his teeth on her bottom lip. Their tongues met, electrifying every sense, and she trembled, unable to stop her body from shaking, and grasped his back.

He pulled away from her mouth and looked at her. "Are you okay?"

"Yes." She moved to kiss him again, but he held her off.

"But you're shaking."

"It's good shaking." She giggled softly and raised an eyebrow. "Really good shaking. I think it would be described as shaking with desire."

"You sure you aren't cold?" He raised his eyebrow and let Rosemary think of all the ways he could warm her up.

"After Norway, I don't think I'll ever really be cold in this life." She kissed his forehead, his cheek, his jaw, and finally landed back at his mouth. She thought for a moment: she was completely naked, and Asher still had all his clothes on. She needed to remedy that.

"Take your shirt off," she said, reaching for the bottom of his shirt.

"In a second," he answered, moving her hand back up to his shoulder. "Let me do a few things first."

"What kind of things?" she questioned, a sly grin claiming her mouth.

Asher locked his eyes with hers, not glancing away, not blinking as his hand traveled down her waist, across her belly, and nestled between her thighs, cupping her sex possessively.

"When I went down on you in my office," he began, his fingers sliding over her wet folds and finding her favorite spots. "And when I touched you in the forest, I couldn't really see your face when you came." He quickly nibbled the underside of her breast. "I'm going to touch you until you come, and I'm going to watch you the entire time."

Rosemary nodded and locked her arms around his neck. She sank into his fingers, letting the feel of it all wash over her and take her to new peaks.

"You're so sexy," he growled. "Your body is amazing." His mouth moved over her belly, biting and kissing, licking and sucking, all the while his fingers slid inside of her and the palm of his hand rubbed firmly against her clit. She could feel warmth spreading from all corners of her body, radiating between her legs where Asher's hand claimed her. She dug her fingers into his shoulders, steadying herself.

It felt so good, even better than when they were together before, because now Rosemary knew the extent of what love with Asher could be. She knew she would want this forever, and not only because they were destined to be together, but because of how she felt in his arms. She was cared for, protected, and desired.

He was her soulmate.

"Come for me, Rosemary," he whispered, upping his tempo. His fingers concentrated on her clit now, swollen with need. She tried to keep her eyes open, maintain eye contact with him, but the pleasure became too great. Her orgasm built and then broke apart, her body wracked with spasms. Asher flung his arm around her waist, keeping her from falling over, but still relentless with his other hand. Wave after wave of pleasure shook her to her core until she was panting to catch her breath.

Asher slowly removed his hand and kissed her mouth hard.

"You are so hot," he said, moving from her mouth to her neck, finding small spots to nibble. "I love every inch of this body," he mumbled and pinched the back of her thigh.

"Ash," she breathed.

"Hm?" He was already moving back to her breast, teasing her nipple into a hard point.

"Let me..." she moaned. "Wait." She put her hands on his shoulders firmly until he stopped and looked up her. She carefully stood on wobbly legs, then pulled him up with her. Her hands went to the hem of his shirt and slowly pulled it over his head.

His chest did not disappoint. Nearly twice as broad as her, Asher looked like a Viking of legends, which made sense since technically...

"What is that?" she asked, suddenly in a panic. At the same spot where the ax had been buried over a thousand years ago, Ash had a huge white scar. It was longer than the palm of her hand and thick, with small white dots on either side of it. She ran her hand over it, feeling the uneven skin against her own.

"Healed," he soothed. "I'll tell you more about it later."

"Ash," she continued, but he shook his head firmly.

"Later. Trust me." He wrapped his arms around her waist and lifted her feet off the ground before tipping them both onto the bed.

Later. She could wait. She could get lost in his arms for a little longer.

Rosemary reached for the zipper of his jeans, but he grabbed her wrists and put her hands over her head. He ran his hands down her arms, over her breasts, and down her legs.

"Ash!"

He blinked and looked at her, smirking.

"Yes, Rosemary?"

"Take your pants off. Now. And then get your dick inside me. I've waited long enough. You can tease me and get me all hot and bothered all night. Right now, I want, no, I need you inside me."

A sly grin captured his mouth as he moved his hands off her and stepped off the bed. He walked around the perimeter until he stood right beside her. Rosemary rolled onto her side, her eyes drifting from his face, down the planes of his chest, to the point where a line of hair below his navel promised more to come.

He shucked his pants and boxers at the same time, his expression pure confidence.

"Better?"

Rosemary nodded her head but didn't take her eyes off his dick. She wasn't one to fawn over a penis. They were fine, visually, in her opinion. It was the work they did that really mattered. But when she looked at Asher, all that flew out of her mind.

"Your dick is wonderful." She wrapped her hand around it, guiding him back onto the bed next to her.

"That's the oddest compliment I've ever received," he said and nipped at her shoulder.

"Wonderful, beautiful, handsome, perfect..."

"Keep that up and it's going in your mouth," he teased.

Rosemary smiled wickedly. "I'll raincheck you on that for later tonight. But when I said I needed you inside me, I had a more particular place in mind."

Asher pushed her onto her back and shifted her legs until they were open in front of him. His hands ran up her inner thighs and he grabbed her hips to drag her towards him. He hovered right at her entrance, watching her intently.

"Please, please," she moaned. "I've been dying for this since the spell."

Asher froze. His brow furrowed.

"What spell?"

"Oh, fuck." Rosemary exhaled. If she just managed to screw up this perfect sex they'd been having so far... She tried to clear her mind to explain quickly. "The night you...gave me the best head of my life in your office... I had done a spell to get you to trust me. But I needed to give you head for it to work. So you flipped it completely. But that night I was dying to fuck you. It was all I could think about. And I have been dying to fuck you ever since."

Ash raised an eyebrow and leaned close to her face.

"You did a sex spell on me?"

"I tried to," she confessed. There was no reason for her to lie.

His brows pinched together, and Rosemary rushed to explain.

"It was before I knew you. I just wanted to tell you everything and have you not freak out. But then, the second you touched me, I lost my mind. Please, don't be mad at me. Please, please, please," she begged. "I'll do anything to make it up to you."

"Hm," he wondered aloud, his expression serious.

Rosemary winced. If she had fucked this up, she'd never forgive herself. Why had she ever tried to do that spell? It was inane. She didn't need Asher to trust her; he was her soulmate. They were meant to trust each other.

Asher hummed a low growl, then flipped her onto her stomach. Before Rosemary registered her new position, he nudged her legs apart with his knees, then thrust inside her in one motion. Rosemary gasped and dug a fist into the comforter.

"Don't do another sex spell on me. Unless you have my permission," he whispered against her ear.

"Yes," she agreed. "I promise."

"Good." His hand snuck beneath her body, finding her breast so he could fondle it. "You feel so good," he growled. "You're so wet and warm." He bit her shoulder and upped his tempo.

Rosemary whimpered with pleasure. She was completely under his control, and the idea of him playing her body so perfectly had her trembling again.

"Do you like this?" Asher asked, rolling her nipple between his thumb and finger.

"Yes," she breathed. "I love it."

He leaned off her, pulling her onto her knees. His fingers found her clit and his thrusts became more purposeful. He took his time, entering her fully before nearly exiting completely.

"Ash," she panted. "Ash, please."

"Please, what?"

"Make me come again. I want to come with you inside me." Rosemary had never been one for talking much during sex, but Asher brought it out in her. She loved his dirty mouth and sought to meet it.

His fingers played with her folds while he brought her closer and closer to the edge. She squeezed her walls against his dick, holding onto the peak as long as she could until her orgasm broke her.

"Ash!" she exclaimed, falling to her elbows. She squeezed him over and over, the waves of her orgasm showing no signs of subsiding.

"I'm going to come inside you," he said, his hands hooking around her hips before he spent himself with a final groan. They stayed there, each locked in their orgasms, until Rosemary exhaled and smiled with relief.

Asher slowly eased out of her and let her fall to the bed in a heap of blissful exhaustion. He stayed on his knees, staring at her.

"What are you doing?" she asked, rolling onto her back.

"You're so beautiful," he said, smiling. He crawled beside her and nestled his head against her breasts. "Your face is gorgeous, but you've got these amazing tits that I am already thinking about licking again, an ass that makes two perfect handfuls, legs I will worship for the rest of my life, and pretty much a golden pussy."

"What on earth is a golden pussy?" Rosemary laughed. She tangled her hands in his hair and kissed the top of his head.

"Basically, the epitome of pussies. Perfect in every way."

"I guess it was your turn to give me an odd compliment. I suppose it makes sense. You've got a wonderful dick and I've got a golden pussy," she mused.

"I need a few minutes before I can do anything but lay here in a daze. But when I get my strength back, I'll be needing that golden pussy again. I have some more things in mind that I think we both will enjoy very much." He nipped at the top of her breast, then burrowed against her neck.

"Deal," Rosemary said, snuggling closer to him.

Chapter Twenty-Two

"You did a sex spell?" Asher mumbled after regaining some sort of consciousness. He wasn't sure how long he'd been laying in a daze against her. Eventually, he needed to get up and chug water so he could continue going nuts on the perfection that was Rosemary. He might be thirty-five, but he felt nineteen at the moment.

"Are we going to talk about that right now?" She scraped her teeth against his chest and then laughed. "Quick answer, yes. I wanted you to trust me. Believe me, I've been very worried about you accepting this whole witch thing since the moment I saw you."

"Since the moment you saw me?" he questioned. "You knew that fast?"

"Ash, we're soulmates, and I'm a witch. I knew we'd be together, and had already been together, the moment I saw you."

"Why'd you panic and leave?" Sure, he would have been confused if she'd immediately dragged him to her bedroom, but truthfully, he would not have minded.

"Honestly? You're a cop. Witches don't have great track records with law enforcement. Also, I occasionally do some very natural drugs. But, you know, arrestable offenses. And I was nervous you'd be boring in bed. I've always pictured cops as big rule followers, you know, lights-off-missionary types. Glad you've dispelled that worry."

"Whoa, whoa, whoa, you occasionally do drugs?"

"Yes."

"What drugs?"

"Witches' eyes, dragon's bane, full moon whispers, but only on the full moon, occasionally green ivy, and I smoke weed about once every six months. Shrooms every few years."

"I don't know what any of those are. With the exception of weed and shrooms. Are those other ones real drugs?" He was starting to believe she was pulling his leg.

"Well, technically yes, if the government knew what I could do with them, they would definitely be on their no-no list. But I don't flaunt my ability to change regular old plants into hallucinogens, so no one knows. Except now you do."

"As long as you don't tell, I won't." He rolled onto his back and put his hands behind his head.

"Ready to really talk?" she asked. She pressed a kiss against his jaw, then moved to her side and cradled her head in one hand.

"If you leave your tits out like that, it's going to be hard for me to concentrate," he admitted, letting his eyes wander away from her face for a minute.

Rosemary pulled the sheet up over her body.

"Hey! I didn't mean cover up."

"What happened to your shoulder?" Her voice had turned serious.

He exhaled. He hated telling this story. He tried to tell it quickly whenever anyone asked, but he doubted that would work with her.

"I was shot."

"You were shot?" she exclaimed. She sat up and stared at him. "When?"

"Little over two years ago."

"How? What happened? Are you okay? Does it still hurt?" She stopped talking. "Sorry. Tell me whatever you want to."

He took a deep breath. "I was working a festival, just a regular day. This guy, Nik, showed up to kill his ex. He managed to kill a bystander, two police officers, one was my partner, and himself. His ex, Alison, survived, so did I. I needed a couple surgeries, physical therapy for a while." He paused. "It's strange to think about because I know when it happened, everything happened so fast, but when I remember it, it's like slow-motion. I heard the first two shots, those hit Alison and the random bystander, Erik. Walter and I ran towards him. Walter rushed Nik. I grabbed Erik and Alison to drag them behind one of the stalls. I heard the gun go off three more times, one hit Walter, one hit the other cop, one hit me. When I turned to see where Nik was, he was turning the gun on himself. Dead in an instant." He turned towards her. "When I replay it in my mind. I think of a million different things I could have done. Walter and I should have rushed him together, then he would have had to decide who to hit. Those extra seconds of decision making could have changed the outcome."

"Maybe. But Alison could have died, too, then. You could never know what could have happened." She pulled him close to her and wrapped her arms tightly around his torso. She kissed his neck. "Oh, Ash. I'm so sorry that happened."

"It will be all right. Someday."

"You are okay, right? I mean physically, your shoulder."

"Most days." He smiled and curled his finger around a stray lock of her hair. "I get some stiffness or bursts of pain once in a while, but nothing too horrible. I can still lift you over my shoulder when I need to drag you to bed." He blew out a breath. "When I woke up from Norway, it felt like I had been shot a week ago rather than a year. That was scary. But it's back to normal now."

"I can't believe it was the same spot." She shuddered. "When I saw your scar...it was like I was back there, trying to save you, but really just watching you die." She squeezed her eyes shut for a second. "I'm so sorry I couldn't save you."

"I doubt anyone could have. When I was shot, I was pumped full of so many antibiotics to stop an infection. Multiple surgeries in a sterile ER are what saved me. You were armed with wild herbs, fire, and your bare hands." He paused and furrowed his brow. "Is Ivan going to come after you like Fáfnir did?"

"I think his motivation is different. I can't imagine he wants to, you know, have me bear children for him. We simply don't live in a society that would allow that. Honestly, I think he's pissed I poisoned him. And..." Her voice trailed off.

"And?" he prompted.

"Don't freak out," she began, immediately causing Asher to feel his alert rise. "Some warlock put a curse on my family in the 1700s and basically if a warlock or witch collects the blood of all the living Bay witches, he or she will be able to steal our powers. And maybe kill us. We're not one hundred percent sure on that. Also, my sisters and I are the only living magical Bays. There has been a run of non-magical boys and spinsters."

Asher took a deep breath. It looked like being soulmates with a witch was going to come with some very scary baggage.

"Ivan Stoch might be here to kill you in revenge or kill you to steal your powers?" he reviewed.

"Yes. Also, he's a metal warlock," she added.

"What the fuck is a metal warlock?"

"We each have inherent magic. My sisters and I are hearth and home witches. I'm a garden witch. Lavender is a kitchen witch, Laurel's a hedge witch, Verbena is a house witch, and Sage is a harvest witch. Ivan's a metal warlock, Morana's a hedge witch."

"Wait," he stopped her. "You know Morana?"

"Oh." Her eyes shifted down. "Technically, I've never met her. But I know who she is."

"Care to elaborate, honey?" He quickly kissed her forehead, hoping to ease any fears she might still harbor over trusting him. All this business was so completely out of the realm of local law enforcement anyway, what on earth could he do?

"Don't be mad," she began.

"Please do not tell me you and your sisters murdered Morana." Murder was not something he would be able to turn a blind eye to.

"What? Of course not. No, Morana had Laurel burned alive in another life. Laurel cursed Morana never to find happiness in retribution, so Morana showed up to both reverse the curse and steal our blood. Laurel trapped her in the Hedge World. She's fine, can't hurt anyone there. We're trying to figure out what to do because we don't have a witches' council in the United States," Rosemary rambled.

"Is there some sort of pamphlet you can give me with an overview of everything magical I need to know? Because honestly, this is all making my head spin." He smiled. "And I would much rather be focusing all my attention on you." He nuzzled his stubble against her neck. "Can we forget about curses and past lives and metal warlocks for a little while?"

"I'm sure Verbena will make you a pamphlet." She giggled. "Pay attention to me instead. Magic can wait a few more hours." She wiggled out from under the sheet and climbed on top of him. "You know, I really like your dominating spirit when it comes to sex." She grabbed his hands and put one of each of her breasts. "But sometimes, I'm going to want to be in charge."

"I will relinquish control to you whenever you want it." He shifted his hips under her, giving her a slight bump.

"Good." She smirked and scrunched up her nose. "You ready for round two out of three?"

"As long as we can make it two out of four. I don't have to be at work for fourteen hours."

"Perfect." Rosemary leaned into his grasp. "So are there any boundaries you want to set?"

"Sex-wise or relationship-wise?" he asked, rolling her nipple between his fingers.

"Both, I guess. Sex magic, too," she answered, arching against him.

"Hm." He thought carefully. "No other people are invited to join in."

"Oh really?" Rosemary raised an eyebrow.

"I don't want anyone else touching you. Or me, for that matter."

Rosemary smiled. "I'm good with us just touching each other." She leaned forward and lowered her voice to a whisper. "I don't want anyone but you touching me anyways. Now that I've been with you, well, the rest of the world would pale in comparison."

Asher fought the urge to flip her on her back and devour her mouth with his. She was in charge, and he would let her be.

"And I want to live with you. Soon," he added. "I want to be able to do this whenever we're both off work, whether it be in the morning, afternoon, evening, or three in the morning. I want to wake up with your cute ass pressed against my dick."

She licked her lips and smiled.

"I like the sound of that." She scooched slightly back and slowly took him in her hand. "Sex magic?"

"I'm going to have to learn a little bit more about it before I dive head first into anything like that."

"Fair." She tightened her grip on him. "You didn't ask before, but I have an IUD."

"Ah, yes." He fought to remain focused. "I should have asked. Sorry about that. No witch birth control?"

"None that works as well as good, old-fashioned science."

"Science it is then."

Rosemary quickly shifted her hips and sank down over him, giving him a shock.

"Whoa," he mumbled as he bucked his hips instinctively.

"Surprise you?" She smirked. She braced her hands on his chest and moved achingly slow.

"I figured..." He took a breath. "I figured you might want a little more foreplay." He grasped her hips lightly, enjoying the pace she had chosen.

"Under most circumstances, yes." She leaned down and scraped her teeth against his jawline. "But right now, I just really wanted to ride you."

"Ride away."

Rosemary's hands moved to his upper arms, pinning them down. He was strong enough to get out of her hold, but why would he want to?

She leaned forward, positioning her breast right in front of his mouth. He couldn't help himself and quickly seized her nipple between his lips before licking it slowly.

"Keep doing that," she moaned, her pace quickening. She moved her hands to his chest, freeing his arms. His hands went to her breasts, one teasing her nipple, the other guiding her to his mouth.

"Ash," she breathed. "I want this forever. I never want this to end. I—" Her voice cracked as her entire body shuddered, her hands wildly grasping at him.

Asher quickly flipped her onto her back and drove into her relentlessly. The feeling of her pussy contracting around his dick was too much for him to take and he came moments later, his hands lifting her hips to meet him.

"Fuck, Rosemary," he panted. "I don't think I'll ever get used to the intensity of being with you."

She wrapped her legs around his waist to keep him from withdrawing.

"I hope not."

Amidst the bliss of being with Rosemary, Asher worried.

What the hell did it mean to be a Guardian? Was he always Rosemary's Guardian, even when they were Skáldi and Gundrun? If yes, he'd done a pretty crappy job in their last life.

"I was thinking," Rosemary began, walking back into the living room from the bathroom. "I still don't know a lot about you. Do you have hobbies?"

"I like to read. In Buffalo, I used to race a lot of the guys I worked with. Like sprint down the street to see who would win. So I have been known to jump the fence at local high schools and utilize the track."

"Badass. Breaking and entering." She slid onto the couch next to him and snuggled against him. She had thrown on one of Asher's T-shirts, which nearly swallowed her whole.

"What about you? Hobbies?"

"Meddling in other people's love lives mostly."

"How?" Asher snuck his hand around her thigh.

"If I can tell two people are into each other, I might give them a little push. Nothing strong that could create feelings where none existed; I don't mess with that stuff. I have, on occasion, done a sort of blanket good-time spell on the town. Just to spice up events."

"Do I want to know what that means?"

"Oh, it's harmless," she insisted. "Makes everyone really horny. Lowers inhibitions a little. Related, the last sheriff didn't really like me and had a whole theory that I was a witch."

"You are a witch," Asher pointed out.

"I know! Maybe on his deathbed I'll let him know he was right." She sighed. "It's so nice to talk about being a witch with someone other than my sisters. I'm not a very good secret-keeper, and having an earth-shattering one my entire life hasn't been easy."

"What else is there?" Asher asked.

"What do you mean?" Rosemary lifted her arms over her head and stretched out long.

"Vampires?"

She giggled. "All right, let's do this. Vampires, as far as I know, they are not real. There are blood witches and warlocks who probably over the years have been confused with vampires. Werewolves, no, shifters, yes."

"What's the difference?"

"Shifters are their own thing. They can turn into their animal spirit at will, not because of the moon. Animans are more common. They're like humans who have special connections with animals. Telepathically. Let me think." Rosemary slid off his lap and slipped her hand into his, pulling him towards the bathroom.

"Mermaids are probably sea witches," she continued, peeling his boxers off.

"Uh-huh," Asher mumbled. Rosemary pulled him into the shower and pressed her body against his, fitting perfectly against his chest.

"Any other questions?" she purred, kneeling before him.

"Nope."

They could talk about the whole Guardian thing later. There was no rush. Absolutely no rush.

Chapter Twenty-Three

"I can't believe I have to go to work," Asher complained as he and Rosemary walked down the stairs of his building. "I feel like I should be getting paid leave. Like people do when they have a child."

Rosemary giggled. "Sorry everyone, I've met my soulmate and her body is *banging*. I need to be banging it for the next six to eight weeks depending on my doctor's recommendations." She slipped her arm through Asher's. "Wouldn't that be nice?"

"Better than nice." He sighed. "Are you sure you don't want me to drive you home?"

"Nope. I have work in an hour and a half. By the time we'd get there, you'd be late for work, and I'd have forty-five minutes before I had to head back. It's beautiful out. I can hang in town."

"It's just...Ivan. He's here, he knows what you look like. I'll put a call in at the motel for him to come in as soon as I get to my office, but what if..."

"What if he comes after me? I'll be in town. When he yelled at me before, he made a huge scene. The people and tourists of Solaris won't let him actually hurt me." She paused. "I'll make sure to grab a ride home with Lavender though."

"No, no, no. Come to the station and I'll drive you home. I'll be able to come up with an excuse to go patrol the Vega Peninsula for a little while."

"Hmmm. I bet you'll start thinking of lots of reasons to patrol the Vega Peninsula."

They stepped out into the bright sunlight, and for the first time, the community of Star Island was going to see them leaving his apartment at eight in the morning.

For the first block, they tried to walk like acquaintances, as if they happened upon each other by accident in the hallway of his building that morning.

And didn't spend the whole night tangled up in each other.

By the second block, Asher had his hand wrapped tightly around hers. By the third block, his arm was around her shoulders and hers around his waist. When they reached the police station steps, Asher kissed her so thoroughly, tourists stopped to stare. Rosemary definitely heard someone gasp.

"See you soon," he murmured, giving her butt a quick squeeze.

"See you soon, tease." She scrunched up her nose as she grinned.

Their relationship was out in the open now; no less than fifteen people saw their fiery embrace. There would be no denying their feelings for each other. Not to any of those witnesses.

Sheriff Asher Evans was dating Rosemary Bay, local florist and relationship meddler. She couldn't help but smile. She'd found her soulmate, he knew she was a witch, and they were dynamite in bed together. Rosemary had been wishing for this since age sixteen. She had dreamed of finding that person she had a deep connection with, spiritually and physically.

She wanted to bask in the glow of love. And now they could.

The painful memories of their past life were starting to fade. She still ached if she thought too long about the sweet faces of their boys, but she was beginning to accept the fact that their life as a family in Norway was hundreds of years ago. She told herself Hakon cared for them, and they were protected. She had no idea if that were true, but with Fáfnir dead, and his clan most likely up in arms from within, her family would have been safe on their small farm. She wished there were records she could pore through and find some nugget of information about their lives, but they didn't exist.

It was a perfect first of July. The tourists would hit the island hard in the next few days, so for now, Rosemary savored the relative quiet of the streets. Every business and house had red, white, and blue flowers outside, the grass was green, and the air was sweet. Rosemary was floating with happiness. She turned to walk toward The Immortal Cupcake. While Lavender wasn't overly interested in soulmate business, Rosemary had to tell someone about the amazing night she just had.

She walked along the edge of the park, quiet in the early morning, when something flashed in the corner of her eye.

"Móna! Móna!"

Rosemary froze. *Mommy! Mommy!* "Leifr? Knutr?" she called out. It was them. Her children. That's what they had called her.

No. It couldn't be them. They'd been dead for hundreds and hundreds of years. Her mind must be playing tricks on her. Maybe it was a side effect of the spell Daisy forgot to mention. She turned back towards The Immortal Cupcake. One of Lavender's pastries would get her back in the right frame of mind.

"Móna!" This time, the voice was so insistent, Rosemary knew she didn't imagine it. It was part of this world, not her imagination.

"Holy shit," she breathed and searched across the park. Where were they? How were they here?

"Leifr! Knutr!" She yelled now, cupping her hands around her mouth. The path to the coast was on the other side of the park. Were they hidden in the trees? She crossed the park quickly, continually calling their names. The path was quiet this early, but they had to be close. Their voices had been too clear to be too far. She started running as fast as she could, wildly searching for her boys.

Why were they alone in the woods? If they were alive now, where were their parents? Rosemary's mother hadn't been Gundrun's—she knew that families didn't always stay the same in each lifetime. Did her spell accidentally awaken their memories of the past? She'd never forgive herself if she put her babies through such a terrifying ordeal.

Or were they ghosts? Had the spell raised their spirits and drawn them to Star Island? If that were the case...Rosemary needed to put them to rest as soon as possible. How awful for her sweet boys.

She tore around the bend and nearly crashed into an older woman with two small children.

"Oh!" the woman exclaimed. "Are you all right?"

Rosemary blinked and looked at the kids. They were two girls with curly red hair in pigtails and wearing swimsuits.

"Yes. I'm...I'm sorry," Rosemary stuttered.

"Can we go to the beach now, Móna?" one of the girls said, pulling on the arm of the older woman.

"Yes, yes." She glanced back at Rosemary. "My granddaughters are impatient. Are you sure you're..."

"I'm fine. Sorry to interrupt your walk." Rosemary made a show of going in the other direction around the bend, then stopped the moment they were out of view. A wave of sadness swept over her.

It hadn't been Leifr and Knutr. Of course it hadn't been. The chances of their souls being alive at this exact time were...well, she didn't know how miniscule, but Asher was the only person from her past life who she knew this time. Her sisters hadn't been in the background, neither had her parents or Aunt June.

Rosemary rubbed her hands over her face and tried to slow her breathing. Her boys weren't here. She needed to come to terms with that. She and Asher...they might have children this time around—she really hoped they did. But there was no guarantee they'd be the same souls. Most likely they wouldn't be.

She would get over it. She had to. Lavender had said it might take a few days or weeks, but one of these days, Rosemary would be able to hear children's voices and not immediately panic that they were hers come back from the past.

She headed back to town determined to regain her good mood. Asher was here, and they were finally together. They were no more secrets between them. Life could begin. After waiting for nearly two decades for her soulmate—Asher, Ash, Sheriff Evans, whatever he wanted to go by—had arrived. Life was good, she thought, unable to hold back a grin.

Hands grabbed her shoulders and threw her to the ground in a heap, turning the world upside down. Rosemary flipped onto her back, immediately trying to slide away from whoever had knocked her down.

Fáfnir! Rosemary felt her body lock up. Leifr and Knutr, she had to get to them. She scrambled away, looking for her boys.

No, it was Ivan. *Ivan* stood over her, his mouth a thin slit and his eyes narrowed. The boys weren't here.

"What the hell?" She tried to get to her feet, but he knocked her over again. "Stop!" she yelled.

"Stay down," he commanded, then crouched beside her. "You're going to tell me where my sister is." He grabbed her wrist and held it next to his face, while his other forearm pinned her. Rosemary wriggled, but he held her tightly.

"Asher knows," she warned. "He knows who you are now. He knows you killed him in the woods and tried to steal me."

"Does he know his perfect little piece of ass poisoned me?" Ivan dug his nails into her arm, biting the flesh.

"He does. He didn't seem to mind much. We were living in a time before legal justice, so he understood why I was inclined to find my own." She tried to wrestle her arm away from him, but he held fast. He grabbed her shoulder and slammed her to the ground, then pinned her legs down. He was a skinny thing but stronger than he looked. Rosemary wasn't thin, but she also wasn't very strong. She had never done a bench press in her life and was really wishing she had at this moment.

"Tell me where the fuck my sister is or I will bleed you out right now, Bay witch."

Rosemary squirmed, trying to break free, but he was too heavy. Her legs were of no use, trapped beneath him, and he had her right hand and chest pinned. She still had use of the bottom half of her left arm though.

She made a tight fist and punched him in the crotch as hard as she could.

"Fuck!" he screamed and rolled off her.

Rosemary scrambled to her feet and sprinted into the woods. She dashed madly, ducking between trees and trying to put as much space between her and Ivan as possible. She knew a way home through the woods. It wasn't close by any means, but she needed to be on her own property where the protection spells were strongest. The florist was behind her, with Ivan between them.

She heard him swear, and a rustling in the undergrowth that let her know she was being followed.

"Shit," she breathed. She ducked behind a tree, taking a minute to gain her bearings and catch her breath. It was a five-mile run or walk home. She wasn't certain of Ivan's endurance, but Rosemary had never been one for running. She might be able to run a mile with the help of her adrenaline, but five was out of the question.

She pulled her phone out of her pocket and shot a text to Verbena, then put the ringer on silent.

> Rosemary: Meet me at the intersection of Stone and Cherry ASAP. In trouble.

She slipped her phone back into her pocket and took off running.

Now she only had to make it a mile and a half. She could do it. She focused on the ground in front of her. The last thing in the world Rosemary wanted was to trip and become easy pickings for Ivan. She wasn't sure if he would actually kill her, but she didn't want to risk it. He was, after all, the same soul as Fáfnir, and Skáldi and Ríg were hardly his only kills in Norway.

"There you are!" she heard him call. He was closer than she thought.

Rosemary racked her brain. She needed something to slow him down. As she ran, she looked at all the trees surrounding her. They were plants. They might not have been traditional garden plants, much wilder and less cultivated. They didn't know her like her own garden did. But nevertheless, they grew out of the island she had lived on for thirteen years. It was worth a shot.

"Oak, maple, pine, and spruce, protect me from the metal warlock who follows me. Grasses, slow him down. Shrubs, make yourself a nuisance," she spat out between sucking in oxygen.

Not much was happening. It wasn't like she expected the trees to pull their roots out of the ground and start moving, but she was hoping for maybe a stray branch to knock Ivan unconscious. That would have been helpful.

She could hear him gaining on her. She tried to pick up her pace, but she was already running as fast as she could manage.

"Idun!" she yelled, panicking. "Idun, I am your faithful servant." She could see Ivan in her peripheral vision. In moments, he would catch her. "Idun, please. I am earth and flowers and spring and herbs. I am made in your image, a woman of the damp ground and nurturing spirit. Please stop him," she panted. "Warlock of metal and hardness. Please."

The world shifted around them, and Rosemary stumbled for a moment before catching her feet.

The forest went silent, not a bird or cricket made a sound. Even the trees went still. Rosemary glanced over her shoulder and couldn't see Ivan. All that was behind her was a thick forest of evergreens without an ounce of sunlight peeking through their needles.

They were not there a breath before.

She slowed for a moment, doing a full spin to be certain Ivan wasn't still in the vicinity, but he was completely gone.

She reached her hand out to touch the brand-new forest, but then thought better of it.

"Thank you," she whispered, and ran on.

"What the hell is going on?" Verbena shouted. She was standing outside her still running-car holding her ritual knife.

"Get in the car," Rosemary sputtered, jumping into the passenger seat. She slammed the door, locked it, then searched the edge of the woods wildly.

Verbena climbed in and gunned it down the uneven road.

"Care to tell me now?"

"Ivan. He attacked me on the path...said he would bleed me out if I didn't tell him where Morana was." Rosemary slunk against the seat and closed her eyes. She rested her hand against her heart, trying to calm it.

"Holy shit!" Verbena's brow furrowed as she increased the speed of the car. "But also, Rosemary, what the hell were you doing walking down a wooded path when there is a powerful warlock on the island hell-bent on revenge against you? That was very stupid."

"I...I thought I heard my children calling to me. It turned out to be some girls calling to their grandma, but it sounded like them." Rosemary fanned herself, then fiddled with the air conditioning. Shit, that was close.

"Oh. Well, don't go chasing after voices again alone, especially with Ivan

Stoch hanging around and threatening you." Verbena kept her speed up and turned toward the Vega Peninsula.

"Where are we going?"

"Home."

"Don't you think Ivan will probably head there? Everyone on this island knows where we live. It's only a matter of time before he figures out our address."

"True, but nowhere on the island has stronger wards up. I've done my best magic there because I can do it out in the open. No hiding my tools and trying to discreetly work magic. If Ivan Stoch wants to attack us at home, he's welcome to try. After Morana, I closed a loophole I hadn't noticed and added a few other things. He might be a metal warlock, but I am a really strong house witch. No one messes with my home."

They pulled into the driveway and quickly ran to the house. As soon as the door slammed, Verbena locked it, chanted over the lock, and started to collect random supplies.

"I'm going to up the protection of the house; do the same," she said, bounding up the stairs.

Rosemary ran into the kitchen. She really wanted to get some fresh herbs, but she wasn't certain going into the yard was the best idea. She would make do with the haul she brought in a few days ago.

She rummaged through the pantry, pulling out the basil, marjoram, salt, rosemary, dill, fennel, and garlic. Next, she grabbed her largest stock pot and filled it with a mix of water, milk, and lime juice. It sounded like a disgusting concoction, but this wasn't for drinking. It was to ward off evil.

She brought the combination to a boil and tried her best to waft the scent throughout the house. The longer she could keep it over the flame, the better it would work, but at the moment, Rosemary didn't feel like time was on her side.

"Verbena, how's it going upstairs?" she called. Verbena didn't answer, but Rosemary was pretty certain she heard some books fall over. That couldn't have been on purpose.

She turned back to her potion, stirring it furiously. She needed to concentrate. Herbs could only do so much. She needed the words to back it up.

"When evil comes upon our door, protect our windows, walls, and floor," Rosemary began. Chants were never her strong suit. Rhyming ones were more powerful, but she always had a difficult time conjuring poetry. "Herbs from my garden, nurtured by my own hand, ward off any that might do ill, by the dirt, the wood, and the land?"

The entire house jolted, and Rosemary dropped her spoon on the floor. She crouched down to grab it and returned to stirring.

"Idun, Flora, Brigit, Lada, goddesses of spring and renewal, please protect this house of devoted believers." Her voice was shaking now. She snapped her fingers, watching the steam swirl around the pot, then flow to the windows. It clouded the glass in the kitchen, dining room, and parlor.

"Hopefully, that means it worked." Rosemary walked to the parlor, creeping along, afraid that her footsteps could be heard outside.

"You think these wards will keep me out?" Ivan yelled. "I've been breaking down wards since I was a child."

The house buckled, this time so violently, Rosemary stumbled and grabbed a chair to steady herself.

"Verbena!" she screamed this time. "Get down here!" She felt her pocket for her phone. She didn't have it. Did she leave it in the car? Or the kitchen? She staggered into the kitchen to check the counters.

"What is he doing out there?" Verbena called, slowly walking down the stairs with both hands on the railing.

"I don't know. I can't find my phone. I need to call Asher. And Lavender and Laurel. And shit! Sage is in the yard alone. What if he goes back there?"

"Remember what she said: if she's near her plants, she's fine." The house shook again, this time the bolts on the door shifted slightly out. "He's not going after her. He knows you're in here." Verbena looked scared. She was never scared. "Rosemary, what are we going to do?"

Rosemary took a deep breath and closed her eyes. She could do this. She called the plants before. Now she was on her own property. It should be easier, right?

All the pots in the cupboard beside the stove flew out and smashed against the opposite wall in the kitchen.

"Shit!" Rosemary yelled. Then it clicked. "He's controlling the metal in the house! That's what it is, the shaking. There must be metal in the foundation or in the floors or walls." She paused and looked around the room. "Can you control the metal integral to the house? Even for a few minutes?"

"Maybe? I can try."

"Start trying. I have an idea."

Chapter Twenty-Four

Asher walked into work less than thrilled to be there.

He wanted to be back at his apartment. With Rosemary. Maybe in the shower again.

That reminded him, he needed to grab a new shower curtain from the market on the way home tonight. He'd ripped the old one clean off the rod last night.

He still needed to broach the Guardian subject with her. She hadn't mentioned it in her list of supernatural beings. At least, he didn't think she had. His memory wasn't reliable when she was naked. He should probably call one of those numbers in the letter before he told her about it. In case his dad had fabricated the whole thing and it was all just one giant coincidence.

"Evans?" Claire knocked on his office door before walking in. "We've got a disturbance at the harbor. There's a bachelor party getting very vocal, and more than one person has called thinking they are about to get violent."

"Who's nearest?"

"We are. Charlie is dealing with a domestic on the Vega Point and Mark is talking to the kids at the summer camp today."

"Okay. I'll be at the car in a second."

Claire ducked out, and Asher grabbed his holster and slipped it on. He thought the chances of him actually needing his weapon were very low, but he didn't want to take any chances.

He prayed it wasn't crowded.

The minute Asher arrived at the harbor, he started to feel strange, even sick. At first, he thought he was nervous to be in a big crowd with several individuals in an agitated state. It wasn't a festival, and it wasn't as crowded as the wine event he'd worked last week, but these men were getting worse, not calmer. He kept his eye on Claire and radioed for Mark to swing by once he finished at camp.

He couldn't quite name what was happening; it was like a string was trying to pull his body away from the harbor. He shook it off as nerves and got to work calming the masses. Asher tried to focus. The faster he could disperse the men, the faster he would get out of there.

He sent half the guys to the diner for food, the other half to the beach to cool down, and with that, the bachelor party was broken up, and hopefully getting over the hangovers that were agitating everyone. The pit in his stomach didn't disappear, though, and he began to worry. The pull was strong, insistent, and it wanted him to travel inland. He couldn't help but wonder if he was being pulled to Rosemary.

"Claire, can you finish up here? There's something I want to check on. Mark will be here in a few minutes to help you wrap things up." There were a few statements left to take, but other than that, they were done here.

"Yeah, sure," she answered quickly, turning back to an annoyed mom with three small children.

Asher quickly climbed into his car and pulled out his phone.

Asher: You OK?

He spun the phone between his fingers waiting for a response. After five minutes passed and Rosemary didn't answer, his mind was made up. He needed to get to her.

Asher drove straight to the florist and parked right in front.

"Rosemary?" he called, pushing through the door.

"Not here," Therese answered. "And ten minutes late. In the summer when we've got a boatload of weddings." Therese huffed. "If you see her, tell her to get her butt to work."

"Sure," Asher half-answered, but he was already on his way out of the store. If she wasn't at work, where was she? Home? The store? The beach?

He decided to follow the pull in his gut. He got back in the car and let his body go on autopilot. He drove out of town, jumped on Pollux Avenue and started heading toward the Vega Peninsula. He picked up speed, realizing he was heading to her house, and put on his siren. He wasn't certain it was an emergency, but it felt like one.

He hated this feeling. It was like knowing the person you loved was in danger and you were helpless to do anything.

"Come on," he mumbled to himself. "Get there."

About a mile away from the Bay cottage, he felt the world shift. The ground was trembling beneath the wheels of his car, and he had to wrestle the steering wheel to keep the car from veering off the road.

He slammed on the gas, tearing down the road. He could see Rosemary's driveway just around the bend. He had to get to her.

The shaking got worse as he got closer, and driving became too difficult. Asher parked his car on the side of the road and started on foot. The road spliced in front of him.

This wasn't natural.

He checked his holster, patting his weapon once. For a moment, Asher felt the rise of panic in his throat, his chest getting tight with fear. He clenched his fists and blew out a hard breath. He needed to keep his head. Rosemary was in danger. He needed to get to her as quickly as possible.

Ivan Stoch was on the Bay's front walk. He paced what looked like an imaginary line, occasionally throwing his hands in the air, which was usually followed by a crash inside. Asher heard Rosemary shout a few times, but she didn't sound hurt. Ivan didn't get any closer to the house, but if the insane hand motions he was making, plus the murmuring in something distinctly not English were any indication, Asher guessed he was trying to break through the protection spells around the house.

Asher did a large loop around the house, sneaking through the more wooded areas and avoiding Ivan's gaze. Ivan was too focused on the Bay cottage to notice anything else around him. Asher walked through the trees until he finally reached Rosemary's herb garden. He stepped over the rows of fragrant plants, and rapped on the back door before pushing through.

"Rosemary?" he hissed. He didn't want Ivan to know he was there. He tried the knob, which at first seemed locked, but then yielded under his grasp. He stepped gingerly through the screen porch and into the kitchen.

Rosemary and Verbena were prone on the floor, their heads covered with their hands. Verbena's eyes were closed and she was chanting quietly, in Latin he thought but wasn't certain. He was about to ask why they were on the ground when a wrought-iron lamp flew across the dining room. He hit the floor and crawled over to Rosemary, covering her torso with his arms.

She jumped when he touched her but quickly threw her arms around him.

"How did you get in here?"

"Went around back. Ivan is pretty focused on your front door."

"The wards are the weakest there, so regular visitors can get through. We've got everything much more locked down at the windows and in the back. I'm glad you got through." She kissed his cheek quickly. "Why are you here?"

"I don't know...but I suddenly felt like I needed to find you. And then I texted you and you didn't answer, I started to panic." He would tell her about being a Guardian as soon as they had time. Right now, home décor was flying over their heads.

"My phone is in the car, I think. Ivan attacked me on the trail. I managed to...get away."

Asher felt his heart rise to his throat. Ivan attacked Rosemary? His Rosemary? He had been prepared to bury the hatchet of their past grievances, but this was unacceptable. Fáfnir was as dead as Skáldi, but if Ivan was going to physically hurt Rosemary, there would be consequences.

"I'm going to talk to him," he fumed, getting to his feet.

"I don't think you should," Rosemary began, holding onto his shirt. "Ivan is really strong. Verbena is using all her power right now to keep him from ripping the metal out of the house. She's letting the little things go to prevent, like, the furnace flying through the parlor."

"He might need a human to shake him out of this. I can't fight him with magic, but I can arrest him. He's been arrested before; he'll be arrested again."

"How on earth are you doing to arrest him for controlling the metal in my house?"

"I'll arrest him for assault. Did he control metal to hurt you on the trail?"

"No, he pushed me to the ground and pinned me," she answered.

"He did what?" Asher could feel rage building in his chest. He stood up and walked through the kitchen to the front door. He heard Rosemary jump up and follow him. She quickly caught up and slipped her hand into his.

"I'm coming with you," she said. "We'll do it together."

He nodded, then called out, "Ivan! It's Sheriff Evans. I'm coming out."

Asher slowly unlocked the bolt, then the chain lock, and lastly turned the knob. He stepped into view, keeping his right hand on Rosemary's hip and ensuring she stayed behind him.

The second they stepped out, the house went silent. No pots and pans or lamps clattered against the walls or the floor.

"Evans, get out of here. My score to settle is with Rosemary. And the rest of the Bay witches. Leave it."

"Mr. Stoch, I'll have to disagree. You are not only harassing Rosemary, but you've also tried to cause her bodily harm. And you've broken several things inside the house."

"What are you going to arrest me for, controlling metal? You'll be laughed out of your job. Get out of here, mortal. Let the magicals talk." Ivan flipped his palms towards them.

"No," Asher answered, his hand pressing against Rosemary. "I will not allow you to continually harass Ms. Bay. She has done nothing to you."

"Nothing? Would you agree with that, Gundrun? You've been a wicked little witch, haven't you?" Ivan used her past name, and with it, Asher felt his blood boil.

"If we are bringing up past grievances, Fáfnir, I believe you need to answer for my murder." Asher pushed Rosemary further into the house, then crossed the threshold. "Fáfnir murdered Skáldi to get his hands on Gundrun. I think she acted in accordance of the laws of the time. If I can get over you ripping me away from my family and the chance to raise my sons, I think you can get over a little poison." He raised an eyebrow. "Gundrun didn't want to be your wife, so she escaped and brought you with her."

"You son of a bitch." Ivan sneered.

There was a loud clang coming from the shed. Asher turned his head as the door flew open. A myriad of gardening tools came flying towards him and Rosemary, rakes, shovels, spades. He dove in front of Rosemary, wrapping his arms around her as she screamed, and waited for the eventual pain of impact.

Chapter Twenty-Five

R osemary felt the rush of the tools through Asher's body. They tumbled into the house, back over the threshold, with him on top of her. His body went immediately limp and heavy, pinning her against the floor.

"Ash!" she screamed. She braced her arms against his chest and wiggled out from beneath him. He was unconscious but still breathing. She ran her hand down his back to feel for wounds, but there were none, at least none that were open. She checked his head as well but couldn't feel anything bleeding or overly swollen.

"Verbena, get over here and stay with Asher!" she yelled, then got to her feet.

She barged over the threshold and past the wards. Ivan was still in the yard, shaking his hands out. He'd been expending a lot of magic the last thirty minutes. It could not have been easy on his body, Rosemary thought.

"Ivan Stoch!" she bellowed. She could feel her magic rushing through her body and radiating in her hands. "You monster!" she screamed.

Rosemary threw her arms into a V and fixed her eyes on all her lovely plants surrounding Ivan. Her yard was full of *her* plants, things she had raised from seeds to seedlings to full grown flowers and shrubs and grasses. Her ornamental trees lined the walk and had been cared for by no one but her since their planting. Her passion had been poured into every one of them. And they would listen to her.

Ivan's eyes flickered towards the haphazard pile of garden tools near her that had crashed into Ash.

"Bind him," she commanded through gritted teeth. She acted quickly, before he could mutter something else and send metal flying in her direction.

It was a small thing at first, just a gentle shifting in the greenery lining the path. The flowers there were wild things, unkempt looking and liberated from any sort of order. But they knew the voice of Rosemary. They knew her energy and the hours she spent nurturing them into their current lovely selves. They knew that when the island had a drought, it was her that brought them water, her that took care no one trod over them.

The vines made the first move, crawling over the stone until they snaked their way around Ivan's legs, tightening until his ankles were wrapped tightly.

"What the hell?" Ivan tried to lift his feet, but they were rooted firmly to the ground. He attempted to lift one of his arms, but a vine snapped up, encircled his wrist and brought it down.

"More!" Rosemary demanded. The whole front garden stirred awake. Geraniums and boxwoods grew to five times their size, forming a tight circle around Ivan. Creeping plants crawled up his legs, twining around his waist, pulling him into their grasps. Branches from the cherry blossom trees shot forward, creating a spider web around him, trapping him in place. Ivan pulled at his arms, his voice becoming nothing but frantic grunts.

Slowly, Ivan drowned beneath the lush greenery until he disappeared into a deep, dense garden.

"Whoa," Rosemary whispered. "Thank you." Her entire body felt heavy and spent.

"Rosemary!" Verbena called and snapped her back to her senses.

She dropped her arms to her sides, inhaling sharply. Had she been breathing? She wasn't certain. She'd definitely never done anything like that before. Her body started to sway and her head felt light. She needed to sit down, have some water maybe. She was so tired.

"Rosemary! Get in the house!"

Asher.

Asher needed her. She had to get back to his side. She couldn't fall over. She turned slowly, not wanting to move too quickly and jar her head into oblivion.

He was still on the floor, eyes closed. Verbena had her hand on his chest, checking the rise and fall and making certain it didn't stop.

"Ash," she said and sank beside him. "Ash, wake up. We're okay. Ivan didn't hurt me. You saved me." She ran her hands over his cheeks, down his neck, and to his heart. "Ash, look at me."

She turned to Verbena. "Call Lavender, Sage, and Laurel."

"Do you want me to call an ambulance?"

"Not yet. Give me two more minutes and then we'll call." Rosemary turned back to Ash, and Verbena ran to find her phone.

"Ash Evans, my soulmate, love of my lives, you wake up and come back to me right this instant. Because we are destined to be together, and in this life, we will have our happily ever after and it will not be cut short. I deem it so, as one blessed by Idun and as someone who just managed some extremely impressive garden magic. So open your eyes and look at your woman. I want you, I need you, and I love you." She leaned forward and kissed his forehead, cheeks, and finally lips.

"Those were very pretty words," Asher answered sleepily. His raised his arm just high enough to rest it on her thighs. "Where is Ivan?"

"Bound with greenery in the front yard. We're going to need to move him momentarily."

"That does sound impressive." He opened his eyes and reached to the back of his head. "How am I not dead?"

"I have no idea. Those garden sheers should have killed you. You aren't even bleeding."

Asher rubbed his hands over his face a few times. "I guess it's true," he mumbled.

"What's true?" Rosemary snuck beside him and snuggled her head against his chest. She needed to move him to her bed and deal with Ivan. But for a minute, she was going to hug her soulmate.

"Do you know what a Guardian is?" Asher turned towards her.

"Yes...do *you* know what a Guardian is?" Rosemary had read a few books that talked about Guardians, but she'd never met one.

"I got a letter from my biological dad. He said he was a Guardian and I am too."

"What?" Rosemary gasped. Asher was a Guardian? Was he her Guardian?

Oh no, she thought. That was why the past life spell brought him. He wasn't technically human.

"I," Asher began.

"Hey," Verbena interrupted. "Laurel and Owen are on their way. Lavender can leave the bakery in about ten minutes, and Sage is cleaning up. We have to move Ivan. And do something about the street."

Gazer Lane was destroyed.

In his attempt to destroy the Bay cottage, Ivan had also pulled up a lot of stray metal and created a ton of holes in the road.

"Well, hell. It was a good run keeping our witchcraft a secret, but I think this might be it. Time to come out of the broom closet," Sage said, surveying the damage. "How are we going to explain this?"

"I can block off the road with my cruiser at one end," Asher offered. "And I have a spare police barricade in the trunk that we can set up at the other end."

"I'm slightly more concerned about the warlock who is basically a shrub in the front yard. Is he going to die?" Lavender asked.

"We should move him," Rosemary admitted. She'd never done that before, and it probably wasn't healthy for him to be under all those plants for too long.

"Where? He can control metal. We can't put him in jail," Verbena pointed out.

The group stood in silence for a moment, everyone racking their brains for some solution.

Rosemary looked at Asher. He was a Guardian? She had just gotten used to the fact that he was a human. Now he wasn't anymore?

Guardians had dangerous lives. During the witch hunts of the seventeenth century, hundreds of Guardians died alongside witches. Plus, a lot of modern witches didn't like Guardians. She didn't want any magicals coming after him.

"I know what to do with Ivan, at least temporarily," Sage said. "But it's going to involve some heavy lifting."

Ivan was not easy to move; it took all five Bay witches, Owen, and Ash, but they got him into the center of Sage's apple orchard. He was still pretty groggy, but by the time he landed in the center of Sage's apple orchard, he was awake.

"What the fuck?" he asked, raising his hand up.

"Not so fast," Sage warned. A branch of one of her trees pulled back, snapped, and slapped Ivan across the face.

"Argh!" Ivan wailed.

"Keep in mind I can do that non-stop for the next six hours."

Ivan looked at the group of them, then plopped onto the ground with his arms crossed.

"We can't keep him here forever," Rosemary said. "And unlike Morana, we can't stash him in the Hedge World until we decide what to do about him."

"Uh, can I talk to you?" Asher murmured to Rosemary.

"Yeah," she turned back to her sisters, "give us a second." They walked away from the orchard and towards the house.

"I have a couple phone numbers. Is this something Guardians deal with?" Asher asked quietly.

"Oh. I don't know. Guardians are sort of their own thing."

"Maybe I should call?"

"Yeah, couldn't hurt." Rosemary crossed her arms and snuck her bottom lip between her teeth. She felt a wave of reality hit her. She suddenly felt like she didn't know Asher at all. "Here, you can use my bedroom."

Rosemary walked Asher into the house and to her room, then went back to her sisters to watch over Ivan. He was her problem, after all. She should be the one to take care of it.

Chapter Twenty-Six

Asher followed Rosemary through the house to the upstairs and into her bedroom. Their staircase creaked under every footstep, but instead of feeling like the house was about to fall apart, Asher had the distinct impression that it was built to last eons.

"That one is my bed," she pointed, "if you want to sit down."

Asher looked around the room, giving himself a second to take in the décor.

The room had two distinct sides, and it was clear who lived on either side. Rosemary's side had pictures of flowers everywhere, taped on the wall, some in fancy frames, and a few attached with pushpins. A blush bedspread with a quilt at the bottom and a mountain of pillows at the head piled on top of her twin-sized bed.

Sage had one calendar hanging next to her bed, a dark green blanket on her bed, and a solitary pillow. There was also an eye mask hanging from the bedpost on that side that said, "LEAVE ME ALONE."

Asher tentatively sat on the bed. It looked antique, and he was partially afraid it would explode into splinters under his weight.

"You should call. I'll go out," Rosemary said quickly.

"You don't have—" Asher started.

"I'm going to. You need to ask Guardian questions, no matter what they are, without worrying what I might think. Take as long as you need."

Rosemary left the room and closed the door behind her.

"Damn it," Asher breathed. He knew he'd fucked up. He should have told her about the Guardian thing. She was the one with experience in the magical world; he had no idea what he was about to be thrown headfirst into. And now Ivan was prisoner in the back yard and he was going to call some, what, magical clean-up crew?

His life was an absolute mess. He wanted to go back to his apartment with Rosemary and pretend all this other stuff had never happened.

But that wasn't possible.

Asher leaned back on Rosemary's mountain of pillows and pulled his phone out. He scrolled through his texts until he got to Natalie's, then opened the letter from his biological dad again and found the number.

Asher's anxiety rose as it rang. Should he have just texted? No, this was probably a landline, he remembered. He was lucky it was still connected.

"Hello?" a gruff voice answered.

"Hi, uh, this is Asher, Ash. I just got a letter from my dead dad telling me to call here with questions." Asher didn't think there was a point in mincing words. He was about to ask this random man a lot of very strange things. Might as well be direct.

"Ash Robinson? Matt's kid?"

Asher felt like ice hit his heart. He had never been Ash Robinson before. He'd been Asher Evans as long as he could remember.

"Yeah, Matt Robinson was my biological father. I'm Asher Evans, though. He didn't raise me."

"Oh. Of course." Asher heard the man let out a huge sigh. "I'm Ted. I guess you're calling about the whole Guardian thing?"

"Yeah. I just managed to protect my girlfriend from a warlock without a scratch. And there's been some other stuff." He paused. There was one question in the forefront of his mind that wouldn't stop bugging him. "Did you know my mom?"

"Met her a couple times."

"Was she a witch?"

"Bev? Nah, she was an animan. It's like, uh…"

"It's okay, my girlfriend can explain. How did she die?" Asher spat out. "Matt didn't tell my parents when he gave me to them."

"She had an aneurysm. Nothing magical about it, just shitty luck."

Asher didn't let his brain focus on that. He could ruminate over the manner in which his birth mother died later. "I don't want to take up too much of your time. Give me the rundown on being a Guardian. There's a safe house? Why?"

"We tend to make a lot of dangerous enemies in this predetermined line of work. We protect good magical people from bad magical people. Usually you have a specific charge, I'm guessing yours in your girlfriend. In a pinch, you can protect most magical people, but it doesn't work on everyone. Don't throw yourself in front of someone you don't know. Chances are, you'll die."

Asher had already learned that lesson the hard way.

"What do I do if I capture an evil warlock?"

A beat passed. "Define evil."

"Tried to murder my girlfriend and her sister, killed me in another life." He left out the part about the Stochs coming after the Bay witches' blood, because he wasn't really sure who this guy was and whether or not he could trust him.

"Geez. Whelp, I can arrange a pick up. Do you have him tied up in your basement or something? These things can get messy fast."

"No, I'm a police officer also. I could legally hold him for assaulting an officer, but he's a metal warlock."

"So that wouldn't work. Hell, I hate those guys. Always assholes. How are you holding him right now?"

"My girlfriend and her sisters are taking care of it."

Ted let out a loud sigh. "All right, here's what we'll do. Where are you?"

"Star Island? Off the coast of Massachusetts."

"Oh, not too bad. I know four Guardians based in Boston. I'll give them a call, let them know you need a pick up. This a good number to call back?"

"Yeah, it's my cell."

"Okay, once I get them sorted, I'll tell them to contact you with a pick up time and you can name the place. Metal warlock might be tricky in a car...maybe we could sedate him..." he mumbled on.

"What do you do to them?" Asher asked. He didn't care much, as a private citizen, what would happen to Ivan. This man had tried to hurt Rosemary. But, as a police officer, he couldn't hand someone over to be tortured or killed.

"We've got a sort of prison for magical folks. It's got wards up to neutralize their powers. We hold them until a council picks them up."

"Wait, a council?" Asher furrowed his brow. He was nearly certain Rosemary said there was no witches' council in the US.

"Yeah, bunch of witches and warlocks. We let them take care of it."

"Are they Americans? The council?" Asher pressed.

"No, actually. They're an Irish group. I know a couple of Guardians over there and they put us in contact."

"Okay. That sounds like a good plan."

"Any other questions?" Ted asked. "I should get going to arrange the pick up for you."

"Did you know my biological dad well?"

"A while ago. Obviously." He paused. "He was a mess after your mom died, made a lot of bad choices. He was a good man, though. Just wanted to protect people. Didn't take care of himself in the process. Made a lot of bad enemies."

"Did someone kill him?"

"Kill him? No. There was a kid about to get hit by a bus and he pushed him out of the way. Got killed in the process." Ted paused. "Don't blame him. After your mom died, he never could have stood by and watch someone die. He was a protector through and through."

Asher felt that declaration like a shot to his heart. He had always wondered where he got his sense of duty from. His adoptive parents were an accountant and a sales rep, but Asher always wanted to help people, protect them. It seemed his nature overtook his nurturing on that front.

He and Ted ended their phone call, but Asher didn't go downstairs right away. He lay back on Rosemary's bed and just breathed. The bed smelled like her, felt like her, and could only be improved by her actual presence. God, he wanted to hide away with her for a year.

He stayed there for a few minutes, processing everything that had happened in the last two weeks.

He met the love of his life. She was a witch. They had kids in ancient Norway. He'd been murdered. He was a Guardian.

It was a lot to take in. Asher felt like he hadn't just started a new chapter in his life. It was a whole new book.

Chapter Twenty-Seven

Rosemary leaned against the tree and stared at Ivan. Sage was nearby, ready to knock him out cold with a branch if he tried anything, but the rest of the Bays and Owen were having an animated discussion closer to the house.

"You were hotter as Gundrun," Ivan muttered.

"Excuse me?" Rosemary answered.

Ivan raised his eyes to meet hers. "You were hotter as Gundrun. You hear me that time? If you looked like this, I wouldn't have killed Skáldi over you. Maybe your father for lying to me."

"Yet you still attempted to kill Asher and me." She wondered if it was morally sound to tell Sage to beat the shit out of him with branches because he was bothering her.

Probably not.

"That was revenge. You did something to my sister and I want your blood."

"Somehow I think your concern over Morana is the least of your reasons."

"You don't know me," Ivan spat.

"That is true! I do not know you. So let me ask, what the hell is wrong with you? You're mad at me for poisoning you to stop you from literally raping me. Get over it. It was hundreds of years ago—you destroyed my life, killed my husband, tore me away from my family, and you're the one who is supposed to get revenge? Why? Because I sped up your death by like five minutes? I was living a quiet life with my family! I didn't care what you did in the world. I wasn't after you or your lands. I would have been happy never to see you again. Do you feel validated in this deep need for vengeance? Get over yourself, you narcissistic monster. You should be ashamed of yourself. Good goddess, Ivan. You're a warlock. Stop acting like a child."

"Are you okay?"

Rosemary jumped at the sound of Asher's voice directly behind her. "What? Yes. I'm fine. Chatting with our attempted murderer." She turned to Sage. "Can you keep an eye on him?"

"Yes. Can I torture him?"

Ivan's eyes went wide.

"If he needs it, by all means." Rosemary turned to Asher. "Any luck?"

"Yeah, let's go talk somewhere alone." He eyed the property.

"We can go in front." Rosemary started to reach for his hand, then stopped. It still felt like there was a disconnect between them.

She led him around the side of the house, past the lilac bushes and the salvia, over the stepping stones she made when they first moved in.

"I arranged a pick up," Asher began as they rounded the corner of the house. "They can be here in about four hours, and they'll take it from there."

"You arranged a pick up?" Rosemary repeated. What did that even mean? Ivan was a metal warlock; he couldn't be taken anywhere in a car or boat. He could destroy it.

"I guess Guardians deal with this all the time," he continued.

"Thanks for handling it." Rosemary forced a smile. "Are you going to go with?"

"With?"

"With the Guardians. When they take Ivan."

Asher's brow furrowed. "Why would I go with them?"

"I don't know, you are a Guardian. It's part of who you are, and it seems like they have lives and callings that you need to get involved with."

"Rosemary." Asher paused. "I'm not going with them. I don't...I don't want to be a Guardian. Hell, I don't want to be a cop. My life is basically a shit show right now. I have no idea who I am anymore. My biological mom was a fucking animan, my biological dad was a Guardian, I'm afraid to be in crowds, I hate going into work, and I've moved away from my entire family. My living family." He ran his hand over his head and blew out a breath. "I'm not leaving you. You are the only thing that makes sense to me right now. A man tried to murder me with garden sheers, and I didn't die. I do not understand any of it, but it's worth it if I get to be with you. I love you."

Rosemary stood in silence, feeling her shields slowly dissipate.

"You love me? Rosemary? Not Gundrun, but actually me."

"Of course. Skáldi loved Gundrun. I love you."

"We don't really know each other," she continued.

"I don't care. I love you. I love the way you talk like you don't care at all if you make someone uncomfortable. I love that you are so fucking friendly to everyone you meet. I love watching you by plants, because you seriously glow. I love the taste of your skin and the sound of your voice and the smell of your hair. I'm not leaving you, Rosemary. I'm sticking with you forever."

"I love you, too." Rosemary slid her hands around his waist and pressed her face against Asher's chest. "I love you so much my heart hurts and I wish the whole world would melt away and it could be only us, at least for a little while."

"Me too," Asher answered. "I'm going to quit my job."

"Okay." She deeply inhaled his scent.

"I'm sorry. I have savings, but I have to figure out what I'm going to do that isn't being a cop."

"Ash." Rosemary tipped her face to his. "I want you to be happy. You'll figure it out. I can help."

Asher pressed a kiss against Rosemary's mouth but pulled away before she could deepen it. "What are we going to do about the street? Even though I'm still employed as the sheriff, I don't think I can explain this away."

"Well, that depends," Rosemary began. She trailed her fingers down his chest and wrapped them around his belt buckle.

"On?" He raised his eyebrow.

"I know a spell…"

Chapter Twenty-Eight

"What are the stakes for?" Asher asked.

Rosemary had insisted she could fix the street if he was cool with a sex spell, and had then run into the house and come out with an arm full of...props.

"The stakes are for, well basically, torches." She handed him an intoxicating basket full of herbs. "Start making a circle with these that's big enough for us to both fit in and stay in throughout the entire spell." Rosemary pulled a rubber hammer out from her back pocket and started pounding the stakes into the grass.

"How athletic are you planning?" Asher asked.

Rosemary burst into giggles. "This isn't a 'let's see how crazy we can fuck' spell. It's about our connection. Make a circle big enough for you to fit in lying down. That should do it."

Asher got on his knees and made a big circle of herbs in the middle of Gazer Lane.

Was he really about to get naked and sleep with Rosemary in the middle of the road?

He glanced over at his woman, who was currently dousing the stakes with oil, and smiled.

He was. And he doubted it was the last time they'd be enjoying each other in a less than private situation.

"All set?"

"I guess." Asher stood in the middle of the circle. It was now or never. Rosemary had told her family to stay in the back, and his cruiser plus the police barricade were blocking the street off. He figured there was about a thirty percent chance someone caught them, but he was resigning tomorrow. If they wanted to fire him for public indecency, well, it would be a good story.

"Okay, here we go!" Rosemary grinned and stepped into the circle with him. She raised to her tiptoes and kissed him hard. "Don't be nervous. It's going to feel like it always does."

"Earth-shattering?"

"Yup." Rosemary licked her lips and closed her eyes. She rested her hands on his forearms and took a deep breath.

"Idun, bestow your blessing on us, my dear patron." Rosemary raised Asher's hands to her face, kissed both his palms, then put his hands on her breasts. "Keepers of the earth, sea, and sky, we come before you, lay down our inhibitions and fears, and ask you to repair the earth before us. Heal the wounds of the earth caused by another, mend our path. We dedicate our dance to you."

Asher was spellbound.

Rosemary's eyes fluttered open. "I love you."

"I love you."

Rosemary unbuttoned his shirt and slipped it off his shoulders, tossing it out of the circle, then ran her hands from his shoulders, past his scar, down his chest and abdomen, curling her fingers under his waistband.

"Take off your pants," she commanded, shrugging out of her own shirt and stepping out of her shorts.

Asher obeyed.

They stood apart for a moment, both stripped bare to their souls. It was as if they had stepped out of time, out of this world and into another. The air between them sparked with magic. Asher wasn't sure what would happen when he reached out for her. He half-expected the heavens to part or the earth to open from the power of it. The entire world felt electric and alive.

Rosemary lay down before him, her legs spread wide, her eyes dreamy, her lips moist.

"Take me. I am yours."

He got to his knees before her, as if in worship. She was a woman of spring and the rich earth, and he would love her through this life and the next and the next...

"Ash." Her voice was like a melody against his ear.

When he slid inside her, it didn't feel the same. Yes, sleeping with Rosemary was always magical and wonderful and mind-blowing. But this time, the air shifted, the soil beneath them pulsed. He could hear the ocean, and the sun warmed his back. It was like he awakened to the world around him.

"Ash," Rosemary moaned again. "Come with me."

He rushed back to his body, his eyes locking with hers. Beautiful Rosemary. God, he didn't think he could ever explain what it meant to love her.

He dragged his hand up her body to cup her face as he felt her come apart beneath him. And he let go.

"Holy shit," Asher breathed once he could again. He rolled onto his back and grabbed a shirt to throw over his crotch in case a neighbor happened by. "Is that...is that what sex spells are always like?"

Rosemary snuggled against his chest. "Of course not. I've never done a sex spell with my soulmate before. But maybe from now on? We'll have to conduct research. Lots of journal entries and what not."

"God, I love you."

"Goddess, I love you." She pressed a kiss against his neck. Rosemary craned her head to the side. "And it looks like it worked."

Beside them was a completely normal road, no jagged cracks, no holes, nothing that said Ivan Stoch had been there.

"Now let's get dressed. I don't think anyone checked to see if Luke was home, and he has a clear view of us from his front porch."

After they got into their clothes and stole a few kisses, Asher and

Rosemary walked back to apple orchard. Ivan couldn't do anything to hurt them anymore. They were together, so they were invincible.

Exactly on time, a van with darkened windows pulled into the Bay's driveway. A group of four Guardians exited, quickly marched to Ivan, and immediately sedated him with something that looked like baby powder.

"How did you get that van?" Sage asked, her arms crossed.

"We brought it. On our boat, which is docked at the Sirius Point." One of the women stopped to talk while the other three got Ivan in the van. "I'm Sue."

"What are you doing to do to him?" Rosemary asked.

"We have measures in place. He'll do some time in our prison for attacking you, messing with human life, all that stuff. Then we'll turn him over to the Irish team."

"Is it the Irish Witches' Council? I thought they were in league with the Brits when it came to magical councils," Verbena asked.

"They've got a separate group over there. They call it the Fianna. It's a mix of witches, warlocks, and Guardians. I think a few animans might be on it. They take care of our big problems."

"Can you wait? We might have someone else for you." Rosemary looked back at Laurel.

"A few minutes. We need to get him on the mainland. That sedative doesn't last forever." Sue paused. "And who is this other person?"

"Morana Stoch. His sister. She tried to murder Laurel," Rosemary pointed at her sister, "a couple weeks ago."

"Nice family," Sue remarked.

The sisters all crowded in a circle, with Asher and Owen on the outskirts.

"I think we should give them Morana. We can't keep her in the Hedge World forever. They at least have a plan in place," Rosemary said.

"Can we trust them? I mean, I have no love for Morana, but how do we know they won't torture or kill her?" Laurel asked.

"I guess we don't. But what are we going to do with her? There's no

American council, we don't know any witches on any of the other councils, we really don't have a path here."

Asher glanced at Owen. He stood directly behind Laurel, his fingertips resting on her upper arm. He looked back to Rosemary. She looked so in control, so sure in her decision.

"If something happens to her, you can blame me," Asher said. "It was my call, I can take responsibility if we need to get her back. Or even him." He felt like he had to include Ivan, even if at the moment he didn't particularly care if they tortured or killed him.

Rosemary turned around to face him. "Are you sure?"

"Yeah. Apparently, it's my calling." He tucked his arm around her and drew her in for an embrace.

"Okay, give me a minute." Laurel settled onto the ground, as if she were going to fall asleep right there. "Find the light, and draw a circle around it," she whispered.

In a flicker, Laurel became Laurel and Morana, both prone on the ground, Laurel's hand wrapped around Morana's arm.

"Holy fuck," Asher breathed.

"She's here!" Rosemary shouted to Sue, who sprang into action and sedated Morana. Two of the other Guardians hopped out of the van and collected her.

"We'll be going then," Sue began. She handed Asher a card. "Call if you need us again."

"Thanks." Asher turned the card over in his hand a few times, then stuck it in his back pocket.

The van disappeared into the darkness of the night as if it had never been there.

Lavender turned to the family. "You know, their older brother is probably going to be very upset that we've turned his siblings over to magical authorities."

"Definitely," Rosemary agreed.

"And he's a chaos warlock, whatever the hell that means," Sage added.

"I guess we're as prepared as we can be," Lavender continued. "I'm going inside. Bedrooms are free for whoever wants them tonight. Don't be loud."

"Are you okay?" Rosemary asked Asher. He shrugged. What felt like thirty-two days later had actually only been six hours. They'd headed back to his apartment so they could be alone, but so far, he'd only been able to sit on the couch and stare at the wall.

"I'm fine. It's been a lot, but..." He paused and looked at her. "But I have you, and that's really all I need."

Rosemary tucked her hands into his and pulled him towards his bedroom.

"Want to have a quickie and then go to sleep? I'm sure the dose of magic you've gotten today is way more than the recommended amount for day one." She covered a yawn.

"If by quickie you mean at least thirty minutes of foreplay, yes."

"Perfect." Rosemary lifted her arms up to hug him, but Asher grabbed her around the waist and tossed her onto the bed.

"Let's get you out of those clothes," he said, smiling. "But let's do it nice and slow. I don't think I've quite explored every inch of you, and that needs to be remedied immediately."

Asher woke up with Rosemary curled against him. Her breath was soft against his shoulder, her hair a crazy pile on the pillow.

God, he was so happy.

He kissed her forehead quickly, then rolled to his side, grabbing his phone. He opened a text conversation to Natalie and his mom.

> Asher: Good morning. I'll call you both separately later today, but I can't hold it in anymore. I've met the woman I'm going to spend the rest of my life with here. Her name is Rosemary and I can't wait to introduce her to you both. Also, I'm resigning today. No more being a cop for me. Got to go, Rosemary is asleep next to me, so I'm not answering any calls. But I love you both. Talk to you soon.

Asher clicked his phone onto silent, set it on the bedside table, and wrapped his arms around Rosemary.

It was a great morning to begin the rest of his life.

Epilogue

A FEW MONTHS LATER

"Is this it?" Asher peered out the side window of his car at the long gravel driveway winding through trees.

"There's the mailbox," Rosemary said. "Yes! Forty-five Moonbeam Way. We're here!"

"I don't know how I feel about living on a street called Moonbeam. Won't it give away that you're a witch and I'm a Guardian?" he teased.

"If we want to avoid a celestial-themed address, we'd have to move off Star Island," she said, giggling. "The elementary school is on Taurus Avenue, for goddess's sake. There's no avoiding it."

He pulled the car down the long drive, following the weaving path through wild forest.

"Well, I like this," he mused. The forest was vibrant green, with birds chirping and small mammals scurrying about. They were close to the tip of the Sagittauri Point of the island, a good place for both of them. Tourists never visited up here because the coastline was rough cliffs giving way occasionally to rock beaches, but never to sand. The waves were wilder here too and were not meant for swimming. There were other houses close by, mostly families who lived on the island year-round, but it was a ten-minute drive to Arpina, the smaller of the two towns on the island. Asher liked the idea of living away from the bustle of Solaris and in a more secluded area.

It might have been a weird time to buy a house, especially with him starting an online masters' degree in Early American History, but he had a good nest egg, and Rosemary had talked Therese into a huge raise once she proved she was irreplaceable. They wanted to find their home together, and it felt right.

The woods opened to a bright expanse framing a white farmhouse with big windows and a large front porch that wrapped around the east side of the house. There was a simple path leading to the front door, but the land was pretty much a blank canvas of grass. Asher parked the car in front of the detached garage and stepped out of the car.

"I love it," Rosemary said, climbing out of the car.

"I heard that!" Verbena called from the porch. "So besides this amazing porch and the two-car garage, plus the thick woods behind you, there are four bedrooms, new appliances, huge space for a garden, and a view of the ocean from the back."

"A view of the ocean?" Asher turned to Rosemary. "Your sister really is the best realtor on the island."

"Probably in the state, but I love our little island," Verbena interrupted. "Take your time out here, I'll be in the living room waiting to show you around." She stepped into the house, leaving Rosemary and Asher alone in the front yard.

"I can't believe we are buying a house," Rosemary said, wandering up the stairs to the porch. "Oh, you really can see the ocean from here!"

Asher walked up behind her, catching a view of the sea over the top of her head. He slipped his arms around her waist and pulled her back to rest against his chest.

"I can. And I can't wait. No more tiny apartment, no more bouncing between my place and yours. No more trying to find you a pair of panties before work."

"The amount of times I've had to go commando in a dress, oof."

"Now," Asher kissed the top of her head, "we can start the rest of our lives."

"Maybe here?" Rosemary leaned back. "The land is absolutely perfect for a garden, and I can line this entire porch with pots of herbs and flowers. And we should put a pair of chairs here, and hammock at the end. Oh! Think of all the new plants I can try now that I don't have to share space with my sisters. And that area, where the grass is blowing, is perfect for a cottage garden, and over there we can put in an apple blossom tree. And Sage could put a few fruit trees in for us." Her voice bubbled with excitement. "Is this the house? Should we live here?"

"Let's at least look inside first." Asher pressed a quick kiss against her mouth.

"Good point. I need to make sure the tub is big enough for us to have sex in. Or that there's room for us to put one in. I've been dying to have water sex with you."

Asher chuckled. "I'm still not ready for ocean sex."

"Which is why we need a big tub!" she exclaimed. Rosemary wrapped her hand through his. "Come on! Let's find out if this is the place!"

She pulled him back around the front of the house with the sweet determination he loved.

Honestly, it didn't matter if this was the perfect house, or if it was just fine. Wherever Asher lived, he'd be with Rosemary, and with her, he was home.

Thank you for reading! Did you enjoy? Please add your review because nothing helps an author more and encourages readers to take a chance on a book than a review.

And don't miss the next book of the *The Witches of Star Island,* HAUNTINGS AND HOUSE WITCHERY, available now. Turn the page for a sneak peek!

You can also sign up for the City Owl Press newsletter to receive notice of all book releases!

Sneak Peek of Hauntings and House Witchery

NINE YEARS EARLIER...

In a cottage home to five witches, there were a few rules that even the old gods respected: a sprig of mugwort tied around a doorknob meant caution to any who crossed that threshold, a harvest moon was good for more than farming, and a younger sister should never, ever compare her fashion sense to her older sister's.

"Is that what you're wearing?" Verbena leaned away from the vanity mirror in her bedroom and caught a vision of Rosemary walking through the hallway.

"Of course, why?" Rosemary answered, hands on her hips.

Verbena glanced down at her outfit. She had on jean shorts, a white tank top that said "HOMEBODY" in black cursive lettering, and purple flip-flops. Her hair was how she always wore it: down, curly in the back, wavy in the front. Getting her hair to do anything else took ages, especially in the summer. She had been a little bold and put on mascara and some pale pink lipstick, but she definitely looked casual.

Rosemary, on the other hand, was wearing...lingerie? It was black and lacy and left little to the imagination in terms of the exact number of freckles she had on her entire body. Her hair was done up like Bridgette Bardot, and she was wearing sandals with straps that wound up to her knees like some sort of Greek goddess.

"You look gorgeous, Verbena. Remember though: I'm twenty-three and you're seventeen. We are going to this little shindig with very different plans in mind. With all hope, I won't be coming home until the sun is on the eastern horizon." Rosemary flitted down the stairs, leaving Verbena with her reflection.

"Try not to pay attention to Rosemary," Laurel interjected.

Verbena cast a glance at another older sister. Laurel was wearing a black, Victorian-style, high-necked dress that fell just above her ankles and Doc Martens. Her hair was freshly dyed black, her face powdered white with intense black eye makeup and dark purple lipstick. She looked like widow from 1890. Who had murdered her husband.

If Verbena had learned anything from being the fourth of five sisters, it was that they all had very different opinions on fashion. And magic. And, honestly, life in general.

Verbena finished up and walked downstairs. She was excited. It was the first year Star Island was doing a Summerfest, and she was ready to have some company other than her sisters. It wasn't that Verbena didn't have friends, only that most of their parents didn't feel comfortable allowing their kids to come hang out at the Bay cottage with a twenty-four-year-old as the guardian. Lavender was beyond the straight and narrow, but she was still in her early twenties. Parents saw her and assumed that the Bay cottage had an unlocked, fully stocked liquor cabinet and bowls of condoms decorating the parlor. In their defense, if Rosemary was her guardian, the vibe wouldn't have been far off. But Lavender took her role as caregiver extremely seriously. Verbena had a curfew of ten-thirty on the weekends, and boys were not allowed in the house once the sun went down, and that included full adult Rosemary. But tonight, Verbena was finally getting a chance to hang out with her friends, and not just until the diner closed and sent them all home.

"Let me stay home." Sage sat at the dining table, her face stuck in a grimace.

"No. I don't feel comfortable with you being home alone at night."

"Lavender, I'm not a baby. I'm fucking fifteen!" Sage seethed.

"Watch your mouth," Lavender replied evenly. "Yes, you are fifteen. You also live in a slightly haunted three-hundred-year-old cottage in the middle of nowhere on an island in the middle of the ocean. There could be an electrical fire. Or an intruder. Or a malicious ghost. You can sulk in the corner, but you have to come."

"I hate this." Sage pushed back from the table and stomped toward the door. She flopped onto the ground to pull on her sneakers.

"You'll grow out of it. Hey, at least we know the food will be good." Lavender had supplied all the desserts for the party, and Mr. and Mrs. Convito, who ran the Italian place in town, were providing dinner. The food would be delicious, but Verbena was much more excited for the company.

She shook her hands nervously as she walked outside. There was something...crackling in the air tonight. She didn't know if it was nerves or something else, but she pushed it away, determined nothing would ruin her good time at Summerfest.

"And then, and then!" Danielle panted, grabbing Verbena's forearm. "Sara told Tom that she didn't want to be exclusive anymore—can you believe it? Who on earth is Sara going to hook up with other than Tom? Paul's with Mari, Caden has that girlfriend from Boston, Jim would never date her, and Robbie is totally in love with Mari. We aren't swimming in available romantic partners here." Danielle rolled her eyes.

Verbena laughed. When your class only had twenty-two kids in it, and fifteen of them were girls, there weren't tons of dating options in high school. Sometimes Verbena wished they had stayed in Ohio after their parents died. She could have gone to a normal high school with more than one hundred kids in her class and stuff like clubs and organized sports that didn't involve a ferry ride. But she had to admit Star Island was pretty great. All the drawbacks were countered with beautiful views, a big piece of land, a gorgeous home, and lots of space for witchcraft without the prying eyes of neighbors. In Ohio their witchy room had been their musty basement, which didn't hold a candle to a sprawling attic. Plus, the neighbors had basically been on top of them. Here they had a bonfire every summer solstice.

"Holy crap," Danielle breathed. "Who is that?"

Verbena looked over her shoulder in the general direction of Danielle gawking.

There—walking out of the diner—was a guy Verbena had never seen before. He was tall and thin, built like he played soccer at whatever school he went to. His blond hair was a little long on top, and he pushed it off his forehead as he descended the stairs toward the party. He had an ease to the way he walked, like he floated on air rather than stomped on the earth like the rest of humanity.

Verbena felt her heart fall to her stomach, and her entire body buzzed like every muscle had fallen asleep. Her hands gripped the sides of her jean shorts, fisting the already tight fabric. She swayed.

Him.

That was *him*.

She'd found her soulmate.

Verbena searched the crowd wildly. She needed to find one of her sisters. Lavender, preferably, but Rosemary or Laurel would do in a pinch. Her soulmate had just walked out of the diner, and she had no idea what to do. She should run away, right? Hide in a bush and observe him for a while? Hide anywhere?

And now he was looking at her. And smiling. And walking in her direction.

Shit. She was done for.

"Hey, Earth to Luke!"

Luke looked up from the soapy water in the sink.

"We're closing for the festival tonight. You should come." His boss, Julio, slipped off his apron and hung it on a hook in the kitchen.

"Yeah, maybe." Luke looked back at the water. He was nearly finished with the dishes, but the floor still needed mopping.

"Star Island isn't New York City, but we still have fun. There'll be a lot of people you haven't had a chance to meet yet," he called over his shoulder. "See you there!"

Luke sighed and switched off the water.

He'd been on Star Island for just under a week, had this job for five days, and in ten days he'd be able to put a deposit down on one of the shittier apartments the island offered. For now, he was camping. But he was lucky—the Star Island campsite wasn't overcrowded and had showers. It was also practically free to camp there, since the person who was supposed to collect money barely ever showed up to work. He'd been there for five nights and only paid for two.

Luke finished the dishes, dried off, and stretched his arms over his head, then got to mopping. The din of the celebration carried over his steady work, beckoning him out of the restaurant and into the night air. Maybe it would be good to socialize a little. All that was waiting for him at the campsite was a pile of clothes that needed handwashing, a threadbare sleeping bag, and a night staring at the stars. Maybe he'd get lucky and someone would buy him a beer. Or better yet, some food.

Luke stepped down the diner stairs and glanced around. There were more people than he imagined this small island could muster for a street festival. Sure, a lot of them were tourists, but still. He'd expected a couple dozen and was met with about a hundred.

He had come to Star Island to turn over a new leaf. He was sick of barely making ends meet in a big city and living in rat-infested apartments with a bunch of guys who tried to steal from him. Luke had landed in the city as a place to disappear from his old life, but there was nothing in the fine print that said you couldn't disappear in a more affordable place with better rent prices. He figured a spit of land in the Atlantic was about as different as he could get from anywhere he'd lived before.

Luke scanned the street, looking for Julio or anyone else who worked in the diner. He counted himself as friendly, but he was tired and didn't necessarily feel like going up to a stranger to strum up some conversation.

A woman caught his eye like he was a fish on a hook willingly being reeled in to his demise. Once he saw her, he couldn't take his eyes off her. It was like the opposite of a car accident—she was too perfect to look away. A mess of unruly brown hair tossing in the breeze, sun-kissed skin glimmering under the streetlights. She smiled nervously in his direction as she chatted with a friend, then turned to really look at him.

His heart switched on.

He had to talk to her.

Luke had never felt so compelled in his life, but the moment he saw that woman, he knew he couldn't let her pass by. She was someone, someone important. He felt it in his bones, his heart, his brain, and, bizarrely, in his teeth. This woman was part of his life. It was like seeing an old friend after years apart, but he was certain they'd never met before.

He closed the distance between them before she could disappear into the crowd and away from him forever. What if she was a tourist? She could walk out of his life as quickly as she'd walked into it.

"Hi, I'm Luke." He wished he had come up with something clever to say to her other than his name, but he hadn't, so that was all he had. He'd try to be charming from now on.

"Hi," she answered slowly. "I'm Verbena."

"Verbena?" he repeated.

"Yup. Like lemon verbena, the herb, candle, soap scent." The girl next to her nudged her. "Oh, this is Danielle." The other girl was grinning ear to ear.

Luke glanced at her for a moment, but his eyes shifted back to Verbena. That name would be seared into his brain for the rest of his life.

"So, Luke," Verbena began, "did you just move here or are you on vacation?" She leaned against a lamp post and tucked her hands behind the small of her back. Her eyes searched beyond him for a minute, then settled back on his face.

Luke couldn't help but do a full sweep of her, head to toe. She was gorgeous. Her legs were long, strong and looked fantastic in her shorts. She was on the thin side. She looked like she might have been a runner of some sort.

"Moved here," he answered, finally. "Few days ago."

"Welcome." She looked over his shoulder. "I think I need to find one of my sisters."

"Can I come with you?" *Shit*, he thought. That was way too forward, but he really didn't want to lose her in the crowd. He needed to talk to her more and figure out where she worked or lived. He didn't have a phone and wasn't planning to have one for a while, but he knew he needed to see her again.

"Oh, hell, I'll see you later," Danielle said to Verbena and stomped away. Verbena tried to smother a smile.

"Sorry. Don't want to lose you yet. If I'm bothering you, I'll go away."

"No! No, you're not bothering me." She smiled and visibly relaxed. "Actually, you want to go somewhere and talk? There are a lot of gossips around here." She motioned to the crowds. "Not much else to talk about."

"Of course," Luke answered, knowing full well if she asked him to swim back to the mainland with her, he'd do it. Hell, he'd walk to California right now if she was next to him. He could definitely leave Summerfest.

"Favorite color?"

"Gray," Verbena answered.

"Gray?" Luke laughed. "Who on earth calls gray a favorite color?"

"Verbena Bay, that's who," she said defensively. "It's so calming. It's the color of the ocean in winter, the sky in winter. No one is agitated by gray. It's a lovely color."

"I'm guessing you really like winter." Luke shifted a little closer to her. She'd taken him to the park a little bit away from the festival in the street. It was quieter here, so they could really talk. People still walked by occasionally, but overall, they were alone.

She'd thrown caution to the wind and foregone finding an older sister for guidance. Luke was her soulmate, she knew it. She was safe with him. Soulmates protected each other. They would never hurt each other. Hell, she was probably going to be dating him by the end of the night.

"I do like winter. It's the perfect season to stay inside and be cozy. And it's quiet here in the winter. No tourists or summer-home people, no loud drunks crowding the beaches. It's really peaceful. Only the real Celestials are here in January."

"Celestials?"

"Oh." Verbena felt color rise to her cheeks. "That's what we called year-round Star Islanders. I think I've earned the title. We moved here four years ago."

"We?" Luke prompted.

"My sisters and I." She thought for a moment whether to tell him that their parents' untimely death had prompted the move, but she decided against it. "We inherited a cottage from our great-aunt. It's been in our family for a while."

"Cool."

Their conversation settled into silence, but it wasn't awkward. It felt like a comfortable, well-earned silence, the calm that two people enjoy after being together for a long time.

Verbena's mind began to wander, thinking about her future with Luke. She was only seventeen. She still had a year of high school to finish. It wasn't like she could move in with Luke tomorrow. But if she could, well, that would be perfect. No more waiting, wondering what her life was going to be like. Her soulmate was here. She didn't have to trip through the rest of her young-adult years trying to figure out what direction her life would take. Everything was settling into place so early.

She slowed her train of thought. Move in with him? Was she crazy? Lavender would slap her silly if she brought it up. He might be her soulmate, but they were teenagers. And Lavender was her legal guardian.

But still, it was so exciting! She'd never have to date or try things out with guys she knew weren't going to be around for the long haul. She was so lucky, getting to meet Luke this early.

Verbena was about ten the first time her mom sat her down and had the soulmate conversation. It was sort of like having the sex talk. It came in waves. She didn't get all the information that day, but she got a general gist. The rest came in other conversations over several years. Verbena was told not to expect her soulmate to show up until she was in her twenties. There were very few witches who knew their soulmates in childhood.

Yet, here she was, the summer between her junior and senior year of high school, sitting next to her soulmate.

"I feel like I should tell you something," Luke started slowly.

Verbena turned toward him, tucking her fist beneath her chin and resting her elbow against the picnic table.

"I swear this isn't a line." He smiled, his dimples making a quick appearance. "I feel connected to you, like we're going to be really good friends, or something."

"Or something," Verbena echoed. She looked at him now, really looked at him. His hair was dirty blond, a little on the long side with some waves in the front. His eyes were hazel with sparks of gold throughout, gleaming like sunspots. He had a relaxed energy to him, as if he didn't have a care in the world. It was so easy, talking to him, being with him. It wouldn't take much for her to lean in and kiss him. For the first time in her life, she was dying to know what someone's lips tasted like.

Verbena moved her knee until it rested against his. Just that simple meeting of knees, skin against skin, and she could feel her heart race.

"Verbena," he breathed. He slid his hand into hers and leaned closer until there was only an inch between their lips. For a moment, they were completely still—a breath away from touching—until she couldn't take it. She pressed her lips against his and buried her hand in his hair. She gasped against his lips, completely unprepared for the raw need that came from deep within her. Excitement and desire bubbled in her chest, turning to white heat. She threw her arms around his neck and grasped at his back, her fingers tangling in the cotton of his t-shirt.

She had never wanted anything as much as she wanted Luke in this moment. Not only to kiss him, but everything—it didn't make any sense. She was picturing all the emotions life had to offer with a boy she'd met a couple hours ago.

This was a whole new horizon. Verbena had kissed a boy before, but nothing like this. This was power and fate and desire and pure need. Her head felt like she'd taken some of Rosemary's herbs, dizzy and giddy.

Luke pulled away from her mouth and let his lips move to her neck, then her collarbone.

Suddenly, Verbena heard the park gate swing shut. Her eyes snapped open.

"What time is it?" she blurted out.

"I don't know," Luke answered, his voice husky against her skin. "Maybe eleven?"

"Shit!" Verbena untangled herself from him and jumped to her feet. "My sister is going to kill me!"

"What do you mean?" His brow furrowed.

"Lavender, my oldest sister, she's my guardian, and she takes the job very seriously. I was supposed to meet her back at the car at ten-thirty. No later. Damn, she is going to be so mad at me." She leaned back toward him, hoping she could sneak one last kiss before heading to the car to be yelled at, but he ducked out of the way.

"Your guardian?" He pushed her to the side and stood up, then paced back and forth in front of her.

"Yeah," she answered slowly. "What's wrong?" She sat on the bench, leaning against the table.

He stopped his pacing and rubbed his hand over his forehead.

"Verbena, how old are you?"

She felt her stomach sink.

"Seventeen," she answered quietly. There was no point in lying. She couldn't lie to him. He was her soulmate. Even if she did, he'd figure it out sooner or later.

"Seventeen?" he repeated. "Fuck!" He turned away, walking back toward the festival.

"Luke! Wait!" she called after him, clamoring to her feet. She couldn't let him go. He was her soulmate. They were destined to be together. They just needed to talk, to figure it out.

She raced to catch him and tried to thread her fingers through his, but he shook her off as if her touch burned him.

"Luke, stop! Come on, please." She ran to keep up with his long strides.

He stopped walking and turned toward her. "Verbena. I'm twenty-two." He shook his head, then jogged away, leaving her alone in the street.

Luke didn't stop running until he reached the campsite. He couldn't risk her catching up with him. He didn't want to be mean to her but...he couldn't be near her. He skidded to a stop at his makeshift home: a hammock strung between two trees with his backpack stashed in the bushes. He grabbed his bag, then turned on his heels and raced toward the showers.

"Fuck," he hissed, letting cold water rush over him. His clothes, hastily removed in his fury, were in a pile outside the stall.

What the hell was wrong with him? Seventeen. Verbena was seventeen years old. She was a child and he'd been about to...he'd wanted to...*oh God*.

He shook his head and turned the water colder, as if to punish himself.

He wasn't like that. He wasn't a guy who believed that if someone looked older they should be treated as such. Luke may have had to grow up fast when he was younger, but he never had an adult prey on him in that way.

"Damn it!" he shouted, water pouring down his face. He'd never felt anything like that before, like they were about to consume each other. He could have kissed her for hours and hours and hours, simply in awe of being in her arms. He wanted her so badly it felt like a need.

His mind raced. Why did he feel like this? He didn't know her. She was just some girl. Why did everything feel so intense?

A moment of clarity washed over him in the cold water. A vision of her —Verbena. But she was different. And he was there, but different. They were somewhere else, someone else. A loud ocean, a brutally cold wind...

Great. Now he was losing his mind too. What was he going to do?

His teeth started to chatter, and he slowly turned the water to cool instead of cold. He needed to keep himself preoccupied. He would finish showering, wash all his clothes and hang them to dry, organize his stuff. Maybe he'd try to build a fire by hand. Sleep probably wouldn't come, but he only had a few more days until he had a paycheck in his hand. He could try to look at some apartments tomorrow, find something small to rent. One thing was for sure: Luke Karnes would not be seeing Verbena Bay for a long time.

Verbena lay in her bed, curled in on herself, trying to stop her body from shaking.

Twenty-two?! Verbena thought he might be older than her, maybe nineteen, but twenty-two? Five whole years older? They couldn't be together, not legally at least, until the end of November. She rolled onto her back, holding her head in her hands.

"This isn't fair," she moaned. She needed him, needed to be with him. He was her soulmate, after all. They were supposed to be together. Two hundred years ago it would have been no big deal that she was seventeen. Hell, they could have gotten married tonight. He would probably have been considered a little young for her. But now...now...

Her mind began to race. Could she entice him into being with her even if it was illegal? She shook her head hard. He could get arrested. And Lavender would kill her.

Verbena choked back a sob. She felt awful right now, like her insides were twisting on themselves, like she'd swallowed a length of barbed wire. How was she going to live like this? It seemed impossible.

A week passed, and it only got worse. Verbena couldn't eat, sleep, or do anything but think about Luke. She tried to sketch ideas for kitchens, something that always calmed her, but she could only draw a house for her and Luke. She had picked up a knitting project, but as soon as the stitches became rhythmic, Luke clouded her vision.

She felt like she was losing her mind.

"Verbena?" Lavender knocked softly on her door. "Do you want some lunch?"

"No," she answered shortly, pulling her quilt around her. It was the blanket she'd had as a baby and toddler, something her mom had tucked her under again and again.

"You need to eat." Now, Lavender sounded insistent.

"Leave me alone, Lavender."

"No. I won't leave you alone. Unlock your door."

Verbena didn't answer. Maybe if she gave her the silent treatment, she would go away.

"Verbena," Lavender began calmly, "open your door right now or I will kick it down and take it off the hinges. You will have no door on your bedroom, and your only privacy will be when you are using the bathroom."

Verbena scrunched her nose. Lavender wasn't one to make idle threats. Verbena slid off her bed and unlocked the door, then got back in bed.

Lavender pushed open the door, her brows creased in worry.

"What happened?"

"I don't want to talk about it."

"I know you don't, but you have to tell me. Is this normal bad, like you had a fight with a friend or a boy embarrassed you, or is this really bad? Like trauma bad?"

She looked at her oldest sister, her brow creased with worry.

Verbena shook her head. "No one did anything bad to me." That was true. Luke may have run away from her, but he didn't do anything terrible.

"Then what is going on? You don't sulk. You don't get moody. You're the one sister I can always count on to leave the dramatics alone."

"I have a lot on my mind. I need to figure it out."

"Can I help?"

Verbena pulled her quilt up to her chin. "No. I have to figure it out on my own."

"Okay. But you have to eat. Something. I'll make whatever you want."

"Seafood paella," Verbena answered quickly. That would take Lavender a couple hours, and she would definitely have to go to the store. The rest of her sisters would leave her alone. Verbena just bought herself an afternoon in peace.

"All right, fancy-pants. You better have two to three servings."

"I will."

Verbena kept her word and ate heaps of dinner, but around two in the morning, when she was still awake, she snuck up to the attic. She tore down books, looking for some sort of heart-hardening spell. There was no way she could handle pining over Luke for seven months before she could do anything about it.

And what if they slipped up? If the wanting became too much? He could go to jail. She needed to take care of this, as a witch.

Verbena had never done a big spell by herself before. She'd done little ones, brightened up different rooms in the house, arranged the furniture in ways to make the room feel inviting or bring good fortune. She always decorated their front porch depending on the season, but that kind of magic was trivial in comparison to what she was looking for now.

Their personal library was huge and unorganized, and after an hour of looking through books on halomancy, astrology, jumping the hedge, and hexing, she collapsed in the middle of the floor and put her face in her hands.

This was hopeless. Verbena lay down on her side and squeezed her eyes shut as hard as she could.

"I want my mom," she sobbed, letting every feeling of loneliness and despair finally escape. Her crying came violently, wracking her body. She hadn't cried with such fervor since her parents died, but it made sense. This was the first time she'd really *needed* her mom. She would have the answer.

A loud bang across the room gave her a start and she sat up, whipping her head toward the noise. The window on the far side of the attic was fogged up as if the temperature inside had suddenly skyrocketed and the outside was freezing. Verbena walked over to investigate.

Letters appeared, written in the fog, as if someone was scribbling advice. *Call Mable for help.*

"Who's Mable?" Verbena whispered.

A book fell off one of the shelves, the pages furiously turning. Then, they abruptly stopped. Verbena hurried to the book.

It was her great-aunt June's address book.

"Mable Silver," Verbena read. Her phone number and address were listed, as well as "Hearth Witch" scribbled beside her entry.

Verbena glanced around the empty attic. The window wasn't foggy anymore. There were no signs of anything.

"Thanks, Aunt June," she whispered.

Don't stop now. Keep reading with your copy of HAUNTINGS AND HOUSE WITCHERY.

And sign up for Colleen's newsletter to get all the news, giveaways, excerpts, and more!

Don't miss book three in the *The Witches of Star Island* series, HAUNTINGS AND HOUSE WITCHERY, available now, and find more from Colleen Delaney at www.colleendelaney.com

Ten years have passed since their first kiss, and fate has waited long enough.

Verbena Bay has built a successful life on her own terms as a talented realtor, powerful house witch, and alchemist. But despite her magical abilities, she's been keeping her soulmate at a distance with the help of morally ambiguous spell work. But when fate intervenes, her carefully controlled world unravels fast. Now, a violent ghost is after her, a family of witches and warlocks is hunting the Bay sisters, and Verbena must face her past mistakes if she hopes to survive.

Luke Karnes has always sought sanctuary on Star Island, far from the painful memories of his past. He's rebuilt his life and hoped that one day, it would include Verbena. But when she confesses years of deception, forgiveness feels impossible. Just when things seem at their darkest, Luke's foster brother arrives, and with him, the voice of their long-dead guardian, pulling Luke deeper into the world of magic—and toward an unexpected future with Verbena.

With deep scars and tangled emotions between them, Verbena and Luke must rely on each other to survive the growing threats from ghosts, warlocks, and dark secrets that refuse to stay buried.

In this high-stakes paranormal romance, love, betrayal, and powerful magic collide, leaving them with no choice but to face their fates together.

Please sign up for the City Owl Press newsletter for chances to win special subscriber-only contests and giveaways as well as receiving information on upcoming releases and special excerpts.

All reviews are **welcome** and **appreciated**. Please consider leaving one on your favorite social media and book buying sites.

Escape Your World. Get Lost in Ours! City Owl Press at www.cityowlpress.com.

Acknowledgments

There's a wonderful feeling that comes when writing the second in a series. Book one is such a flurry of excitement over this world and the characters you've created, but book two means you are sticking with it. The world now has a place in not only your heart, but the hearts of readers. With that said, thank you to every reader who is sticking with The Witches of Star Island. I hope you are enjoying your time with the Bay sisters. I am having a blast writing them!

To my husband: no matter what this life throws at us, these past twenty-three years together have been nothing short of magical. Thank you for holding down the fort during my late nights (and Saturday afternoons) at the library and putting up with me reading tarot cards for the neighbors in the backyard. I cannot imagine a better partner.

To my children: why on earth are you reading this? I definitely didn't approve any such behavior. You're grounded.

To my editor, Tee: I will carry your compliment about Gundrun and Skáldi forever. Thank you for working so hard with me on the ending! Your support has meant the world to me.

To my writing friends, Abigail, Desirée, Jen, Katy, and Tova: I don't think I could do any of this without your support. Someday, we'll all meet at a gorgeous writers' retreat and get absolutely no work completed.

To my village: Thank you to my mom, siblings, neighbors, friends—everyone who helped out with childcare while I wrote and edited this book. The support was invaluable.

And lastly, to Bar Harbor, Maine: I know you aren't a person and you aren't in the middle of the Atlantic, but if you've ever wondered how I picture Solaris in my brain, it's here. This place is quickly becoming one of my favorite spots to visit and I can't wait to go back.

Now, if you'll excuse me. There are three more Bay sisters who need my attention.

About the Author

COLLEEN DELANEY is an author, librarian, gardener, and occasional baker. She likes being outside in every season except winter, which she prefers to enjoy from a window. She currently lives on the shores of a Great Lake with her husband and four time-consuming children.

www.colleendelaney.com

instagram.com/colleendelaneywrites

x.com/cdelaneywriter

tiktok.com/@colleendelaneywrites

youtube.com/@ColleenDelaney

threads.com/@colleendelaneywrites

About the Publisher

City Owl Press is a cutting edge indie publishing company, bringing the world of romance and speculative fiction to discerning readers.

Escape Your World. Get Lost in Ours!

www.cityowlpress.com

facebook.com/CityOwlPress

x.com/cityowlpress

instagram.com/cityowlbooks

pinterest.com/cityowlpress

tiktok.com/@cityowlpress